· Terry Spear

…ances…a howling good time."
—Long and Short Reviews for *A Silver Wolf Christmas*

"There is nothing like a marvelously captivating paranormal romance by Terry Spear to get you in the holiday spirit."
—*Tome Tender* for *A Highland Wolf Christmas*

"A holiday treat—romance that sizzles and entertains."
—*Fresh Fiction* for *A Highland Wolf Christmas*

"A witty, passionate paranormal romance that will lift your spirits… Ms. Spear is an amazingly gifted storyteller."
—*Romance Junkies* for *A Highland Wolf Christmas*

"Intriguing, suspenseful, and romantic…the chemistry is amazing."
—*Fresh Fiction* for *A SEAL Wolf Christmas*

"Edge-of-your-seat-action… Spear's wonderful gifts as a writer [are] on clear display."
—*RT Book Reviews* for *A SEAL Wolf Christmas*

"Delectable…a 'Recommended Read' for Christmas and all year long!"
—*Romance Junkies* for *A SEAL Wolf Christmas*

"Sensuous, heartwarming romance, enhanced by an adorable wolf pup and wintertime fun."
—*Library Journal* for *A Very Jaguar Christmas*

Also by Terry Spear

Heart of the Wolf
Heart of the Wolf
To Tempt the Wolf
Legend of the White Wolf
Seduced by the Wolf

Silver Town Wolf
Destiny of the Wolf
Wolf Fever
Dreaming of the Wolf
Silence of the Wolf
A Silver Wolf Christmas
Alpha Wolf Need Not Apply
Between a Wolf and a Hard Place

Highland Wolf
Heart of the Highland Wolf
A Howl for a Highlander
A Highland Werewolf Wedding
Hero of a Highland Wolf
A Highland Wolf Christmas

SEAL Wolf
A SEAL in Wolf's Clothing
A SEAL Wolf Christmas
SEAL Wolf Hunting
SEAL Wolf In Too Deep
SEAL Wolf Undercover

Heart of the Jaguar
Savage Hunger
Jaguar Fever
Jaguar Hunt
Jaguar Pride
A Very Jaguar Christmas

Billionaire Wolf
Billionaire in Wolf's Clothing

Dreaming of a White Wolf Christmas

Terry Spear

Cover design by Aleta Rafton
Cover images © Lauzia/iStock, Cybernesco/iStock, Roman Mikhailiuk/Shutterstock, Stefano Cavoretto/Shutterstock

Published by Sourcebooks Casablanca, an imprint of Sourcebooks, Inc.
P.O. Box 4410, Naperville, Illinois 60567-4410
(630) 961-3900
Fax: (630) 961-2168
www.sourcebooks.com

Printed and bound in the United States of America.
OPM 10 9 8 7 6 5 4 3 2 1

To Fran Breece, who always asks me when I'm going to write another White Wolf book. Enjoy! And thanks for being a wonderful friend and fan!

Prologue

Boundary Waters Canoe Area Wilderness, Minnesota
Two years ago

CLARA HART FELT LIKE SHE WAS BEING FOLLOWED. She and her four friends had trekked through the wilderness, stopping for lunch and setting up the two tents for the afternoon, then exploring a bit more before making dinner and sharing stories around the campfire. She hadn't been camping in years. Even then, she'd only gone as a Girl Scout. She didn't think her adoptive parents had ever camped out. They preferred ritzy resorts—fine dining, the best of accommodations.

Except for the eerie sensation that they were being watched, Clara was having a ball.

"Hey, see anything?" Eleanor asked, teasing her as Clara peered around at the woods again.

"Nope."

Fisher laughed. "You've been saying something's following us for miles. When was the last time you'd been camping again?"

Clara threw her camp pillow at him. He grabbed it and threw it back to her. "You know," she said, "it could be a bear or a cougar. Be sure to take something to eat in your tent tonight so the rest of us won't have any worries."

Smiling, the redheaded guy shook his head. "You're

paranoid. As noisy as we've been, nothing would come near us."

Maybe she'd watched too many scary movies. Fisher was probably right. But Clara couldn't quit checking out the pines surrounding them, just in case he wasn't.

"She's just getting psyched to write her next romantic suspense novel set on a camping trip with friends," Fisher said. "And everyone dies, except a man and a woman who hate each other's guts and fall in love over the ordeal."

He was the total geek of the bunch, a computer wizard, but he'd taken up canoeing and hiking when his girlfriend said she was dumping him if he didn't immerse himself in the real world every once in a while. The twist was that she had to work and he had to come without her on this trip.

"Why don't you write real stuff?" Charles asked.

Eleanor slapped his shoulder. "I like her books. You just keep writing them. Ignore Charles. He wouldn't know a good book anyway, if he ever read any."

Later that summer night, the full moon was bright and the stars were sprinkled across the darkening sky as Clara and her friends were ready to settle down in their tents. She closed her eyes, but she couldn't sleep. She lived in the suburbs of Houston and was used to hearing doves cooing and blue jays fighting over suet in the feeders in her backyard during the day. At night, everything was quiet out where she lived.

Here in the wilderness, she listened as a wolf howled off in the distance, its song eerie and beautiful. An owl hooted nearby, and a breeze whipped the pine and fir branches around, making her feel as though Bigfoot was walking through the forest to join them.

Eleanor and Melanie appeared to be sound asleep in their tent. Clara wished she could be too. They planned a couple more canoe trips and several more hiking excursions over the next few days, so she needed to be well rested. Her exercise was usually limited to a gym, so though she was in great shape, hiking on uneven terrain made her aware that not all her muscle groups had been getting a good workout. Until now.

Unable to sleep, Clara quietly slipped on her boots, then rummaged through her bag until she found her camera and pulled it out. Camera in hand, she grabbed a flashlight and a small tripod, then headed outside. She set everything down on the ground and stretched, smelling the crisp, pine-filled air. She loved it out here.

She set up her tripod, set her camera on it, and angled it at the sky. If she couldn't sleep, she might as well take some pictures of the stars with the pines reaching up to touch them.

Then she heard the sound of a small dog whimpering. Thinking a puppy had found its way to their campsite, she grabbed her flashlight and turned it toward the woods. Maybe it had smelled the hot dogs they'd cooked over the campfire earlier. They had seen other canoeists and hikers with dogs, so maybe someone was camping nearby.

Clara didn't see anything at first, just the glow of the moon and the stars scattered across the darkness in a beautiful, sparkling array. Then she heard movement in the brush, and she shined the flashlight on the bushes. A fluffy, white puppy with huge feet stared back at her. She loved animals and knew how to interact with them so she didn't scare them off. She watched him while he observed her.

"What are you doing out here?" she whispered to him. They couldn't leave a puppy in the wilderness to fend for itself. He looked about five or six months old, so not old enough to take care of himself.

He finally approached the campfire and smelled the ashes where the juices from the hot dogs had dripped into the fire.

"You look like you could use a little meat on your bones." Clara walked over to the tree where they'd secured their food up high to keep it away from bears and other wild animals. She pulled down one of the secure bags and rifled through it for a package of beef jerky, keeping an eye on the young dog the whole time. He seemed so well behaved, sitting like an obedience-trained pup, though he wore no collar. But it made her think he'd gone exploring and the smell of food had brought him here.

She held out a piece of beef jerky to him, though in retrospect, she realized she should have tossed it to him no matter how well behaved he seemed. She hadn't thought she'd have any trouble with him. She was wrong. He was so hungry that he grabbed the jerky, biting her fingers. He only cut the skin a bit, making her bleed, but he could have injured her badly. She cried out, and he stared at her for a moment. Then, as if he knew he was a bad dog, he tore off into the woods, the beef jerky firmly secured between his jaws, and was gone.

Furious with herself for not being more careful, Clara still felt bad about the puppy, knowing he was hungry. She had to put the food away and take care of her injury. Trying not to hurt her bitten hand, though any movement was painful, she tied the food bag high up in the tree again. She considered leaving more beef jerky out for him, but it might attract bears.

Then she wondered if maybe the puppy was what had been following them all along and that's why she kept feeling like they were being watched. With flashlight in hand, she tried to locate the puppy, but she couldn't find any sign of him. She didn't want to travel too far from camp either. She could just imagine losing her way on top of being bitten!

Her hand was throbbing like crazy, and she finally gave up the search. After returning to the tent, she found the first aid kit and camp lantern and carried them outside so she didn't disturb Eleanor and Melanie, who were still curled up in their bags, sleeping soundly. Clara assumed the puppy would return for more beef jerky if he got hungry. They could work on locating his owners if they could coax him to come with them.

By the light of the lantern and her flashlight propped up against the log she was sitting on, she poured antiseptic on the wounds. The stinging and burning was like a million jellyfish tentacles ripping through her nerve endings, and she clenched her teeth to avoid crying out. The notion that being in the woods like this could increase her chances of the wound becoming infected made her curse her foolhardiness all over again. Then she had an awful thought… What if the puppy was carrying rabies?

Hoping she hadn't made the worst mistake of her life, Clara bandaged her fingers and turned off the lantern. She made two trips to carry everything she'd brought out back to the tent. Making sure everything was secure so no one would trip over it if someone got up before she did, she returned to her sleeping bag and zipped it up to her chin. Her injured fingers throbbed like hell. Now she *really* couldn't sleep.

A couple of hours later, she suddenly felt her muscles twitching and her whole body heating—like she was running a fever. *Damn it!* She was so hot that she wanted to yank off her clothes.

She fought the urge to strip naked, but she was burning up and feeling so weird that she finally unzipped her sleeping bag and started to strip off her sweats and socks, as if her brain was telling her she needed to cool down before the fever consumed her.

For an instant, everything seemed to blur, and she realized she could see some light in the tent, when before she couldn't without her flashlight. Was the sun already rising? Great, and she hadn't had any sleep. Yet she was no longer hot.

She meant to reach for her flashlight, but what she saw made her want to scream out in terror. But the sound wouldn't come at all. She couldn't grab her flashlight. Her arm had turned into a white dog's leg. Ohmigod, she was hallucinating!

She ran out of the tent and stood by the fire ring. Looking down at herself in the full moonlight, all she saw was one big, white dog with a fluffy white tail. *What. The. Hell.*

Yet, despite the fact that the experience felt real, she knew she had to be hallucinating. She smelled the sharpness of the fragrances: the pines and firs, the scent of the river nearby, the strong aroma of food—their food. She could smell the ashes in the fire ring, the drippings of the fish they'd cooked for lunch, and the hot dogs and marshmallows too.

The sounds were startling: the movement of the leaves and swaying pine branches; the hooting of the owl, which seemed clearer, closer; the running of the river over stones, the water dipping and rising again as if she could "see" the movement.

When she reached the river, wanting to take a drink—which, in her right mind, she would never have done without purifying the water first—she saw the most beautiful white wolf drinking at the edge on the opposite bank.

Her jaw dropped. Wolf, *not* dog.

Which immediately made her think of the white puppy. And the howl she had heard.

She frowned. How could the puppy have gotten across the river if it had been with this wolf? And what in the world were Arctic wolves doing in Minnesota? They didn't have them here, did they?

The wolf rose to its full height, and she didn't think it was a female. Not as big as he was. Beautiful, white fur all fluffed out like he'd had a shampoo and a blow-dry treatment.

She realized he was looking at her. Staring like she was staring at him. This could be a really bad thing. If this was real.

She tore off and heard him howl, the most beautiful howl she'd ever heard. More wolves howled in response from farther away, and she figured a whole pack of them would race after her next.

The next thing she remembered was climbing into her sleeping bag and she was out like the proverbial light.

When Clara woke in her sleeping bag the next morning, she recalled the most bizarre dream she'd ever experienced. Her fingers felt fine. Had she even been bitten? Had the wolf pup even come into camp last night? Or had she imagined the whole thing? Why hadn't she taken a picture of the pup? She'd never managed to take a picture of the stars either.

She glanced at her sweats lying next to the sleeping bag, realizing she really had stripped naked. Her hand was still bandaged, which proved she had been bitten. Yet her fingers didn't hurt. Not even a tiny bit.

Everyone had already gotten up and was making breakfast—oatmeal and coffee. She could smell the meal as if she was sitting fireside. She could hear the crackling of the burning firewood and her friends commenting that they'd never seen her sleep so long in the morning, although they were talking softly so they wouldn't disturb her sleep.

She pulled off the bandages, intending to show her friends what had happened to her last night, to explain why she'd been sleeping like the dead after the wild hallucinations she'd had. But her hand didn't have a mark on it. That was way too weird.

She could understand being so hot last night in the sleeping bag that she'd taken off her sweats, but bandaging her hand over an imaginary bite wound? She still recalled how painful it had been when she'd poured the antiseptic over the injuries.

If nothing more, she had one hell of a tale to tell everyone over breakfast. She tied her hair back in a ponytail like she always did before she hiked, thinking she needed to cut it shorter so it wasn't always whipping around in her face. Then she quickly dressed. When she left the tent to join her friends at the campfire, she knew they'd give her grief for being the last one up. Mainly since she usually gave them grief because she always started the fire in the morning and always told them they waited until they smelled the coffee before they rolled out of their sleeping bags. She couldn't believe she'd slept in either.

"Here's Sleeping Beauty," Fisher said. "You always beat us out here, so what happened? I was expecting my cocoa latte, but all I woke to were cold ashes."

"Well, I had one crazy night." Clara got her coffee, sat down on a log next to the fire, and told them what had happened to her: the puppy bite, dreaming she'd shifted, seeing a white wolf across the river.

Everyone was smiling at her.

"I tripped over her sweats this morning, so she was naked in her sleeping bag last night," Eleanor said.

Clara felt her cheeks flush with heat. She hadn't meant to tell anyone she had stripped naked.

Then Fisher very seriously said, "Hell, Clara, they were werewolves, and now you're one."

"So you shifted and it knocked the mahogany coloring out of your hair?" Eleanor asked. "I didn't even know you were a true redhead until now."

Melanie nodded. "I love your natural color."

Thinking her friends were teasing her, Clara untied her hair and looked at the silky strands in the early morning light. The vibrant cinnamon color of her natural hair was back. Her jaw hung agape.

"I thought the coloring you used was hair dye," Eleanor said. "That it couldn't be washed out. You had to grow your hair out or color it with something else. When in the world did you change it?"

Eleanor was correct. Clara had dyed her hair a darker color—brown with a hint of red—to add drama to her hair. Were her eyebrows also the lighter red again? She couldn't believe it, yet she had the proof right between her fingers.

After a day of hiking and pitching tents for the camp before dusk, they prepared dinner, but the topic of conversation returned to the werewolf business.

"We really should post guards to watch Clara's behavior," Fisher joked.

She snorted.

"If she's running around naked at night, I volunteer for first watch," Charles said and winked at her.

"Very funny." Tonight, Clara was sleeping normally and would be the first one up, just like usual. She looked up at the moon, and it was as full and bright as last night.

Everyone was talking about their walk and canoe trip tomorrow, but Clara couldn't shake the feeling that what she had done last night—all of it—had been real.

They all finally went to bed, and thank God, she drifted off right away. Until she felt the urge to pull off her sweats. And lost the battle. She was running as a white wolf…again.

Terrified, she realized the truth. She wasn't dreaming. She wasn't hallucinating. Fisher was right, even though he'd only been joking.

The wolf puppy that had bitten her hadn't been a full-blooded wolf at all. He'd been a werewolf.

And her life was spinning out of control.

Chapter 1

Nearly Christmas, two years later

Owen Nottingham, Arctic wolf and private investigator, had made daily treks into the wilderness ever since he'd seen the white wolf across the river. He knew she had to be an Arctic *lupus garou* just like him. But the fact she was running with humans had to mean she had lots more control over her shifting or she couldn't be with them on a long-term hiking and canoeing trip. Maybe she'd been born as a *lupus garou*. Maybe her wolf roots went so far back that she was a royal and completely in control of her shifting at all times.

One thing was for certain—she wasn't one of the Arctic wolves who had changed him and his friends. He would never forget that day seven years ago when he and his PI partner David Davis were hunting for bear in Maine, never having come close to finding one in the five years they'd been trying. They'd spotted a bear, and the hunt was on. Never in a million years would he or David have thought his good friend would end up having a heart attack.

Nor that the Arctic wolves the guide had on the hunt weren't all wolf and that they were all from the same *lupus garou* pack. Neither the guide nor Owen could do anything to save David's life way out in the woods. Owen had been willing to pay any price to save his friend. Whatever it cost. He'd envisioned the guide calling in a helicopter and air evacuating David to a hospital.

Owen had to admit that he'd agreed to it. Anything. Like making a pact with a devil wolf. The wolves wouldn't have bitten them if he hadn't asked for the guide's help. Owen hadn't known what was going on at the time. Only that the wolves had bitten both of them—David, to give him their enhanced healing abilities to repair his heart, and Owen, because he couldn't witness what they were without paying the consequences. Which meant becoming one of them or dying.

After that, the pack took them in. They had to because David and Owen had no control over the shifting, but they were captives just the same, until one of the pack members had helped them to escape. So Owen knew all of the members of that pack. Those were the only Arctic wolves he'd ever met, beyond his own small pack.

More than anything in the world, he wanted to find her. Wanted to get to know her. Locating her could mean finding a mate for either him or one of his bachelor male partners in the PI agency. He still envisioned her standing near the river's edge—half hidden in the brush, watching him, wide-eyed—and wondered where the hell she'd come from. He knew she'd been a she because she was smaller than the males. She had to be a shifter. Arctic wolves didn't live in this part of the country.

Still, he'd tried to locate her after that, to no avail. She and her friends had taken a canoe trip after a few days, and he never knew what had become of her. He wasn't even sure which of the women she'd been.

He was afraid he'd be looking for her until he was old and gray and might never see her again.

Owen opened up the new PI office that morning in White River Falls, Minnesota, the Christmas wreath jingling on the door. He was eager to make a go of a brick-and-mortar business again after seven years of working online, unable to set up a real office.

None of the other investigators believed they'd get a call first thing that morning, so they were coming in a little later. He finished hanging his sign on his door and stringing more Christmas lights on the miniature tree in his office. The whole pack—three bachelor males, and one couple and their two sons and a daughter—had decorated the seven-foot tree in the lobby so it looked cheery and welcoming sitting next to one of the front windows.

When Owen had settled down at his desk with a cup of coffee and a Christmas tree–decorated donut, he began checking his emails. He had only read one when he got the call that would be the first job they received at the office. He was enthusiastic about solving the missing person's case promptly, hoping for their first good review.

Ever since that day in the woods, Clara Hart had been a very different person, her whole world turned inside out. Her friends were no longer her friends, and her adoptive parents had disowned her. She'd changed her name to her pseudonym, Candice Mayfair. She'd moved from the suburbs of Houston to the wilderness in South Dakota. It was beautiful, perfect for her to run free and be herself. Or rather—her *other* self. The wolf part of her that howled to be free, especially during the occurrence of the full moon. But at other times too, except during the new moon. She'd finally realized this by keeping a calendar of the moon phases at hand at all times to document the trouble she was having with fighting the urge to shift. She'd also purchased dozens of books about werewolves that definitely were not written by real werewolves.

She finished hanging her Christmas wreath on the door, placed a Christmas throw rug she had hooked on the kitchen floor, and added a few more nutcrackers on the mantel. She'd set up her Christmas tree the day after Thanksgiving as she'd always done. At least that was something that hadn't changed. Though last Thanksgiving, she'd had to wait until she turned back into her human form to finish decorating.

After two years, she had finally come to grips with what she was. That she wasn't going to suddenly be her normal self again. She'd sometimes dreamed she was, but then she'd get the urge to shift and that shattered the illusion.

She suspected everyone she'd known thought she'd gotten into drugs or alcohol, because she'd disappeared from their lives. At first, she'd given excuses for why she couldn't see them. But then she realized she had to isolate herself from anyone she'd known in the past. They didn't understand what was wrong with her. And she couldn't explain.

Drinking didn't stop her from shifting either. She'd learned that the hard way. Being tipsy just made it harder to remove her clothes and shift, which meant she was caught in her clothes as a wolf for several hours one night, thankfully in her own home. So, no more drinking to try to control the shift. She'd also had the uncontrollable urge to howl sometimes when she ran as a wolf, and she was certain that would be a disaster. What if a wolf pack responded? She could be in real trouble.

She'd settled into her life, such as it was, and she'd found that writing about the subject she knew best—werewolves—was a good outlet for her. Using her former talent at writing romantic suspense, she'd started writing Arctic wolf romances. Unlike in other books where werewolves were hideous monsters out to eat people, her characters were misfits like her. She'd never encountered another like the male and the pup she'd seen that night she was camping. She knew they had to be out there somewhere in the Superior National Forest in Minnesota. She'd never been back there. Why would she be?

She had no idea if werewolves ran as a pack, a family unit, or whatever. What if the beautiful male was mated?

Candice had made a niche for herself on her fifteen acres where she still could get Internet, with a small town nearby for groceries and anything else she needed. She could avoid people. Except online. Which worked great.

The worst part was her parents disowning her. When her father had a stroke, the full moon had been in full swing. Candice had been so angry, furious with her inability to control the shift. She'd even driven partway home when she'd had to pull over on a dirt road, park, strip, and shift. She knew then she just couldn't manage the trip. When her mother had gone in for a pacemaker, the moon was nearly full. Her parents' medical emergencies never came up when the new moon or waxing and waning crescents came around. And she couldn't explain how she couldn't travel anywhere as a wolf. That she was liable to turn into a wolf in the emergency room.

Her folks must have thought their adopted daughter didn't care anything about them, so she was out of their lives. It didn't matter that she'd come to see them straightaway when it was safer to do so. They believed she hadn't wanted to help them when they needed her, and she'd felt horrible about it.

She'd learned they'd both died in a car accident, and it broke her heart. She had no one to blame for being unable to be with them when they really needed her but herself. She'd hand-fed a werewolf puppy on a camping trip and had paid the price.

Owen was glad he and the rest of his buddies were officially back in business. Sure, they were still out in the boonies, had a wolf door for an easy escape, and conducted most of their business online, but they officially had an office again after seven years of trying to get their shifting under control. At least, it was a first step.

This morning he had his first real client. In fact, the first for any of them. His partners, Cameron MacPherson, David Davis, and Gavin Summerfield—all formerly of Seattle—were coming in later that morning, so he was it, and he got the job.

He was glad they lived in northern Minnesota where they had the freedom to run unseen. They couldn't have settled in Seattle where they'd had their PI office. They'd tried, but a gray wolf shifter pack had learned of their presence in the city and threatened to kill them if they stayed. Not only did Owen's pack have trouble controlling their shifting, but they also were Arctic wolves and couldn't easily blend in with the surroundings the way the gray wolves could. Not to mention that wolves were naturally territorial, and the gray pack had ruled there for many years. All of this was news to Owen and his partners. They hadn't known shifters existed before their trip to Maine.

"I'm Jim Winchester," the man said over the phone. "I'm an assistant to Strom Hart. His offices are based in Houston. He's in need of a PI who can look for a missing person—his niece, Clara Hart. You have a month to find her and return her to Houston so she can claim her parents' inheritance, or it will be forfeit."

"Okay. Do you have any idea where she is?"

"That's the thing of it. If it were up to me, I'd hire a local PI. But the boss says she wasn't the same when she returned from a camping trip up your way. He wants you to start looking there. See if she ended up moving up there. She quit her job, sold her home, and took off. She wouldn't let her parents know where she was living."

"Okay. If I don't find her, who would the inheritance go to?"

"Strom Hart. He's the brother of John Hart, the deceased, and is Clara's uncle. John died two weeks ago; his wife, a couple of days before that. Mr. Hart thought his brother had disowned his daughter. But when the will was read, he learned his brother had not. The provision was that Mr. Hart would have one month to search for her and deliver the message to her, and if he couldn't find her or she didn't return to Houston, the money would go to him as the next living relative."

"I see. Have you asked anyone else to look into this matter?"

"No. It's all in your hands. He'll pay the going rate.

Deliver her before the month is up, and she can claim her inheritance."

"Okay. I just need you to tell me a few things—last known address, phone number, where she was staying in this area. Her last place of employment, and if you know any of her friends, a list of their names. Also, do you have a photo of her?"

"This is the most recent picture I could find of her. She's been gone for two years. In anticipation of you needing some other information, I'm sending that along too." In an email, Mr. Winchester forwarded a photo of the woman and some of the information Owen had requested. "Her dad checked with her place of employment, friends, anywhere he could think of. She just disappeared without a trace."

The assistant hadn't given him a list of friends' names though. "I take it you don't know the names of any of her friends?"

"No. Sorry."

Owen opened the picture of the woman. She had dark, reddish-brown hair, long and curling over her shoulders. Her eyes were a vivid violet, and her glossy peach lips were smiling. She appeared happy in the photo.

What had made her give up everyone and everything and vanish from her former life? Drugs? A cult? Boyfriend? The wrong crowd?

Owen wondered if she'd changed the color of her hair since then. He suspected if she hadn't wanted to be found, she would have.

"Can I ask how you learned of us?" Owen hoped their online site had finally gotten some notice.

"Online, based on your location. You are the closest

PI office to where Clara was visiting before she…quit her family and friends and job so suddenly," Mr. Winchester said. "Mr. Hart could use one of the big-city PI agencies, if you think they'd do a better job."

"No, no, I'm the man for the job. I'll get right on it."

Owen made the arrangements to have Strom billed for the charges while he worked the case. He had every intention of finding the woman as soon as he could. They could use all the good reviews they could get. And a quick resolution should give them a five-star review. Though he wondered how much inheritance they were talking about and how much motivation that would be for this Strom Hart to ensure his niece was never found. Maybe that's why he'd hired Owen's firm instead of going with a big-time Houston PI.

Owen wished he could have asked for something of hers so he could get her scent. He imagined the uncle would have fired him on the spot.

He ended the conversation and called Cameron to tell him the good news. "Got a viable case." He told Cameron what he was looking into.

"If you need any of our help, just holler," Cameron said.

The money went into the pack's funds so they could all share in the proceeds, so it wasn't like one of them would get a job and the money would be all his. They all helped one another.

"I sure will. Thanks, Cameron, and tell Faith her new website is working."

Owen checked out Strom Hart and Clara's deceased parents and was shocked to learn both brothers were billionaires in their own right. For a moment, he thought he was charging too little for the job. He smiled. Then he got down to business and called Clara Hart's old workplace, a law firm in Houston.

"You would need a court order for me to release information about where Clara Hart is living now. But yeah, we had to forward her last pay to that location," said Lyn Rose, the law firm's administrative assistant. "What is this concerning?"

"An inheritance. I need to find her to let her know she needs to claim it before it goes to her uncle." Owen wouldn't normally have said so much, but he wanted to impress upon the woman—if she was at all a friend of Clara Hart, and he suspected she was from the way she had talked about her—that she'd better share any information she had.

"An inheritance? Oh wow. A big inheritance? Well, she deserves it, as much as she cared about her parents. Tragic car accident, but her mother shouldn't have let her father drive when he was on the medication he was on. Not that I don't know how that goes. My dad had lung cancer and was dying, for heaven's sake, but my mother still let him drive. Why? Because he was always the one who drove everywhere when they went places together. You know, like he earned the money in the family, and when Mom worked, it was just her pin money. Not to use to pay household bills. I tell you, things have sure changed since then. Yeah, we're emancipated, but now the guy wants us to make as much as him and never quit working.

"Well, you probably can't tell me how much her inheritance is worth. That's okay. Yeah, she was the best little helper. If I needed her to do anything, she was right there assisting me, though her job called for her to be a file clerk, nothing else. She would rather be doing something than not. I still can't tell you where she lives now, but I can share something with you that isn't classified as confidential."

"That is?" Owen eagerly asked.

"She's a romance author. Surprised the daylights out of me when I saw she had her own website, and I began buying her books. She's really a great storyteller too. Love them. Just wish I could find one of those dreamy, hunky wolves she writes about."

"Wolves?"

"Yeah. She wrote romantic suspense before, but she switched a couple years ago. There's something about her werewolves that just sucks me in. They're great. Anyway, she goes by Candice Mayfair. That's her pen name. Just look her up. She has a message box you can query her at that goes right to her email. That's how I got ahold of her to tell her how much I love her stories, and then what do you know? I learn she's the same sweet woman who worked here in our office as a file clerk. Send her a note. She'll write back. She always does. Good luck!"

As soon as Owen thanked the administrative assistant and did an online search for Candice Mayfair, he came face-to-face with a red-haired beauty with piercing green eyes, her curly hair in a short bob. "Clara Hart?" He couldn't be sure it was her. If it was, the find would prove to be Owen's lucky day. He'd never solved a case so fast.

Owen quickly searched her biography page, but it didn't have a phone number, email, or snail mail address listed. He would use the webpage contact note and hope she answered him back pronto.

Thinking about how he could show her some real

wolf loving for her wolf stories, he smiled and started typing the message: *If you need a real wolf to base your characters on…*

Then he deleted the message. Hell, what could he say to get her response? He called Cameron's mate for some advice. "Hey, Faith, I need to run this by you."

Candice had been writing for two days straight, working on her publisher's book deadline, when she wrote the ending, smiled, and set the book aside. She would start proofing it tomorrow after she'd given her brain a break. Now she'd do what she always did when she finished a book or reached a good stopping point in one. Clean house. Check her backlog of emails. Pick up some more groceries. And take a run on the wolf side.

She finished vacuuming and dusting, swearing every window must let in all the outdoors, and then started a batch of gingerbread cookie cutouts to celebrate the Christmas holiday season and finishing another book. While they were baking, she finally settled down to check her emails. Fan mail always came first, and one from her website got her attention right off. She opened it and read:

> *Hello, I'm Owen Nottingham, private investigator for White River Investigations, White River Falls, Minnesota. My client, Strom Hart, hired me to locate you. Your parents, John and Cynthia Hart, left you an inheritance, and you need to see the lawyer about it so you can claim it. I need to verify that*

you are the right woman first. Is there any way we could meet and get this taken care of so you can collect your inheritance? Strom Hart will be the one to receive it by the end of the month otherwise. His assistant, Jim Winchester, said Mr. Hart is your uncle.

Candice reread the message, not believing her eyes, tears filling them. She quickly looked at the date of the message. Two days ago! She knew she shouldn't have neglected her emails, but when she was into a story, she couldn't break away.

She ground her teeth, raised her fingers to respond, and heard a knocking at her door. No one came here. Never. Ever. Not even salesmen.

She glanced at her phases-of-the moon calendar. The waxing gibbous was just beginning. She should be fine. Just to be on the safe side, in case the person at the door was trouble, she pulled a can of mace from her desk drawer and headed for the door. She peered through the peephole. Waiting at the door was a handsome black-haired man with rugged features and intense blue eyes. He was dressed in a black suit, a red shirt, and a dark-purple tie covered in red, purple, and gold Christmas balls. She raised her brows.

"I'm Owen Nottingham," he said to the door, holding up his PI license and driver's license. He couldn't know that she was watching him, so he must have hoped she was there, observing him. "I tried getting ahold of you through the contact form on your website about your inheritance. Your contact form might not be working, so I had to locate you in person."

So this was the man who had sent the message. Was he for real? He had to be. He wouldn't have come all this way to see her if he wasn't. But how had he found her?

Candice opened the door, the bells jingling on her Christmas wreath, and the man glanced down at the can of mace in her hand. He smiled, his gaze holding hers with such intensity that it was as though he could see clear through to her soul. "Really, just a PI doing my job."

A chilly breeze carried his scent to her. Wolf scent. All at once, she felt so light-headed that she grabbed the door to keep herself upright and dropped the can of mace on the tile floor. It clattered, but she couldn't have reached for it if her life depended on it.

Oh. My. God.

This couldn't be real. He couldn't be real. No wonder he'd been talking to the door. He must have heard her footfalls as she'd approached.

He took a deep breath at the same time, and when he smelled *her* scent, his eyes widened in surprise. His hand shot out to grab her arm and steady her. For a minute, she tried to control her breathing and her heart rate, neither of which she could steady. She felt like she was going to pass out.

"Hell, you're the wolf I saw across the White River, aren't you?"

Her jaw dropped, and her knees buckled. He swept her up in his arms and she wanted to object, but he slammed the door behind him with his hip and carried her into the house. He was the wolf she'd seen across the river that day on the camping trip in Minnesota two years ago, sipping from the water? She still remembered it like it was yesterday. Him looking up and seeing her staring at him while she'd believed she was hallucinating.

Until the next night, and then she knew she hadn't been dreaming at all.

Chapter 2

Owen couldn't believe his luck. Candice Mayfair was the beautiful white wolf he'd seen that day so long ago. Not that she looked like a wolf now. He only knew for sure she was the wolf because he recognized her scent. After the initial shock of seeing an unfamiliar and intriguing Arctic she-wolf, he'd gone after her that night.

The whole pack had been on a run, but they knew to stay far from any campsite. He and the other guys had swum across the river to explore a bit. Cameron and his mate had stayed on the other side with the kids. Owen had even swum back across the river to find the mysterious female and discovered that her scent led right to one of the tents. Since she had gone into the tent, he knew she had to be one of their shifter kind. He'd even hung around the next day, waiting to catch a glimpse of her, but there were three women, and he had no idea which was her. A blond, a brunette, and a red-haired woman—none of whom looked like the picture he had of Clara Hart.

Being a white wolf in summer had made it difficult to blend in, so he'd had to keep well out of sight.

Candice Mayfair was definitely the author of the books on the website, though she didn't look like the photo her uncle had of her, if she was Clara Hart. She had the same compelling eyes, different color, but they got Owen's attention, grabbed hold, and wouldn't let go.

He carried her to her couch and set her down, staying close, his hand still on her arm until she seemed to regain her equilibrium.

"The wolf pup was yours," she accused, jerking her arm away from him.

"Wolf pup?"

"Yeah, wolf pup. Don't pretend you don't know about your own wolf pup."

Then all the pieces began to fall into place. Campers. Campfire. Food. Corey, the wolf pup she had to be referring to, hadn't just found food like they'd thought. Candice must not have been a wolf until that night.

"You fed him? Corey? His mom wondered why he smelled of beef jerky that night. We thought he'd found some at the campsite. Don't tell me... He bit you." Which would be the only possible way to have turned her. Owen couldn't believe it. Boy, would Corey be in trouble now. They were never to bite anyone unless they had no choice. "I'm so sorry, Candice. We're all newly turned, really. Not as newly turned as you though. It's been seven years for us." He waited for that to sink in, for her to give him a chance to speak about the pack and how she needed to be one of them. She *was* one of them.

She must have had to live with this alone the last couple of years, which had to have been awful. Suddenly, the business of who she was—if she was Clara Hart or not—wasn't half as important as righting a wrong with a fellow Arctic *lupus garou*.

She folded her arms. "You should have trained your son better than that."

"Son? No, he's Cameron and Faith MacPherson's son. I don't have a mate. No kids. I'm single." Was he making it too obvious he was *very* available? That happened when you didn't want to date anyone because your wolfish half might come to the forefront at a really bad time.

She lifted a red brow and gave him a hint of a smile. All he could think of was kissing her. A wolf, she-wolf, Arctic wolf.

Hell, he was rambling. Unless they turned someone, none of the guys who had been turned would ever have a wolf mate. Not a white wolf anyway, unless they were lucky enough to find others like them. He had to convince her to meet the pack. Not that she would want to be anyone's mate, but she should be part of the pack. She had been turned by one of them. She needed to learn what they knew about all of this. He couldn't imagine her being on her own and having to deal with it all alone.

Owen noticed the warm fire glowing in the fireplace and the cheery scent warmers wafting ginger-and-cinnamon Christmas fragrances into the air, making him think of home and hearth and spending Christmas with a she-wolf of his own. The place was nice and clean like his home, though he was certain Candice hadn't expected visitors. Then the smell of burning gingerbread suddenly caught his attention and hers, and she rushed to the kitchen.

When he hurried in after her, he saw a tall Christmas tree sitting in one corner. The tree was covered in gold, red, and purple balls, just like his tie. Lights sparkled all over the tree, and Candice had a collection of reindeer in various sizes, along with nutcrackers, sitting on the fireplace mantel, under the tree, and on a curio cabinet. Really homey and holiday festive. Her decorated home was warm and cheery, not ostentatious like his. But what could he do? All the guys wanted to outdo each other with the decorations.

He wondered if Candice had friends over to enjoy the beautiful decorations. Or had she isolated herself because of the problem with her wolf half? Like they had done. At least he and his pack members had one another to share in the laughter and concerns—the shifts that had happened when they hadn't had time to strip off their clothes, their near disasters when they were running as wolves and got caught on camera, and other catastrophes.

"I don't normally feel faint over anything." She yanked out the cookie sheet covered in gingerbread cookies. Shoving the sheet onto the stove top, she muttered about not taking her eyes off her cooking for *anything* next time.

"Believe me, I normally don't either," he told her. Smelling her beautiful scent had made him feel a little light-headed too.

Her chin tilted down, she gave him a look indicating that she didn't believe him.

"Hell, if you hadn't been holding on to the doorjamb and I hadn't been holding on to you, we might have both ended up sitting on the floor."

He swore she was fighting a smile as she grabbed a mixing bowl out of the fridge and set it on the counter, then pulled out another cookie sheet and a bag of flour and put them beside the bowl. Then to his surprise, she seized an apron and handed it to him. "Here. You made me burn my cookies, so you can help me make them again."

He opened up the apron and read the message on it: *Dear Santa, I've been very naughty…* He laughed because that was in a Christmas wolf story she'd written, which he'd been listening to on audiobook on the drive here. Except in that story, the heroine was wearing lacy, red silk panties, a matching bra, and high-heeled shoes after going to a Christmas party. She'd slipped out of her classy gown to keep from making a mess of it. Owen couldn't help but envision Candice wearing the red slips of silk and lace, the spiked heels, and this apron.

She glanced at the apron and yanked it out of his hands, her face turning as red as her hair. She shoved the apron in the drawer, then pulled out another. This one featured an image of Christmas balls. Safer. He smiled.

She frowned at him. "How did you find me?"

"It wasn't easy. I first looked for you using your real name, not knowing you're using your pen name for everything now. Once I knew your pen name, I found you on several social networking sites. No address on any of them. We use a top-notch professional investigative database available only to licensed PIs, and I found your current address in that."

Owen looked down at the bowl of dough. Now he had to bake cookies, and he had no idea how to do it.

"Tell me what this is all about again. An inheritance? My parents wouldn't have left me any money. They disowned me because of this little problem of mine."

For an instant, Owen wondered if he really did have the right woman. "You're Clara Hart, right?"

"In the past. Not today."

He took a relieved breath. "Okay. Well, as long as Strom Hart recognizes you as his niece and you have proof of your former identity as Clara, we should be good."

"We?" Candice sprinkled some of the flour on a

cutting board and plopped a ball of dough on top of it. She started kneading.

He frowned at the speckled dots of flour that had somehow managed to end up on his black dress jacket. Here he was, trying to make an impression as a first-class private investigator, though he was usually more comfortable in jeans and a lumberjack shirt. He tried to brush away the flour spots and only managed to streak them all over the black fabric.

"Here, roll out the dough like this." She took his hand and placed it on the rolling pin handle, and then she offered him the other handle. "Roll it out, and then cut out the cookies with the cutters." She motioned to the tin cutters.

Owen looked down at the dough and glanced at the cutters.

"The Twelve Days of Christmas," she said.

"Aren't you supposed to drink Christmas drinks while you're baking cookies?" He thought if he had a warm, fuzzy drink, he might even be half good at this. Using the rolling pin, he began trying to smoosh the dough onto the board to make it as thin as he thought it needed to be.

A piece of the buttery dough flipped off the rolling pin and onto his tie. He glanced down at it, not believing he was making such a mess of himself.

"Oh, for heaven's sake. That's what the apron is for." Candice frowned at his flour-speckled jacket, took hold of his arm, and moved him away from the counter so she could unbutton his jacket.

Never wearing an apron back home when he cooked, he hadn't thought he'd make a mess of himself here.

He'd been sure of it and had set the apron aside. He sure hadn't expected her to unbutton his jacket.

Then she removed it and set it aside on a barstool. She began to work on unfastening his tie next, slipping it out of its knot and setting it on the counter next to the barstool.

Hell, all he could think about was her removing the rest of his clothes. His cock was already stirring to life. She smelled good: sweet and spicy, woodsy, and some kind of exotic floral mixture. She-wolf, of course, and gingerbread cookies.

He was waiting for her to remove his shirt when she looked up at him, her green eyes all-knowing. She grabbed the Christmas balls apron and slapped it against his chest. "Wear it so I don't have to clean all your clothes."

He wondered just how messy he could get while wearing the apron. His sleeves? Then she'd remove his shirt and...

She proceeded to clean his jacket and set it aside, and then she cleaned his tie while he went back to smooshing the ball of dough into something more manageable. No matter how much he tried, he couldn't make it perfectly level. Some places were fat, some skinny. He took a moment to stare at the dough to figure out what to do with it. He could imagine some of the cookies baking too fast and being way too crisp, and some being thick and doughy and not cooked all the way through.

"Are we having trouble?"

Yeah, that was an understatement. Owen pointed with the rolling pin at the unevenly rolled-out dough. "Some are for those who want fewer calories, and some for those who want a fuller bite."

Candice laughed, then took the rolling pin from him, saving him from any more humiliation—or maybe she just wanted to make sure the cookies turned out right and to finish this before the day turned into tomorrow.

She set the rolling pin aside, re-formed the dough into a ball, and rolled it out uniformly. She wasn't even wearing an apron, but she didn't have a drop of dough or flour on her.

"You've probably been doing this for a long time." He imagined it would take him years to get it down pat.

"With my mom. We used to make them every Christmas. I always helped her. Until..." She shook her head.

"The camping trip and the unfortunate incident. You need to meet our pack. Talk to Corey about what he did. You're part of it, you know. One of us."

She snorted. "It's hard enough keeping my 'condition' secret. How much harder would it be to keep the secret of a whole pack of Arctic wolves?"

"We manage it just fine. We have for seven years. In any event, you're still one of us. We can help answer any questions you might have." What he really wanted to do was prove being with another wolf was very different from being a lone wolf. "Would you like to run after this? As wolves?"

She handed him the partridge-in-a-pear-tree cookie cutter and placed her hand over his to show him how to apply pressure on top of the leveled-out dough, keeping it steady to make clean edges. He liked the way she touched him, thinking that if he wanted to learn how to bake cutout cookies right, he would be a really slow learner. She would have to repeat each move, her hand on his, leaning close, moving into his space, rubbing up against him. The oven was heating up, but so was he.

He helped her cut out the rest of the cookies and really was having fun. “So about running tonight?”

Candice turned to look at him, her lips parted in what appeared to be surprise. “How long do you intend to stay here? You know there’s a snowstorm on its way.”

“Which was why I felt compelled to come here to tell you about the inheritance, in case the electricity went out and you didn’t receive my contact email. And now I can try to convince you to come with me to see the pack. If nothing more than to let us know how you feel about being turned. Get it off your chest.” He glanced down at her breasts covered in a soft green sweater, the color matching her eyes. She had one hell of a nice chest.

“I don’t need to get anything off my chest. I dealt with it, like a big girl.” She slipped the baking sheet into the oven. Once she was done, she put the rest of the dough in the fridge and began to fill the sink full of sudsy water. She washed the utensils, the cutting board, and the rolling pin, then set them aside to dry.

Owen washed his hands. “Can you control your shifting?”

“Better. But not fully during the full moon or waning and waxing gibbous.”

“Yeah, we all have trouble with that.”

She frowned. “You’re kidding. Does it mean we’ll have no control over it forever?”

“For years, at least. From what we’ve learned. We can’t shift during the new moon. That’s when I’ll take you to see your uncle.”

"That won't give us a lot of time, with the deadline to claim the inheritance so close."

"I don't know any other way of handling it. In the meantime, you could get to know us."

She glanced at his dress shirt. "Do you always dress so formally on a PI job?"

"I was trying hard to make a good impression. It's not every day a guy meets a famous author."

Candice made a derisive sound.

"Well, it's true. How do you ensure no one learns the truth about you?"

"You mean when I sell the manuscript?"

"Yeah. Book signings. The like."

"All done online, as far as selling and publishing the manuscript. I do book signings during the new moon only."

"Maybe we could help you with a signing."

"How's that?" She seemed interested, but also wary.

"None of us can shift during the new moon, but those who have werewolf lines going back a few generations can shift at will during the new moon and avoid shifting during the full moon. We could maybe solicit a couple wolf shifters to come to some of your signings as wolves during the new moon."

"Some were born this way? You're kidding."

Owen felt bad for her, knowing she'd had no one to help her deal with this. "Yeah, see, there's a lot you need to know. I looked at your books online and noticed that you only write about white wolves."

"Right, because..." She leaned her back against the counter and folded her arms. "Don't tell me there are other types."

"Yeah. There are."

The timer went off, and she whipped around to take the cookies out of the oven and set them on top of the stove. "Red wolves? Gray wolves? I know Arctic wolves are a subspecies of gray wolves, but some of the other kind are werewolves too?"

"Yeah, even something else that we're just learning about."

"Coyotes?"

"Yeah. And jaguars."

She turned her head to the side, her chin down in a get-real look.

"Really. Who knows? There may be lions and tigers—"

"And bears, oh my."

He laughed.

"It would be cool to have real wolves at the signing, but I'd be afraid they might scare off potential readers."

"True. How long before the cookies cool?"

"Half an hour, all night, doesn't matter. Then I put frosting on them. Okay, so you say you've been managing this shifter business for seven years. You and your partners? You couldn't have fed a ravenous wolf cub, like I did, and have him bite every one of you."

"Uh, no. My PI partner, David, and I were bear hunting—"

She tilted her chin down and gave him the look that meant she didn't like hunters shooting wild animals.

"We never bagged one. In all the years we tried, we never came close. Until that day." He explained about David's heart attack and nearly losing him and the guide's pet Arctic wolves that had accompanied them to track the bear, instead of the guide using dogs.

"Wow. So the wolves who turned you and David

weren't exactly bad guys. They saved David's life in the only way they could, and they were trying to protect you and themselves from you giving them away."

"Yeah, except we wanted to resume our old lives, and we needed to tell our PI partners, Cameron and Gavin, what had happened. They only knew we had vanished on the hunt, so they came to Maine looking for us. The alpha female of the pack bit Cameron, and he accidentally shared what he was with Faith, turning her. At that point, Gavin was the only one who hadn't been turned. Later, I was sleeping so deeply as a wolf that Gavin got worried. He touched my chest to see if he could feel my heart beating. I felt something touching me, and half asleep, I whipped my head around and bit Gavin on the wrist. I felt terrible about it. We assumed he'd want to be just like us sooner or later, but if at least one of us could have driven us home without the trouble with shifting, it would have helped. What a nightmare it was for all of us to travel back to Seattle with so little control over our shifting!"

"Seattle?"

"Yeah. That's where we were born and raised and had our office. Wolves are extremely territorial, and when we arrived home, it didn't take long for a gray wolf shifter from a local pack to catch David and me ordering Starbucks drinks. We smelled him and were shocked that another wolf was there. He eyed us warily, didn't bother to order anything, and slunk right out of there. We thought we'd scared him off. We had barely picked up our drinks when a car rolled up, and two men got out. One was the gray pack's alpha male and the other his second-in-command. The alpha pack leader told us in a low, growly voice to get out of their territory—and pronto. We explained we were all from there and had a PI practice there, but he said to sell and move. No other pack was moving into their territory unless they wanted to die. Especially a newly turned Arctic wolf pack.

"Well, since we were newly turned, we weren't as knowledgeable about fighting other wolves, and we didn't know how big their pack was. So we made the decision to move. We kept running into other gray wolf packs as we made our way back east, and we finally ended up in northern Minnesota where there were no shifters and, in the winter, lots of snow."

"Wow, I would never have thought wolf shifter packs would be territorial like that. I'm glad you were able to find a place to settle where everyone's safe. I guess I got lucky too."

And in meeting Clara here, Owen knew he'd gotten damn lucky.

Owen's phone rang—a call from Cameron. He looked over at Candice and said, "Let me take this, and then we can go for a run." Into the phone, he said to Cameron, "Hey, listen, I'm here. Candice is an Arctic wolf like us. I'll explain later."

"Uh, okay. Soon."

"Yeah, we're going for a run," Owen told him, ending the call. He wasn't taking no for an answer as far as running with Candice as a wolf. The chance of meeting another Arctic female wolf was so rare that he wasn't going to let this opportunity to know her better pass. As a newly turned lone wolf, she would never have experienced running with another shifter wolf. Besides, Owen had every intention of convincing her to go with him to meet the pack. That meant meeting Cameron, Faith, and their kids, but also his footloose bachelor partners, and he wanted her to get to know him first. Maybe she'd be more interested in them. He could live with that, if she found happiness with their pack. In any event, she shouldn't be on her own.

But Owen still wanted the chance to be with her a while before he took her to see them.

"All right. I want you to know I'm not a pushover or anything, but I planned to run tonight anyway. It will be…different, running with another wolf. We run, then after we return and ice the cookies, you can take some back to your friends. When the new moon is here, I'll see my uncle and the lawyer and take care of that."

That was a start, but Owen still felt he had to convince her to meet the others. She shouldn't be running as a wolf alone. If she ever wanted a full-time guy in her life, settling down with a human wouldn't work. Changing someone could present all kinds of problems, as she well knew.

"You won't meet the others in the pack?"

"Maybe later."

He thought that meant never. She seemed satisfied with being a lone wolf. Then again, before she met him, she'd had no other choice. If she was anything like him, she had to adjust to the notion of being a wolf with a pack, so he needed to take it easy.

He started to unbutton his shirt before she changed her mind.

"Whoa, Mr. Alpha Wolf. You can strip off your clothes in the guest bedroom down that hall. Oh, and I *just* vacuumed. Try not to shed too much fur in the house." She hesitated, then retrieved her can of mace and raised her brows a little as if to say she was armed and dangerous, in case he had any notion of giving her grief.

Owen smiled back, loving her tenacity. She walked through the living room, disappeared into another room, then shut the door.

Feeling he'd won a small victory, which thrilled him, he headed for the guest bedroom decorated in forest greens and a moose motif. He quickly took off his clothes, shifted, and raced out of the bedroom and down the hall.

He met her coming out of the master bedroom as a wolf, and he recalled the day he'd first laid eyes on her standing across the river watching him. She was just as beautiful now, mostly white, but she had a soft tinge of gold on her lower body. She stood her ground, but she looked a little…startled. Maybe because he was a much bigger wolf. Even though she knew he was human too, he was certain she wasn't used to encountering other wolves this close up. Which was another reason she needed to join the pack.

He thought she would love Faith and Cameron's pups.

Owen moved toward her to greet her like wolves would do in friendship. She stepped back. He knew this was going to be a real learning experience for her, despite her having been a wolf for two years. She'd had no wolf socialization.

He took another step forward, and this time, she remained in place, ears perked, eyes on him, while he touched his nose to hers. Then she responded, and he took a relieved breath. He would have to take baby steps with her until she learned some of the wolf cues they all knew. Then he headed for the wolf door and she ran after him.

After that, they raced all over White Wolf Mountain in the snow, and Candice seemed to really enjoy her run in the wild. Owen ran alongside her for a while, wondering if she had ever howled. Maybe not. She might have been afraid to gather real wolves to her. And she would have no reason to howl. Yet it was part of who they were.

There was nothing out here but snow and more snow. He stopped, raised his chin, and howled. Then he looked at her to see if she'd give it a try. But she suddenly turned her attention to the west side of the mountain, ears perked, listening. He heard it too then, the low rumbling of snowmobiles in the distance—three of them.

Owen and Candice were on the back side of the mountain, and it would take them nearly an hour to make it through the thick snowdrifts to her home. Both of them headed that way, intent on avoiding the snowmobilers and the disaster their recklessness could create. The wolves couldn't outrun the snowmobilers, should they catch up to them. Not unless Owen and Candice reached the trees and the snowmobilers couldn't maneuver through them easily enough. He hoped that the humans wouldn't follow them.

The heavy snowfall was too recent, and the wind had begun to pick up. The slope was steep enough to provide the momentum for an avalanche. Even a small slide could prove deadly. One that might carry a snowmobiler off a cliff or into a tree could be just as dangerous as a heavier slide burying the rider. If they were smart, only one of the riders would traverse the slope at a time.

Owen and Candice still couldn't see the snowmobilers on the other side of the mountain, but they heard one of them suddenly turn toward the summit, most likely in a daredevil high-marking contest, accelerating and gaining momentum until he could no longer push his snowmobile upward due to the steepness of the grade and was forced to turn and ride back down.

He would have left his mark, and if they dared, the others would seek to make a higher mark than his. Owen hoped they were equipped with avalanche transceivers. They'd also need to know how to locate the distress signal to rescue someone who had triggered an avalanche and was buried. All Owen cared about was ensuring that Candice and he didn't end up in a slide if the snowmobilers set one off.

The second snowmobiler rose to the top, and though Owen shouldn't have cared about anything but their own safety, he was curious who would make the highest mark. Total guy competitiveness coming to the forefront, though Owen wouldn't do anything so foolish and endanger his life and others'. If the other two were sitting there watching from close by, they could all be buried if the snow began to slide.

The second snowmobiler started to descend the mountain, and then all hell broke loose.

Owen heard the sound of the snow sliding downhill, the way it roared as it gathered speed, and the snowmobilers gunning their machines to move out of its devastating path. He thought he and Candice were far enough on the other side of the mountain to avoid the onslaught. They waited in case anyone needed their help. Even though they were wolves, they would have to act quickly. Chances of survival for a victim buried under the snow dropped drastically after fifteen minutes. They wouldn't have time to return to the house and call for an emergency crew.

Then they heard one of the men shouting and no others responding.

Owen took off running, hoping the guy would accept the wolves' help.

Chapter 3

Candice couldn't believe she was going to attempt to rescue snowmobilers who seemed to have a death wish when she was running as a wolf. But she wasn't letting Owen do this by himself. She just hoped that no one would want to scare off the evil wolves that suddenly appeared as if they were sharks coming at the sound of the dinner bell ringing.

Her heart was pounding even harder than when they'd first heard the snowmobilers. She knew how dangerous people could be around wolves. Then the avalanche happened, and her adrenaline had shot through the roof. It continued to flood her bloodstream as she worried about the men, the unstable snow, and Owen's and her safety if others saw them as wolves.

When they finally reached the slide area, one man was probing the snow frantically with an avalanche pole. The other two weren't in sight, and Candice feared that the snow had buried them completely. The sole snowmobiler who had escaped the avalanche hadn't spied them yet because he was too busy trying to locate one of his friends. Being white against the white snow helped camouflage Owen and her for the moment.

They moved cautiously across the slide, listening for movement only they could hear, and smelled for the other snowmobiler's scent. Candice was also looking for abnormalities in the snow indicating anyone might be beneath it. Then she noticed a disturbance in the top layer a few feet away and prayed that someone had moved under it, trying frantically to claw his way out, and caused the collapsed debris.

She headed for it. Owen stayed close to her, watching the other man periodically while she concentrated on listening, looking, and smelling the snow. She heard something moving beneath it and started digging with her paws, frantically trying to reach the man. She couldn't imagine anything worse than being buried alive.

Owen started to dig near her, but far enough away to give her room. The snow was flying out behind them as they hurried to uncover the top of a black helmet. They kept digging around the man's helmet to free his face so he could breathe. And he did, thank God, gasping for air. Then they began to dig away at the snow covering his chest, trying to uncover him enough so he could wriggle out a bit and help himself if he wasn't injured too badly.

He didn't move though, just stared up at them as if he couldn't believe what he was seeing.

They turned to look in the direction of the other man, who was standing with the pole in his hand, just staring at them. So, they'd been discovered, but they still had to help to dig the man out. The first man hadn't even begun to use his shovel, which meant he probably hadn't located the other man yet.

Owen barked as if trying to tell him that they had unburied his friend and to come dig him out the rest of the way.

Candice also started to bark, then continued clawing at the snow. She wanted to go after the third guy too, but if they could unbury one, that was better than none.

The first man suddenly came running with the shovel in hand, and she was glad for that.

Wary of him, she and Owen ran in a wide circle around him to keep him from drawing near them as he approached his friend. He reached the place they'd been digging, saw that his friend was partially unburied, and began frantically using the shovel to dig him out. "Hang on. Just hang on!" he called to his friend.

For the moment, he forgot all about the wolves, which was just what they'd wanted to happen.

Candice and Owen ran to the place where the man had been probing with the pole. Thinking she heard someone under the snow trying to call out, Candice put her nose practically on the snow, perking her ears up and twisting her head to hear better. It had to be the third snowmobiler. She began to dig like she had before, and so did Owen. Together, they made a great wolf rescue team. Wouldn't the humans be amazed? But they couldn't let them know they'd helped. She could imagine being caught and then studied. Maybe even "trained" for future rescue missions. Maybe the men would believe the wolves were wolf dogs and someone's pets.

She couldn't help but feel appreciative that Owen was with her. She didn't think she would have had the nerve to help humans in a disaster like this if she'd been alone. Working alongside him, she felt more equipped to deal with the emergency. She hadn't thought to bark like a dog, so she knew she still had some learning to do about their kind. He definitely was ahead of her in that.

They finally found part of the snowmobile, and the guy wedged underneath it. As soon as they'd unburied him enough that his face was freed and he could breathe fresh air, he began gasping to fill his lungs.

Thankfully, the snowmobile had partially protected him from some of the snow, and he had a pocket of air that had helped him hold on for a while longer. They dug around his face and shoulders where the snow was up to his neck. He was lying on his back like the other man had been. Like that man, he was staring at them as if he couldn't believe what he was seeing. They barked to let the first man know they'd found his remaining friend, then continued to dig because he was so busy trying to extricate the other man.

Candice hoped the unharmed man hadn't lost his cell phone and had called for help. She didn't see his snowmobile anywhere. She was glad she and Owen had made a difference in the men's survival. Either or both of the men could still succumb to their injuries, but at least they were alive and breathing on their own. She licked the snow off the red-helmeted guy's face while Owen continued to dig out the snow around the man's chest. She started digging again farther down, trying to find his legs. At least the avalanche hadn't buried the snowmobilers too deep. She'd heard of victims' bodies that couldn't be recovered until spring thaw.

The wailing of sirens alerted them that emergency crews were on the way. Her heart skipped a couple of beats. Candice was grateful that the unharmed man had been able to reach emergency services. Reception could be dicey out here sometimes. The arrival of the rescue teams also meant she and Owen had to leave before the rescuers saw them. She continued to work with Owen, allowing it to be his call on when they had to disappear.

Since he'd been a wolf longer, she assumed he would know better. She didn't want to run off before they absolutely had to.

"Hey!" someone called from the other side of the mountain. "Where are you?"

The man who was still digging around his friend shouted, "We're here! Over here!"

"We're on our way!" a rescuer shouted back from just around the bend.

Candice glanced at Owen, who was hurriedly digging deeper. Both of them were now in a pit where they'd been working on the snow. They weren't very visible to anyone, but she didn't want to be caught here. What if men went in search of her and Owen later? What if news crews tried to capture images of the rescue dogs that had saved the men? Especially when wolf biologists identified them as a couple of Arctic wolves and not dogs.

Owen was so busy that she thought maybe he had forgotten he was a wolf. She woofed at him.

He nodded and leaped out of the pit, waiting for Candice to follow him before he raced off. She jumped up beside him, ready to run.

"Wait," the partially buried snowmobiler called out weakly to them, as if they had reassured him that they would get him out, but now they were abandoning him to his fate.

She woofed at him, jumped back into the pit, and licked his face to reassure him he'd be all right. Then she jumped back out.

He had trained emergency rescuers coming for him. She and Owen couldn't do anything more for him than they had at this point. Still, she hated leaving him when he seemed to feel she was someone he could rely on, someone who had made him feel as though he'd live through this ordeal. Hopefully, he would be smarter the next time. Or not. If he could beat death once, why not again?

Owen bounded down the mountain away from the emergency crews and buried men, but also away from her home. She was right on the big wolf's heels. She didn't know where he was going until she realized he didn't want to head straight back to her place. *Great.* She was all for rushing there, and she would have, figuring she'd be safer inside her home no matter what. How would she have explained the trail left by a rescue dog that looked like a wolf that had headed right to her wolf door and gone inside? Then again, without visual evidence, no one would be able to verify the men's stories if they claimed wolves had rescued them. Who would ever believe it?

That gave her a bit of relief.

Maybe the snowstorm would obliterate their tracks. She realized, without question, that Owen was staying the night with her. *In* the guest room. Though she didn't want to join a pack, she loved how caring he was and how protective, even if it meant risking his own safety. She trusted his instincts and followed him away from her home, across an icy river—their paw pads helping to keep them from slipping on the frozen riverbank—and then swimming to the other side. She couldn't imagine doing this in her human form. It was nearly dusk, and she was exhausted when he led her back home. She'd begun to think he'd lost the way and she was lost with him.

She could hardly wait to push through her door. She paused and waited for him to join her. Then she licked his nose in thanks, and he licked hers back, their gazes holding for an instant. She woofed and dashed off again for the house. Realization dawned that if someone had captured them, she wouldn't have been alone. That his pack would have known there was trouble when he never reported back in. That someone would have come to their rescue. If he'd been caught and she had remained free, she could have called his friends for help. If men had captured her, she knew beyond a doubt that Owen would have come to her rescue, no matter the danger to himself.

She realized that was what a pack was all about.

Sure, she'd written about pack dynamics in her werewolf romance books, but it was one thing to imagine what it would be like with a hunky hero at her side and quite another to be living that during real danger.

Owen couldn't believe the trouble they'd found themselves in. The buried snowmobilers never would have made it if he and Candice hadn't been there to help them. He'd hated taking Candice into the dangerous situation though, not wanting to risk her life. But he knew she wouldn't have returned home without him, and he'd figured that two of them could work at rescuing the men better than one. They hadn't even been sure at first if anyone had made it out alive. He was just glad one man had been able to call for an emergency crew, and that he and Candice hadn't gotten caught.

He was still playing the whole scenario out in his mind, unable to let go of it. The avalanche sliding down the hill. The snowmobile engines running full out. And then all he'd heard were the wind whipping the tree branches around ahead of them and the blowing snow surrounding them. No matter how much he'd wanted to protect them both from discovery, he couldn't have let the men die. He'd had to try his best to give them a chance to live.

As soon as they reached Candice's place, Owen intended to shift, dress, and pack his bag. Then he'd leave and find a nearby hotel to stay for the night. He'd return tomorrow and again try to convince her to go home with him. To meet the pack. To learn that they were a good group of people, and maybe she'd want to join them.

They finally reached the clearing where her house sat. Owen was amazed at what a fast runner she was, even though he was much taller than her and she had to be exhausted after the workout they'd both had. She dove in through the wolf door first, and then he followed. She raced off for her bedroom, and he was heading for the guest bedroom when he hit the red-and-white snowman throw rug covering the wooden floor. The rug went sliding—and so did he. Unable to stop himself, he slid into the kitchen island, jamming his right rear leg against the cabinets. *Damn it!*

If he lived here, that rug would have to go up on the wall for decoration, or somewhere else out of the footpath. Not that it would normally cause problems, he thought. Just when dashing through the house as a wolf, which he wouldn't usually be doing. Glad she hadn't seen him take the spill, he got to his feet and felt a twinge of pain around his ankle. Hell, he'd twisted it slightly. He hoped the sprain would disappear quickly.

He reached the guest room and shifted, but as soon as he did, Candice called out to him, "Are you all right?"

Candice came out of her bedroom wearing jeans, a white sweater, and socks, boot slippers in hand, fully intending to make them dinner. When she saw the throw rug scrunched up next to the kitchen island, she knew exactly what had happened.

Ever since she'd started decorating for Christmas, she'd meant to hang the rug somewhere and put down another one that was a lot more slip-resistant. She lifted the rug off the floor and set it on a chair in the living room for now.

"Yeah, I'm all right," Owen hollered.

"I'm going to fix dinner. Do you have anything to wear that isn't quite so formal?" She thought maybe he kept something casual in the car for emergencies.

"I've got other clothes in a bag in the car. I always take spare clothes. If the car had broken down somewhere along the way in this weather, I could have been in real trouble without warm winter gear. That is, if I couldn't just shift." He limped out of the bedroom. Not a bad sprain, she thought, but a slight one.

Candice held out her hand palm up for his keys. "Let me grab your bag. How badly did you sprain your ankle?"

"It's just a twinge." He handed her the keys.

"Which can worsen if you're trying to trudge through the snow to reach your car." Where he'd parked, it was still pretty deep, and she didn't want him to have to walk through the snow if he didn't have to. "I have an ice pack in the freezer… Just sit and I'll secure it for you."

"I'm fine, really."

"Sit," she said as if speaking to her dog.

Owen took a seat at her counter, his mouth curving a little, his blue eyes smiling.

"On a recliner...any of the three that are part of the sectional couch. You'll need to elevate your foot."

"It's not that—"

She gave him a look that said she was in charge of this situation, then pulled out the ice pack and handed it to him. "I'll be right back." She hated that he'd hurt himself, especially when it was her fault. She hurried outside and unlocked the blue SUV's door. His bag was on the backseat, and she smelled that he'd had coffee on the trip, cheeseburger, fries, but no trash. Impressed he was such a neat guy, she grabbed the black bag and relocked his door, then went back inside.

"Need any help changing?" The words were out before she realized what she was saying.

Owen smiled so wickedly that she dropped the bag on the sectional recliner next to his and sat at the other end to pull off her boots.

"I planned on going to a hotel tonight," he said, unbuttoning his shirt and setting it aside. "Do you know any close by?"

He was seriously hot, with well-molded abs and biceps, plus a light dusting of dark hair trailing down to his dress pants. He had to stand up to pull them off, and she jumped off the recliner to help him.

He chuckled. "I really can do this all on my own."

"And then if you injured yourself further, you could sue me."

He laughed. "Okay, I'm all yours." He held on to her

shoulder while she unfastened his pants. Once he'd stepped out of them, she laid them on the other recliner and helped him into a pair of jeans.

They heard emergency vehicles' sirens close to the mountain, leaving the area. "Good, they're on their way to the hospital." Candice helped him put on his socks and noticed he winced when she pulled the one on, no matter how gently she tried. She pointed toward his snow boots. "You don't need to wear those. You can have dinner and elevate your foot and put some ice on it. I'll fix dinner in a minute, and then you can stay the night."

He pulled on a sweatshirt and sat back down. "Thanks, Candice. I appreciate it."

She set a Christmas tree lap blanket next to him and then situated the ice pack around his ankle. "Remove it—"

"Right. I know the drill. Some people have left ice packs on to take care of a sprain and ended up with major frostbite."

"Exactly." She headed into the kitchen. "I still can't believe we managed to locate those men."

"You know what the statistics of survival are when snow buries them like that, right?"

"Not good. If they'd had to wait for someone to come dig those men out?" She shook her head. "We had a similar case like this last year. The guy's friend actually reached him and managed to dig him out enough so he could breathe. He was lucky, having been under only about ten minutes and having had a pocket of air. But he was suffering from hypothermia and hypoxia. He survived though." She opened the freezer door. "Steaks all right?"

"Way to a man's heart."

She laughed. "I knew my hearing and sense of smell were good, but I never suspected that I could hear a man buried under the snow. At first, I saw the strange depression in the snow in that one area. I figured one of the men might have been moving around underneath it."

"I agree. It was a miracle. What would we have done if all of them had been buried?"

"Kept on digging."

"But without a cell phone? Without one of them being able to make the distress call? It could have ended a lot differently."

"I agree. Do you want baked potatoes? Spinach?"

"Both sound good. I need to call Cameron and let him know I'm staying the night."

"Do you have to?" She didn't want his friend thinking something more was coming of this, like she was leaving her home to join their pack, or that she might even be interested in something more—like mating a wolf. If real werewolves were anything like she pictured them to be.

"Yeah. I need to let him know about the accident. Even though nothing happened that would cause the pack alarm, we still keep one another informed in case we find ourselves in a potentially dangerous situation. Plus, he knew about the snowstorm headed this way and tried to talk me out of leaving until it had passed, but I wanted to tell you about the inheritance as soon as I could. Cameron might worry that I'm trying to return in the snowstorm."

Candice realized how nice that must be, to have others watching her back. And she hadn't even thanked Owen for coming to talk to her.

"Thanks for coming here with the news. I was busy finishing up a book, and I hadn't read my messages for a couple of days. I really appreciate it. I still can't believe my parents left me anything."

"I wish it was the phase of the new moon already so I could take you there now to resolve it." He pulled out his cell phone, but before he could make the call, it rang. He glanced at the ID. "Well, Cameron's calling me instead." He answered the call. "Yeah, Cameron, we just got back from the—"

Candice stuck the steaks and potatoes in a baking pan and put them in the oven. She was going to fix them something to drink when she heard a pause in Owen's conversation and turned to see what was wrong.

His eyes were wide, and his mouth open in surprise. Now what? "Television? Hold on."

The mention of the television made her think of news reports. She should have figured that the news would be reporting the accident already. But Owen hadn't even told Cameron that they'd been at the scene, so why would he say anything to Owen about it? Not unless the news reporter had mentioned two Arctic wolves rescuing two snowmobile victims in South Dakota.

Owen turned on the TV, and there on the mountain stood a female reporter, talking about the situation during the final stages of the rescue. The news crew had come well after Owen and Candice had left, so that was good.

Then the reporter was interviewing the uninjured snowmobiler.

"Yeah, yeah, I swear they were wolves. White wolves. You know, that live in the Arctic. I was still probing around in the snow, trying to locate Kent, when I saw the two wolves digging out Wally. I didn't know what to do. Chase them off? Had they planned to eat him? I figured if they could get at Wally, then I could run over and chase them off before they bit him. I hadn't even found Kent yet. Then they barked at me, as if they were dogs and wanted me to come rescue him. I grabbed my shovel, and they gave me a wide berth. I figured they thought I was going to hit them, which I was prepared to do if they attacked me. But why not come after me if they were hungry? Why not just eat me? Less work, right?"

Candice was barely breathing. No one would believe the men. What were the odds that two Arctic wolves would even be in the area? And further, that they would have rescued two snowmobilers?

"Are you sure they weren't big, white dogs?" the reporter asked.

"Nah, I know a dog when I see one. Hell, here's a video of them."

Candice's heart did a triple beat.

"Wally said the wolves saved him. He wanted me to take a picture of them to show to his parents. I did one better and videotaped them at work. No one would ever have believed us otherwise."

"And there you have it. Man's earliest best friend. In this case, two Arctic wolves, possibly wolf dogs, rescuing two of the snowmobilers who were victims of the avalanche you see here today."

Candice couldn't believe her eyes when she saw the short clip of the video the snowmobiler had taken. She figured he'd be tweeting it for the whole world to see next. Not that anyone would recognize her in her wolf form, but what if tons of people descended on the area, looking for the white wolves that had rescued the men to take pictures of them too? What if hunters descended on the area, wanting to kill the white wolves?

What if wolf biologists came to capture the white wolves to study them? What if...what if she needed to move now? She could just imagine being cooped up in the house for weeks when she couldn't bring the shifting under wraps. Especially with the full moon on its way. That was the only thing that made living out here by herself worth the trouble. She could run as a wolf without any problems.

She also couldn't believe Owen's pack was already aware of the situation. But she supposed any mention of wolves got their attention. Was Cameron angry with them for helping the men and risking discovery? Or just worried about them? Were he and his mate their pack leaders? She wondered how that would work. Did the wolves marry?

"Okay, Cameron. I'm staying the night, which is why I was about to call you. And tell you about Candice... Hell, the damn snowmobiler was supposed to be digging out his friend. Who would have thought he'd grab his cell phone and shoot a video?... Okay, thanks. We went all over hell and back, so we didn't leave a trail straight to the house. Crossed an icy river even. We're supposed to have snow tonight, so hopefully that will help cover the tracks... All right."

Owen glanced at her before continuing his conversation with Cameron. "Uh, yeah, about that. I hate to mention it, but one of your kids bit Candice two years ago while she was camping in our territory... Yes, the romance author who writes about Arctic werewolves. It isn't just an ironic twist of fate that she happens to be one of us. Remember the incident with the beef jerky? That was it. Had to be Corey because Faith smelled beef jerky on his breath. He said he found it by a campsite, and nobody was around. Candice said the wolf pup broke the skin on her hand. He might not have realized he'd bitten her. I'm trying to convince her to come home and see the rest of the pack. Not only because she's an Arctic wolf like us, but because she's actually one of us because of Corey." Pause. "Okay, I'll let her know. Thanks. Bye."

"Let me know what?" Candice moved into the kitchen to ice the ginger cookies.

"Wait, I helped bake them. I want to help frost them too."

"You're not trying to butter me up, are you?" She smiled. "Or, you just want to lick the rest of the bowl?"

Owen got off the couch to join her. "I just figured this was the fun part."

She laughed. "All parts of making cookies are fun. Eating them especially. What about your ankle?"

"It's not that bad."

"What did Cameron tell you that you need to let me know?"

"That they're dying to meet you, and that you and Corey need to have a talk."

"I hope Cameron isn't going to make too big a deal of it. It was too long ago to worry about it." She began to bring out the ingredients for the icing. "Okay, I'll set this up for you at the bar so you can sit there and decorate." She was having fun with him here. She'd never imagined she'd have company—a wolf at that—who would help her make cookies after rescuing victims of a snowslide.

After Candice mixed the icing, she handed Owen a

container of sugar sprinkles and the bowl of icing. She assumed he could figure this part out on his own.

She was trying not to think of the fallout from the wolf rescue video. But she couldn't help herself. On her cell phone, she pulled up the video the snowmobiler had made of them and shared on YouTube, showing Owen and her digging out the one man as fast as wolves could dig, snow flying all over the place. And yep, they looked like two white wolves, a male and female. A mated pair.

"Can I see it?" Owen asked as he coated every square inch of cookie with frosting and then piled on the sugar sprinkles.

The sugar was nearly as thick as the cookies. Maybe she should have given him some direction, but she liked seeing him having fun with them.

"Shows our good side," he said, watching the video.

Candice groaned. "I never imagined the guy would stop to pull out his cell phone to video record it."

"Have you seen the one where the man stopped to prop up his phone to record himself saving a victim from a car crash? So yeah, I can see it. Who would have believed two Arctic wolves rescued his buddies if he hadn't recorded it? No one. Already over a million views, and the shares keep going." Owen looked up from the cell phone. "You ought to share it with your fans. Are you going to expand your wolves to red and gray now? Jaguar shifters?"

"I guess that will be the next thing." She lifted a maids a-milking cookie off the tray and took a bite. "Wow, nice and sweet. Great job."

He looked down at the cookies. "You don't think I put too much frosting on them, do you?"

Chapter 4

Later that evening, Candice and Owen had dinner, and she talked about what growing up in the Houston area was like, compared to living near the mountains now.

"It's a lot different. I think the hardest part was getting used to snow and ice—preparing for power outages and the like. Then again, we had power outages in Houston sometimes from storms. It's quiet out here. No traffic to speak of. Town's about half an hour away, but driving ten miles to somewhere in Houston could take me that long with traffic. No dating. No seeing family, unless they're wolves too. No socializing unless it's online. And then everyone thinks you're perfectly normal. Hopefully, no one in town realizes the only time they see lots of me is during the new moon."

"Probably not, unless they're hunting werewolves."

"That would be just great. Good thing no one knows about us, right?"

"No, really. We had trouble with werewolf hunters shortly after we were turned. Talk about shocking. They had been searching for Bigfoot, not that it's real, but they saw the woman shifting who had bitten Cameron. Then they were after us."

Candice closed her gaping mouth.

"Yeah. I mean, how many werewolf hunters would really be out there? Probably a slim chance there would be any more. We just got lucky."

"What happened?"

"In our world, we change them or…well, eliminate them. We can't allow anyone to expose us for what we are."

"Wow." Candice couldn't believe it. She had never considered what would happen if anyone actually caught her shifting. She always did it at home. Which brought to mind her encounter with Corey. "What if the little boy, Corey, had shifted in front of me at the campfire?"

"He couldn't have. The kids can't shift unless the mom does, not until they're older and can be reliable about it. Corey couldn't have unless his mother had."

In her stories, werewolves shifted at thirteen, to give them time to mature a little bit. She frowned. "How did she have her kids? As wolf pups or kids?"

"Kids. Though because of the trouble with shifting that we were having, she very well could have had them as wolf pups. It might have been easier on her too. It was during the new moon though, and she had them in a hospital. The other good thing is that our blood indicates we are what we appear to be. If someone took a sample of our blood when we're wolf, they'd find all wolf DNA. When we're humans, all human DNA."

"Wow. Okay. Good to know."

"Also, since humans take so long to develop, our wolf half-growth is slowed down. Normally, a yearling wolf, one that's a year old, is a little smaller than a full-grown wolf and hasn't filled out. Yet they're much more adapted to the wild. Our kids are still young at five years old in their human form, and their wolf half is still a pup."

"Corey was how old in his human form when he bit me then?"

"Four. He's six now, but in his wolf form, he's still a pup. We hadn't really thought of what it would be like with the kids in their wolf forms since we were turned and didn't go through that process. We also homeschool our kids."

"All right, so back to the case of the werewolf hunters. What happened?"

"Two tried to kill us, and we managed to save the third hunter. A red wolf by the name of Leidolf, the leader of a Portland, Oregon, red wolf pack, who was born a *lupus garou*, joined us, turned the other hunter, and made him one of his pack. The other two hunters tried to kill us and we had no choice but to take them down instead. Leidolf helped us to learn about ourselves. We were totally clueless."

"Like I've been."

"Exactly. Which is why, even if you don't want to join our pack, if you come visit us, you could learn more about what it's like to be a *lupus garou*."

"A...what?"

"Werewolf. That's the fancy name for us."

Candice tried to think of anything else she could ask him about being werewolves, but after making dinner, cleaning the dishes, and drinking a hot, caramelized café mocha with him, she was ready for a whirlpool bath to soak her muscles and then retire to bed. She wished she could offer him a bath like that too, as hard as he'd worked to free the snowmobilers, but she didn't want to give him ideas.

Then again, she could offer. She'd just read a book or watch something on TV for a while in the living room while he used her tub.

She had to admit she'd been feeling like she was the last werewolf on earth—although she knew there had to be a family of them because one of them had bitten her. She hadn't thought bachelor male wolves were out there—Arctic wolves like her—who had the same problem as her. No possibility for an Arctic wolf mate. Unless they socialized with the pack that had turned Cameron, Owen, and David in the first place.

She got the impression from Owen that they would rather *not* deal with that wolf pack again. He had to understand she had some of the same reservations about meeting the wolf pack that had turned her, even though it was an accident. Turning somebody to have a mate wasn't a good idea either. She could just imagine turning a guy and then him hating her for having done so. There would be no going back either.

"Cameron won't be too upset with his son about turning me, will he?"

"It's been two years, so unless Corey has turned others since then, probably not real mad, but he would be even less angry if you saw Corey and let him know how you felt that he had turned you and upset your whole life. The kids were born *lupus garous*, so they don't know any other way of life. It's hard for them to understand what it means to be human first and then have to live with the change."

Candice let out her breath. "I'll think about it." She didn't want the boy to be in trouble for an accident that happened so long ago, but he needed to know how real changing someone was. Just telling him he'd done it wouldn't be the same as seeing her in person. "Would you like to use my whirlpool bath to soak your muscles?"

He raised his brows a little.

"I'll just watch a show in here while you take a bath."

He smiled then and shook his head. "A quick shower will be fine."

"All right. If you need anything, feel free to knock on my door. You can snack on anything you'd like in the kitchen if you become hungry. Towels are in the linen closet near the guest room. Otherwise, I'll see you in the morning."

"'Night, Candice. Thanks for everything—dinner, the cookies, helping me rescue the men. Thanks for running with me too. If not for the snowmobilers, it would have been a perfect wolf run."

"It was good we were out there, or they wouldn't have made it. Not both men, anyway. We worked well together, I thought. Now I just hope the guy's video doesn't cause trouble for us."

"As long as no one tracks us back here and the snow fills up the tracks tonight, no worries."

"Except if others begin to watch for me when I go running later." That was a real concern for her.

"You can always join us." Owen looked hopeful she'd still change her mind.

"That's more wolves. More of a chance to get caught."

"It hasn't been a problem for us. Well, I'll let you go to bed and see you in the morning."

"I have another ice pack chilled in the freezer if you need it later."

"Thanks. My ankle should be as good as new tomorrow."

She did love that about wolf genetics. They healed so much faster. She had to be careful about seeing the doctor with problems because of it. "'Night, Owen."

"'Night, Candice."

And then she headed to her bedroom.

She'd taken a lovely, hot bath, enjoying the feel of the silky, peach bubbles against her skin until the water began to cool and she turned off the jets. Then she heard crunching footsteps in the snow outside near her bedroom window. She couldn't imagine it would be her wolf guest, not when he had a sprained ankle. She hurried out of the bath, dried off, and threw on some sweats, socks, boots, and her jacket.

She yanked on a white wool cap, glad her hair was dry, then grabbed her can of mace and headed for the back door to see what had made the crunching noise in the crisp snow. But what she saw made her pause—a flashlight briefly shining against her closed blinds. She hesitated.

Then she turned on the patio lights, opened the blinds on the upper part of the back door, and peered out. She didn't see anyone, but she knew what she'd heard and seen. It had sounded like a two-footed creature. Human. Considering he'd flashed a light in her windows, she knew it had to be.

She readied her can of mace, unlocked the door, and pulled it open. She stared out into the dark, but couldn't see anything in the woods. Glancing down to see if there were any human footprints, she found only the wolves'. Had the man tracked their wolf prints here?

Candice hadn't even considered doing it after they got home, but she should have shoveled the snow off her back patio. Yet, she couldn't have gotten rid of the tracks leading to the wolf door.

She shut and locked the back door, and though she

hadn't wanted to bother Owen, she thought he should know that they might have trouble. Who would have made the effort to follow them all the way here? Across a river and back through it again even?

All she could think of was a news-hungry reporter. That's all she needed. Maybe it would be good to leave for a time. Just so that if she needed to run as a wolf, she could do it where others like her felt it was safe. She didn't imagine the pesky news reporter would follow her all the way to Minnesota.

And eventually, everyone would stop looking for the white wolves.

Owen was surprised to hear a soft tapping at his door. "Yeah?" He hurried to throw on a pair of boxer briefs before answering. Candice stood in the doorway with a can of mace in her hand, dressed for the snowy outdoors. "This reminds me of earlier, when you answered the door with that can of mace. I didn't do anything wrong, did I?"

"Someone followed our wolf tracks." She whipped around and headed down the hall.

He hurried after her, but she turned and glanced at his black boxer briefs. "You might need a few more clothes than that if you plan to explore outside. If you think your ankle can handle it."

Turning back toward his room, Owen replied, "I'll be right there, though it would serve the trespasser right if I ran outside as a wolf and greeted him."

"Why hadn't I thought of that?" She'd been thinking about hiding their secret rather than exposing them more.

Owen headed back to the guest room and dressed.

He'd never expected this turn of events. Candice seemed spooked, and he hated that anyone would bother her, but he was glad he was here to help alleviate her worry. He soon joined her in the still-dark living room as she went to the back door and peered out the window.

He moved in beside her but didn't see anything. "Think he's still out there?"

"Maybe. Watching the house? Seeing what we might do? He should be afraid we'd let loose the wolves."

"They only rescue people, remember?"

"They're wild animals. Unpredictable," she said.

"True."

"How's your ankle? I really don't want you traipsing around out there. I just wanted you to know we might have company."

He pulled his Glock from his jacket.

She stared at it.

"PI with a license to carry a concealed weapon. I'll take a look around."

"What if *he's* got a gun?"

"Do you think he intends to break into a place he thinks might house a couple of wolves?"

"Probably not. He was just trying to see where they lived."

Which was what Owen was thinking. He wanted to be prepared, just in case. "You stay here. I'll take a quick look around."

"Your ankle?"

"It's fine."

"If we do have a snoopy reporter hanging around out there, maybe it wouldn't hurt for me to go with you to see your pack for a few days."

He smiled at her, then grew serious, knowing she didn't feel she had any alternative. "Okay, sounds like a plan. Lock the door after me."

"Are you sure you don't want me to come out too?"

"Nah. I'll be fine. And if I don't have someone walking in the snow next to me, I'll be able to pick up the sound of someone else's footfalls better."

"All right. If you're not back in half an hour, I'm calling the police."

"Wait about an hour, just in case. If we don't have to involve them, so much the better. At least until the snow covers the wolf tracks overnight." When Owen went out into the snow, he didn't need long to discover where a man with size 10½ shoes had stood in the forest. The man's flashlight would have followed the wolf prints to the patio, and then he could have shined it on the back door and seen the wolf door. He hadn't actually come up on the patio. He probably didn't want to leave *his* footprints there.

Owen walked around a bit and found that the guy had followed his own tracks back out of there. Though Owen couldn't imagine that the man had crossed the river in the night and risked drowning. He had to be freezing as it was. Owen would check it out tomorrow. The guy might even be an icicle by then. Couldn't be helped.

He returned to the house where Candice was fretfully waiting at the door, watching him walk up onto the patio. "He's gone," Owen said as she let him into the house.

"A man?"

"Size 10½ snow boots, and probably about frozen if he crossed the river where we did."

She opened her mouth to speak, and Owen quickly said, "I'm not chasing him down to rescue him."

She smiled. "Thanks. I promise I won't get you up again."

"No worries. If you need me, just holler."

"Thanks. Good night." And then she returned to her bedroom.

That worked out well. Not that Owen was glad someone was snooping around her house, looking for wolves—and he couldn't imagine it would be for any other reason. But he hadn't been sure how he was going to convince her to come home with him, and now she was agreeable.

Despite not intending to go out in the middle of the night to look for the man who had been trespassing, Owen couldn't stop worrying about whether someone was out there freezing to death. He finally said to hell with it, stripped out of his clothes, shifted, and headed for the back door.

As soon as he was outside, he began to smell for the man's scent. Owen didn't find just the man's. He found Candice's too. Her recent scent. Like now, not earlier. Owen was really glad he'd decided to go out and look for the man. Surprised she'd do so, he realized she really had a heart of gold. He wanted to keep Candice safe too.

The snow was already falling, collecting on his top coat of fur. It wouldn't reach his skin where the second coat provided great insulation from the cold. All wolves did well in the snow. But Arctic wolves' legs and ears were shorter, so they did even better in the frigid weather.

He couldn't believe Candice would go after the man without asking him to come too. Then again, he could. She was certain he practically had a broken leg, and he had said he wouldn't go out to rescue the man. Owen had to admit his ankle was bothering him, but he wouldn't stop until he found her.

He must have trudged through the misty snow for more than half an hour when he saw her standing near a road. Then she turned and saw him. She gave a little woof and dashed through the snow to greet him, nipping his neck as if in scolding, or maybe a love bite. He wasn't sure which. He licked her face, choosing to believe she'd given him a love bite. Then they headed home, but he didn't race back because he was trying to protect his ankle. He would be fine by tomorrow, if he could just rest it the remainder of the night. When she realized he wasn't keeping up with her, she ran back to him and stayed next to him as if she were his wolf mate, giving him solace. He could sure get used to this.

When they reached the house, Candice ran into her bedroom. Owen headed for his. But she called out to him, "You were supposed to be resting your ankle."

He shifted in the hallway. "You were supposed to be sleeping," he called back. He entered the guest room, threw on a pair of boxer briefs, and walked back into the living room, turning on the light and wanting to know what she'd discovered.

She came out wearing blue fleece pajamas covered in white fluffy sheep. She looked so huggable that he nearly forgot why he'd come out to see her. "He got in a red pickup truck and headed for town. He was wearing an old olive-green winter army parka with a fur-trimmed hood, ski pants, and snow boots. He never knew I followed him, because he used his flashlight to stick to the tracks he'd made in the snow and was looking forward the whole time. He didn't look like he was suffering from hypothermia or anything."

"Good. We'll leave in the morning and be gone until we can settle this business with your uncle and the lawyer. By the time you return, the news of the wolves will be old news, and you can get on with your life." Or hopefully decide to stay with his pack.

"Thanks for going out to look for him. I couldn't sleep, knowing he could freeze to death out there."

"Me either."

Candice didn't look like she believed Owen had heard her leave and run to catch up to her.

He smiled. "No, I wouldn't have woken you either. I wasn't surprised to see you'd gone out though. Well, not *too* surprised."

Owen *was* surprised when she closed the gap between them and pulled him in for a hug. "Thanks."

He wanted more than the soft, cuddly wolf in a hugging embrace. He bent his head to kiss her, and she lifted her head. He thought that meant she was agreeable, and he wasn't waiting to find out.

At first, he pressed his mouth gently against hers, but when she didn't seem to want to stop at just that, he pushed for more, his hand at her back, keeping her close against his body, his other caressing her soft, fleece-covered back. He was already turned on, and he knew she could feel how much so. He could smell her pheromones responding in eagerness and felt his jump-starting too. His hand moved up to her neck, and he caressed her soft skin as he deepened the kiss.

Candice kissed him back with abandon as if she'd missed this part of her life as a wolf, and yet, she'd never felt anything like it—a wolf-to-wolf encounter of the most pleasurable kind. He realized the only interaction she'd had with wolves had been a bad one—Corey biting her. Owen was glad to give her a new experience. A good one. To demonstrate what could happen when two wolves showed any affection for each other, how their pheromones would drive the need.

He was damned intrigued. She seemed to be too.

His heart was racing wildly, her pulse just as fast. He hadn't expected a firestorm of need to hit him all at once, but then he realized he was in the same predicament as she was. He'd never kissed a wolf before.

She opened her mouth to caress his tongue with her own before moaning softly. This had to stop. Before they went too far. She probably didn't know that their kind mated for life, just like real wolves did.

Candice pulled her mouth away from his, her beautiful eyes darkened with lust, and Owen was certain his were just as dark. She didn't pull her body away from his, as if enjoying the intimacy just a little while longer. He caressed her shoulders, waiting for her to make a decision. She let out her breath on a heavy sigh. "We'd better go to sleep. And you'd better rest that ankle."

When she pulled away from him, he missed the heat and softness of her body snuggling against his. "Tomorrow then." At least tonight he wouldn't have nightmares about a human frozen in the snow near their wolf-blazed trail. He hoped he'd only think of kissing the white wolf he'd seen so long ago.

Which had him wondering if he was doing the right thing. Taking her to see his bachelor friends. Wolves, the lot of them. How could they resist a female wolf as lovely and smart as Candice? They wouldn't be able to, he was certain.

This could be a real test of their friendship. He hoped bringing her to their new home wouldn't break up their cohesive pack. They needed each other. But he needed a female wolf in his life too, and so did they.

Candice couldn't believe she'd kissed Owen. And ohmigod, she couldn't have imagined anything sexier than the way he kissed. It wasn't just that he was one hell of a kisser. Her senses were so attuned to him. She smelled his delectably aroused body scent that triggered her own. She enjoyed feeling his heated, hard body pressed against hers, showing exactly how much she intrigued him. She'd read how pheromones would intensify the interest for other animal species that could actually smell them, but she hadn't really been able to envision how that worked. Not until she'd experienced it herself. Would she feel that way about other wolves? About Owen's other bachelor wolf friends?

Philosophically speaking, she wondered if they all had the same interesting pheromones, or if they were unique for each of them. If one would faithfully sing out to her and keep her from being interested in the others. Then she realized that if they'd never had wolf girlfriends, she might cause all kinds of trouble for the pack. She sure hoped not. She had enough trouble of her own.

Chapter 5

Owen had risen before dawn while Candice was still sleeping. He showered and dressed, then went out to check around the house to make sure the intruder hadn't returned. The snow had filled all the tracks, leaving nothing but the ones he was making.

When he returned, Candice was up and dressed, her bags packed. He heard a snowblower in the driveway, and Candice explained, "Oh, that's Stanley. He does my yard work in the summer and blows the snow off the driveway in the winter. The county will have cleared the road. Did you find any sign of the guy?" She returned to her bedroom and then brought out a couple more bags.

"No sign of him. Do you want me to fix something for breakfast?" He took her bags to the front door.

"We ran out of eggs and bread for toast. Why don't we go to the local coffee shop and bakery? We could eat breakfast there and head out. They have excellent food, everything from full-course breakfasts to home-baked goods."

"Okay, sounds good."

"About the driving…"

"I'll drive. You can just leave your car here. I'll bring you home when you're ready to return. Just in case you can't hold your form. I rarely have trouble now, except sometimes a couple of days before, during, and after the fullest full moon."

"Are you going to tell my uncle that you found me?"

"That's kind of a problem. I don't want to charge him for expenses when I've already found you, but he's going to wonder why you can't return at once to claim your inheritance. We'll have to make up a story for why you can't, so I can tell him I've found you and he's done paying for my services."

"Okay, so how long is the drive to your place, and where will I be staying?"

"It's about thirteen hours, depending on road conditions and traffic. Each of us has our own log home. You're welcome to stay with me. Or, if you'd prefer, you can stay with Faith and her family and have some female company."

"That might be awkward for Corey...and maybe the parents if they feel guilty about me." She hauled out the last bag while Owen packed the groceries she needed to take so they wouldn't spoil.

"Good. Then I want you to stay with me."

She smiled at him, and he figured she'd wanted to hear that she wasn't going to be an imposition. Some people didn't like change in their living arrangements, particularly if they were used to living alone. "I'll need to take my computers. I'll have to write while I'm at your place. I need to proof a manuscript I just finished before I turn it in. We also need to take the gingerbread cookies, to show you made them and to share them with the others."

"They won't believe it. Yeah, I cook. But I've never baked cookies or pies or anything." He hauled out her PC, and she grabbed her laptop. "If you need me to read over your book, I can. A second pair of eyes might help."

"Thanks. As long as you don't critique my werewolf world too much."

"You mean because your wolves aren't true to our way of life? It's fantasy. Your world, your way."

After they were packed, Owen started the car, and *Loving the Arctic Wolf* by Candice Mayfair began playing in the MP3 player. He quickly turned off the sex scene where the heroine was wearing the *Dear Santa, I've been very naughty…* apron while cooking dinner and the hero was distracting her.

They were both quiet for a moment as Owen drove them to the Yoke Café and Bakery, not sure how to explain that he'd been listening to her book.

"That—" he began while she commented at the same time, "You—"

"Are listening to your book? Uh, yeah. Great way to get to where I'm going and learn a little about you at the same time. I'd never listened to an audiobook before."

"That's not me."

"Oh, I don't know. Your heroine had the *Dear Santa, I've been very naughty…* apron in this book, and it reminded me of…"

"I mean…" She was blushing beautifully and seemed to change her mind about what she was going to say. "I hope you're enjoying it."

"Hell yeah. I've listened to this part three times already because I missed my turnoff and had to listen to it over again."

She laughed. "Two more times?"

"Yeah, it was a really good part. I might even learn a thing or two."

"Yeah, right."

He just chuckled. “Hey, I wondered about the money situation with your family. If they’re so well-off—”

“Why do I live in a modest-sized house? Well, my dad worked his way up the ladder in the oil industry. My parents had nothing starting out. They didn’t come into money; they had to earn every cent they made. They were careful how they spent it. They had a really nice home, but I was expected to earn my way too. That’s the only way to appreciate what you have, you know. If you have to work for it.”

“Okay, gotcha.”

“What about your parents?”

“My mother abandoned me when I was twelve. My dad was in enough barroom brawls that I decided I wanted to be on the side of the law, not constantly in jail. Cameron, Gavin, David, and I lived in the same general area. We went to school together and were best friends from the beginning. I was at Gavin’s house more than at my grandparents’. Gavin’s dad was a war hero, having saved five men when their Humvee hit a mine in Afghanistan. He joined the police force after that, but died in a bank robbery shoot-out. We were devastated.

“Cameron’s dad was a womanizer, carouser, gambler, and all-around deadbeat who died in a car accident. His mom died in the same accident. Cameron didn’t have any other family, so Gavin’s father took him in. Gavin’s father was like the father we all needed and looked up to. His death decided it for Cameron and Gavin. They both wanted to join the police force. David had always loved adventure and was waffling between joining the army or the police force. We all decided on joining the police, then later, we started a PI business.”

"What about David's family?"

"Well-to-do, but too busy with their social lives. His father died of a heart attack when he was fairly young, which should have clued us in that David might experience heart problems. His mom married a wealthy landowner, and they moved to Australia. David had been close to his dad, not his mother. Her new husband really didn't like David. David's dad had a trust set aside for him, so when he turned twenty-one, David was wealthy. I came into money when my grandparents died. So, we really didn't have any issues with our families learning what we had become. Thankfully."

"What about Faith's family?"

"Her mother had died. Faith was trying to locate her father and his research when she learned a red wolf pack had taken him in and turned him. He's mated to a red wolf from the pack, and they take trips all over. Sometimes they stay with Cameron and Faith to see the kids."

"Wow. Okay."

The log cabin restaurant was warm and well lit, with several cars parked outside and patrons filling more than half of the tables and booths for breakfast. Christmas music was playing in the background as the aromas of fresh-brewed coffee and sweet cinnamon and chocolate pastries wafted in the air. Christmas wreaths and lights hanging overhead provided holiday cheer.

Candice took a seat at one of the red vinyl booths. "It's busier than I've ever seen it."

"Because of the food and atmosphere, I imagine."

They looked over the menus on the table, and then the waitress came to take their orders, wearing a red-and-white Santa hat.

Owen ordered steak and eggs and a coffee. Candice ordered chocolate-chip pancakes and hot tea.

When the waitress left to place their orders, Candice asked Owen, "Did you tell everyone I was coming?"

"Yeah. They're thrilled to meet you. Corey's anxious to say he's sorry."

"I don't want him feeling bad about it."

"He'll be okay. It's one of those life lessons. It's important to make amends."

Candice's phone rang, and she looked at the caller ID but didn't recognize it. The call was from Minnesota. "Anyone you know?" She handed the phone to Owen.

"Faith."

She quickly answered the call. "Hi, this is Candice."

Owen was glad Faith called Candice. She might be more able to influence Candice to stay than any of the guys would be.

Candice was looking down at the table while Faith spoke, but then she glanced up at Owen and smiled. "Thanks. I can't wait to meet you too… I'll tell him. Thanks again. Bye."

Owen was dying to know what Faith had said to her. "Well?"

"She said if you did anything to dissuade me from meeting the pack, she was putting you in the doghouse."

He laughed, but he knew Faith meant it. Not literally, of course.

Another group of people entered the restaurant. Owen wouldn't have noticed them if one of the men hadn't been wearing what Candice had described to him the night before—snow boots and an olive-green winter army parka with a fur-covered hood. The man's hair was military short, dark brown, and he had blue eyes. His gaze shifted around the café while he checked everyone out.

Candice squeezed Owen's hand, confirming that's who she thought the man was too. But unless he was a wolf and could smell their scents, he wouldn't know they had been at the cabin that night. Unless he had seen Owen's vehicle outside the café and recognized it as the one that had been parked at Candice's home. That worried her a bit. She could just imagine him coming over to ask them about the wolf tracks that led back to her house.

The sheriff walked in right after that and greeted a few people.

"Know either of them?" Owen asked.

"No. I hardly know anyone because I don't go into town much, and I sure don't advertise what I do."

Then the blond-haired, brown-eyed sheriff went straight back to where the other man was seated. "Rowdy Sanderson. What the hell are you doing back here, of all places? I thought you were in Montana solving murder cases. How's the homicide business treating you?"

Candice looked at Owen. He was wondering the same thing. How did a homicide detective get involved in tracking down wolves?

"Can't complain. I was up here seeing a cousin before he left to visit a friend. I was..." Rowdy sneezed. "I was curious about the wolves at the avalanche site yesterday, Ed."

"Well, you and everyone else. I've already had trouble over that. Someone was asking if I'd pay him a bounty to take down the wolves. After they saved two people? I don't think so. Someone else wanted to take pictures of the wolves and punched the hunter. Gave him a bloody nose. As much as I hated to do it, I had to arrest the photo hobbyist. A reporter caught the whole damn thing on video. Now animal-rights folks are mad at me for locking up the other guy and not the hunter."

"You don't have any idea if someone living in the area raised them?" Rowdy asked.

Then the two men paused to give the waitress their orders.

Owen and Candice's meals had been served, and Candice was pouring maple syrup over her pancakes while Owen salted his steak. It was a good thing they had such good hearing, or they wouldn't have made out the sheriff's conversation with Rowdy.

Candice reached over to Owen and squeezed his hand. He nodded to let her know he was as surprised as she was to learn a detective was looking into the wolf situation.

After the waitress left cups of coffee and a decanter at the sheriff and the detective's table, the sheriff said, "Nope. Don't know of anyone who owns wolves or wolf dogs in the area. But I'd say it was a sure bet."

"Are you looking for whoever is taking care of them?"

"Nope. As long as the wolves don't hurt anyone, livestock, or pets, I'm not mounting a hunt for them. Unless we start receiving complaints—and we've had dozens of sightings of them since the accident, but no real trouble—I'm not doing anything about it."

"Were there any real sightings?"

"One of two Samoyeds on leashes with their owner."

Owen could imagine some Photoshopped pictures cropping up next.

Rowdy sneezed two more times and then blew his nose into a hanky. "Sorry. I think I caught a bit of a cold last night."

"Serves him right," Candice whispered to Owen.

He nodded.

"Mr. Lexus said the wolves were really his dogs. His Samoyeds look a lot like the wolves. They are white, but if you look at the video of the rescue, those are wolves. Maybe wolf dogs, but definitely not purebred Samoyeds," the sheriff said. "They're way too tall."

"Wolf dogs," Owen said, snorting.

"Have you had any incidents with wolves causing trouble here in the past?" Rowdy asked.

"Nope. And seeing Arctic wolves is even more unusual. An occasional gray wolf is seen in South Dakota, but Arctic wolves?" The sheriff shook his head.

"Well, that was really remarkable, seeing them dig those men out like that. If they hadn't, the snowmobilers would never have made it. I still can't believe that yahoo was taking a video of them when he should have been digging out his friends. I understand the men are in stable condition."

"Yeah. We had a landslide a while back, and the man who was buried wasn't so lucky. Oxygen deprivation. We couldn't revive him."

"Well, hell, what does Mr. Lexus think? That he can have his dogs take credit for saving the men's lives? What if you have another case like this and call on him to bring his dogs to help?" Rowdy asked.

"Exactly. Lives could be lost because of it. He's already been talking this up on Facebook. I wouldn't be surprised if he started trying to train them in rescue operations to keep up the charade. They're smart dogs, but that doesn't mean they can do what those wolves did."

"If they can manage it, maybe some good will come of it."

Owen finished his food and looked to see if Candice had. She pushed her plate aside and nodded. "Ready to go," she said softly.

"Let's go." He paid the bill, and then they left the restaurant, trying not to catch the sheriff or the detective's attention.

"Hey, do you know a Candice Mayfair?" Rowdy asked.

Chills raced up Candice's spine, but she slowed her pace to hear what was being said.

"From what my dispatcher says, the lady is a romance author."

"Romance author, eh?" Rowdy leaned back from the table as the server brought them their plates of stacked pancakes.

"Yeah. Writes that weird stuff. Werewolves. All the rage, you know."

"Werewolves?"

"Yeah. Helen reads all her works, says I should to support a local author." The sheriff snorted. "Hell, I don't even read the paper."

Candice stepped outside with Owen, her heart racing. She motioned to a red pickup as they walked briskly to Owen's vehicle. "That's his truck right there. The one I saw last night."

"I'm glad we're leaving for a time. A reporter might have a nose for news, but a homicide detective would also know how to look for clues. And watch to see if we left the house as wolves. I can't believe a homicide detective is trying to learn about the wolves. Discovering that you write about werewolves didn't help. How much do you want to bet the detective will look up your books and realize you write about Arctic werewolves?"

"Yeah, and maybe even believe I'm raising a couple and that's why I only write about Arctic ones. I wouldn't be surprised if he put a motion camera out there to watch the house while he isn't around." As soon as they got on the road, Candice brought out her notepad. "If you don't mind, I need to ask you a few questions."

"An interview?"

She laughed. "Not quite. I just want to keep my facts straight. Okay, so do werewolves have sex as wolves with each other?"

He smiled. This was going to be one interesting trip back home.

Chapter 6

CANDICE NEEDED TO GET HER MIND OFF THE HOMICIDE detective and where it belonged: on creating werewolf romances. They had a long drive ahead of them, and she figured she'd put the time to good use since Owen was driving. When he smiled at her, she hoped he didn't think she was being too silly for asking, but what did she know? Wolves did it in the wild, or at least the mated alpha pair did. Then she frowned. He opened his mouth to speak, but she blurted out, "It's not only the alpha mated pair that have sex, is it?"

Now how wrong would that be?

Owen smiled again. "Well, truthfully, I've never had sex with a wolf. And I haven't chased after Cameron and Faith to see what they're up to when they want some alone time as wolves."

"You take care of the kids?"

"Pups. When Faith shifts, so do the kids. So yeah, I do. Or the other guys do. We all take turns."

Candice thought that was amazing. "Were you watching Corey the night he bit me?" She couldn't imagine how the pup had gotten across the river without help.

"No. He was with his mom on the other side of the river. Cameron too."

"Are Cameron and Faith your pack leaders?"

"Sort of. Cameron has always been pseudo in charge of the detective agency. He convinced us all to go into it together. We've been friends forever. We call it a pack, but I don't think we really consider him and Faith in charge of it. We just work and play together. Makes it easier that way."

"Okay, so what is it like being with a human versus a wolf? I mean, well, just the kissing part." As soon as she spoke the words and saw the dimple in his cheek and the curve of his mouth, she felt her face flush with heat.

"You want to know what it's like being a wolf with a human? The difference between night and day."

"Well, I don't mean to be fishing for compliments or anything but—"

"You noticed it too, didn't you? How our pheromones stir each other's up? How they make the experience headier, more complex, more...intriguing?"

"That's just because we can smell the pheromones. Right? I mean, it would be the same if we kissed any other wolf, wouldn't it?"

"Leidolf, the red wolf who helped us out and shared *Lupus Garou* 101 with us, said there has to be a real mutual attraction between the wolves. Humans experience something similar. One man may smell divine to you, and another is a total turnoff. Or elicits no feelings at all. Like maybe a close relation. You might like the way a father smells, but that doesn't make you sexually attracted to him. It has to do with procreation of the species, finding the wolf that is not only suited to you by temperament, but also carries the right genetic material for the offspring."

"Hmmm." Candice continued to jot down notes.

"The other thing is that once a wolf sets his or her sights on another, and they commit to each other, and I mean a sexual commitment, that's it. They mate for life."

She closed her gaping mouth, then finally said, "Wolves do that for the most part. Though some take another mate if they lose theirs. But the human half wouldn't feel obligated, would they?"

"It's tied into our wolf half, the need to take care of the wolf kids—something I didn't think would happen to me, being the bachelor that I am. Not that I ever thought I'd marry someone and then turn around and divorce her, but that was always an option. Somehow our wolf instincts override our human instincts in that area. Once a relationship is consummated, there's no going back."

"That's hard to believe."

"It's like our ability to heal or see and hear better. I always thought I was in good shape until I became a wolf, but I couldn't be in better shape than this."

"Have you ever shifted when it was or could have been a problem?"

"At first, yeah. We had to keep a really low profile. You?"

"Some. I moved to South Dakota during the phase of the new moon. Okay, another thing I was wondering about. Have you ever had a confrontation with real wolves?"

"No. You?"

"No. I wonder what they would think of us because we have both human and wolf scents."

"They might stay away. It's hard to tell. They're territorial and have to have enough prey for their pack, so they could try to kill a trespassing wolf."

"This doesn't wear off, does it?"

"No, I'm afraid not. You will have better control over it as the years go on. We asked Leidolf if there's a cure for it. I don't think he appreciated us asking. He was born like that, like others of his kind. It's not a curse or a virus. It's who they are. And what we are now too. If you didn't know already, we have increased longevity. You probably wouldn't have noticed this early on."

"Really."

"Yeah. Wolves used to only age a year for about every thirty years, but it's down to around five now. A researcher is looking into what's caused the change and how to fix it, if it's fixable. I'd say we're lucky to have any increased longevity at all."

"Wow. But you say some werewolves were born like that?" Candice asked.

"Yeah, they've been full *lupus garous* for generations."

"So how did you feel about being turned when it first happened?"

"After seven years, I've gotten used to it."

Candice tapped her pen on her notebook. "At first, it was unsettling to me, to say the least. If there were such a thing as a cure, I think I'd miss this part of my life now though. Like you mentioned about exercise and being in good shape, I can run for miles and not even notice it. I return home after a long run and begin writing my stories. It's a great way to start my day. At night, it's a great way to de-stress. When I used to go to the gym, it was a hassle. I had to take time out of my work day just to drive over there. With all the traffic, that definitely wasn't a way to de-stress. It took me forever to unwind after arriving home and return to work on the story. I normally run both in the morning and at night, and I feel great."

"Same here. It took a while to grow used to the changes, the lack of control over my physical being, and just dealing with the enhanced abilities, like thinking things were closer than they were because our hearing is so much better. After a few months of having lived like this, I wouldn't have wanted it any other way. If I didn't have a pack to rely on, I might have felt differently. I'm not a lone-wolf sort of guy."

"I have missed being with people. Have you ever considered going to another pack and meeting some wolves just to date?"

"I have, but I haven't done anything about it. I haven't been interested in going to another state just to try to meet a woman. If I happened to be on an assignment in the area, and it just happened, then fine. But you have to remember that we're different from other wolves."

"Because we're Arctic."

"Right. We don't blend in with the surroundings like gray wolves do. Also, we're newly turned. Some might not be interested in hooking up with a newly turned wolf."

"I hadn't thought of that. So you're kind of stuck then." She let out her breath. "Like I am. And turning someone isn't really an option. Well, it's an option, but not a really good one."

"Right."

"I bet when you go on an assignment, you're completely focused on your job. Somehow I don't see you as the kind of guy who mixes pleasure with business."

"I wasn't, until I met you and got to make gingerbread cookies."

She laughed. "I made you make them."

"I had fun. And I thought they tasted really good."

"They did." Then she began working on her story and added the avalanche and snowmobilers for more drama, glad she was getting away from an annoying homicide detective investigating her and the Arctic wolves. Yet, she was a little apprehensive about meeting the other wolves and the little boy who had bitten her.

Several hours later, Owen and Candice finally reached the wilderness area where the pack's log homes were located on a small lake in northern Minnesota. "That's Cameron's home," Owen said as they drove past the place. It was all dressed in Christmas lights, with the tree standing inside next to the front window, the colorful lights shimmering and looking festive. Owen hoped she didn't think he'd overdone the decorating at his place. Then again, he hadn't expected to be bringing home an Arctic she-wolf to stay with him when he took on this assignment. He was usually pretty good about picking up after himself, so he hoped the place was neat when they arrived there.

He was glad his home would be warm and welcoming, once he turned on the sparkling lights. His cabin was dark when he parked, making him want to start a cheery fire in the fireplace, turn on the lights draped around his Christmas tree, and make her feel at home.

"We'll drop off your bags and the groceries before we see anyone." Owen intended to call Cameron to let him know they'd gotten in okay, but he thought Candice would probably prefer to meet with Cameron's family tomorrow after the long drive they'd had. It was already half past seven. "What do you think? We could just have dinner at my place and get together with Cameron and Faith and the kids for lunch tomorrow."

"Yeah, that sounds good."

"I have to warn you that the kids will be super excited about meeting you. And yes, even Corey. Maybe especially Corey. I thought we could run as wolves tonight and in the morning, then join them about noon."

"Sounds good to me. After driving for so long, I'm ready for a run to stretch my legs."

He couldn't wait to show her their territory so she would feel more at home. It was a beautiful area, full of pines, maples, quaking aspen, birch, and oaks that helped to shield them from the world. "Okay. The other guys are working jobs, so they said they'd meet you a little later in the week. They're already giving me a hard time about it, saying I knew they'd gotten jobs that took them out of state for a few days before I brought you home."

"Did you?"

He laughed. "It will give you time to meet Cameron's family before you have to meet with the rest of the pack. That way it's not so overwhelming."

"And you can get to know me better first."

He smiled. "You bet. We're all wolves. What can I say? Until a wolf is claimed, there's always a chance she might fall for some other guy."

"And if the situation were reversed and you were one of the other guys, you'd have felt the same way."

"You'd better believe it. I'd finish up the job I had out of state pronto. I'd have returned before the other guy had even arrived here, greeted you at the door with flowers and candy, and made you feel welcome."

She raised a brow.

He laughed. "Okay, so I guess I need to do something about that, right?"

Smiling, she shook her head, and they got out of the car. The one-story cabin was about as big as her home, with a big front patio, rocking chairs, a swing for two, and a large deck out back overlooking the lake.

"We still haven't come up with a story about why you can't return to Houston right away to collect your inheritance." Owen began hauling her bags into the house. Then he started to turn on all the Christmas lights inside and out.

"I could pretend I'm in another country on a world book-signing tour. I could make up pictures showing various locations where I've been. Photoshop myself in all over the world. I could pre-post blogs and make up some for days past." She grabbed her laptop and another bag and paused to look at the lights. "Just beautiful." Then she followed him inside.

"Will anyone miss you in the places where you supposedly are doing signings?"

"I do drive-by signings at bookstores whenever I can. I don't have official book signings, but I do autograph books for fans. I could say I was in England, Scotland, France, and Germany, and then had gone to Australia and New Zealand. Well, maybe that would be a little long. But no one will miss me. I drive all over, signing books in the stores every time I can, and my fans always want me to visit where they live."

"What if your agent learns about this and becomes upset?"

"I don't have an agent. I've done tons of these before. Just never overseas. I can look for bookstores in smaller places, so there's less of a chance that anyone follows me from there." She set her laptop and the bag on the kitchen counter and stared at the seven-foot tree. Wow. She thought hers was nice and cheery, but his was rich, huge, and elegant—woodsy style. Green-and-red-plaid bows, colorful lights, wooden ornaments, and feather-covered balls, with little faux birds' nests and birds sitting in them all made her feel as though he had decorated the tree in the forest.

"All right. I can help you with that. Just give me an itinerary, and I'll help you set it up. I can call Strom when you're ready. I doubt he'll look into it, but just in case."

"Okay. As soon as we finish unpacking, I'll start to work on it." She headed outside with him and grabbed another bag.

"Why don't you just use your laptop to start it? I'll grab the rest of your things and then fix dinner."

"Thanks." She paused beside the car as she saw the lights trimming the whole house from every angle—the windows, gutters, and rooftop. Even the trees were aglow with white lights. "Wow, just beautiful. I never put any lights up outside. It seems like too much work just for me." She couldn't believe how much he'd decorated the place. She'd expected a Charlie Brown Christmas tree, if that. If her mother hadn't decorated their home, her dad certainly wouldn't have.

"There's a bit of a competition between the guys. Wolf posturing."

She laughed. "Money involved?"

"Nah, just a little friendly competition. And the kids love it too."

Candice thought the guys were cute to want to impress the kids. She also couldn't believe Owen was willing to help her with this charade. Then again, he was like her, an Arctic *lupus garou* who had to keep her true nature under wraps. She was beginning to believe this could work. For a while, she hadn't been so sure. Yet, she hadn't wanted to pretend Owen was still looking for her while her uncle was paying for Owen's services.

When she reentered the house, she glanced around the spacious home. The kitchen was open to the dining room and living room like hers, but Owen had expansive bay windows looking onto the lake, while her large windows viewed the mountains. She could imagine how pretty it would be here when the fall and spring colors emerged, reflecting off the water. Wanting to see more of the view, she opened the back door and stepped out onto the deck. An aluminum boat dock jutted out into the water, and a bright-orange canoe rested on the shore. Now that's what she'd love to do. Go canoeing. She could add it to one of her stories even. She smiled. This would be great as a new setting for a book.

A boathouse was off to one side, and she wondered what kind of a boat Owen had. A huge wreath hung on the side, and Christmas lights trimmed the boathouse and the dock, the lights sparkling in the water. Just beautiful.

"Don't you have to remove the dock?"

"I'll be taking it out in a couple of days. It's a one-man job to install and remove; don't even have to get in the water to remove it. The sections are lightweight and can be stacked by the boathouse. I would have brought it in already, but it's been mild so far. Plus, a spring runs into the lake that helps to keep the water from freezing early. It's deep, so it takes longer for the ice to take over. Our dock bubblers help us to keep the water from freezing around the docks also. I have a sailboat too," Owen said. "I hauled her out of the water for the winter, but I love taking her out for night sails or seeing the sunrise."

"Perfect for a romance story."

"Then you'll have to hang around and go sailing with me so you can experience the real thing." He motioned to the house. "I can set your PC up on the table next to my computer desk. I have another comfortable desk chair you can use. Sometimes the guys come over and we play video games. Or you can use my desk. Whichever is more convenient for you. Or I can set it up in your guest room if you'd rather. Maybe you need more quiet to write."

"Nah. I write no matter how much noise is going on, or even when it's really quiet. I'll sit at the table next to your desk. I'll only be here for a couple of weeks until the new moon arrives." But she was already thinking of returning in the summer to sail with him. "Do you mind if I just sit on one of your recliners while I do this on my laptop?"

"Go right ahead. There's an outlet next to the recliner." Owen got busy starting a fire. He put away the groceries she'd brought and then began preparing the meal. "Are stuffed bell peppers okay?"

"Sounds delicious."

Owen called Cameron and let him know they had arrived, then confirmed tomorrow's lunch date before signing off.

"What made you decide to take up writing?" Owen pulled out a pot for the bell peppers and filled it with water.

"Oh, I've been writing stories since I was a kid. I would write stuff at night after work. I was a file clerk at a law firm. I got really lucky with a publishing contract about five years ago, but back then, I was writing romantic suspense, no paranormal. My focus shifted once I was turned. I had a new appreciation for the paranormal and began writing werewolf romances. A write-what-you-know thing. Not only that, but it was a way for me to deal with the issues I was having. I have fifteen books out now. When I could no longer work at the law firm—trying to control the urge to shift wasn't working—I had to work at something that I could do at home without creating mass hysteria. That meant writing full time and really having to make sure I made it work. You must have had a real time of it with the kind of work you do."

He started cooking the hamburger for the bell pepper filling. "We all had a lot of funds saved, and some of us also had inheritances, so we pooled our money and worked together to make this a viable option. All of us guys had been PIs, so we knew the business. And a lot of the research is done online now. We just officially opened our office after not having one for seven years. I was glad the four of us have jobs to show opening a brick-and-mortar business was worth it."

"I bet."

"Not sure I should mention it, because I imagine a lot of people who learn you're an author tell you they've started to write a book or have a great story to tell, but..."

"You've written a book," she said.

"I've written a little bit of one."

She raised her brows, smiling.

"I wrote when I was a kid too. Later, when I was waiting to hear on leads while working on cases or doing a stakeout, I'd record story ideas."

"Do you plan to do anything with them?"

"I... Well, I never get beyond the first chapter before I start something else."

She laughed. "Hey, maybe we can take a canoe trip around the lake sometime."

"Great way to work out. I'll put it on the schedule of fun things to do while you're here."

She glanced at his Christmas tree. Leaving her laptop on the couch, she walked over to see the wooden ornaments up close. Intricately hand-carved wolves, bears, moose, foxes, Santa Clauses, and elves. Topping the tree was a hand-carved fairy, the details just beautiful. "These are lovely."

"Thanks. When I'm thinking about a case, trying to come up with another angle, I whittle away."

She walked over to the bookcases on either side of his TV and saw that he was a big mystery reader. "Have you ever considered writing about some of your cases? Writing a mystery story?"

"I've thought about it, actually. I was writing more in the line of fantasy. But after listening to your book, I was thinking a romance story with a mystery plot could even be more fun. Maybe you could give me some writing tips."

She smiled, having known he'd ask. She hoped she could be honest without hurting his feelings if his stories needed tons of work. "I'd love to. Anytime you need some help, let me know." A half hour later, they sat down for a dinner of stuffed bell peppers, boiled red potatoes, and whole green beans. Afterward, they got ready to run. She loved running with him. It wasn't the same as running alone at all. Normally she'd be wary of her surroundings in a place where she'd never been before. In fact, since she'd moved to her new home, she'd never ventured far from the house, so she could race home if she felt threatened by humans.

Here, it was different. Owen knew the lay of the land, and he was comfortable with his surroundings. That made her relax too and enjoy not only the new scenery, but also running with him. She was still watchful—they always had to be—but she wasn't as worried as she normally was. Even back home, she'd enjoyed taking a wolf run with him, despite the dire circumstances of having to rescue the snowmobilers. Before that, running with him had been pure joy. Even after that, with her heart pounding with trepidation, she'd felt better not being alone.

She could imagine worrying about the snowmobilers on her own and not having any backup. She loved her home and the forested area surrounding it. But now she could see how important it was to have friends who were just like her—who could commiserate with her and help her out if she was in trouble. She wasn't sure she could go back to the way her life had been.

It was like going to a movie theater alone, then sitting next to a wolf and sharing the experience with him the next time, laughing at the same comedic points, sitting on the edge of the seat during the dangerous twists and turns, and relaxing during the lulling moments. Talking about the experience afterward, agreeing and disagreeing. She realized she'd really missed that human interaction. Being with just a human wasn't the same either. Her perspective had changed so much. Being with fellow wolves who could understand those feelings was a real boon.

Candice continued to explore and sniff out the scents—a fox, two raccoons, a number of deer—while she pondered her once-again changed life.

She'd given up hope of ever being with someone again. Anyone. Not even girlfriends. To learn that her longevity had increased made doing something about that all the more important, now that she could. Knowing Owen meant all the difference in the world. And meeting the others in his pack did too.

She paused to observe the night sky, the stars, and the growing moon.

Meeting the pack was more important to her than anything money could buy, she realized. The situation with the inheritance had been a miracle. It had made her come face-to-face with the pack that had changed her life. The money or properties didn't mean half as much to her.

She turned her head and found Owen watching her. Then she began moving again, sniffing the scents, memorizing his territory, and thinking about her parents.

Before her parents died, all that had mattered was going back to see them when she could. Unfortunately, those visits had become strained. Her parents had been angry with her for not coming to see them when they could have really used her aid. The care packages she'd sent, the flowers, nothing could have replaced her being there.

Now they were gone. Candice had to believe they were still watching over her like they had when she was growing up, providing a good home that her own parents couldn't have given her. If that was so, could they see now she was a wolf sometimes? Know that was the reason she couldn't go home? She wanted to believe so, for her own peace of mind.

She looked up at the stars, imagining her parents up there, some of the brightest stars lighting her way.

As she began to walk with Owen again, she recognized they were drawing nearer to his place. She swore she heard movement in the shrubs close by, not caused by the wind. Something small, an animal. Owen was off to her left, the animal to the right. She didn't want to scare it off, but she was curious about what it was. It sounded larger than a rabbit. A fox, maybe? One of the raccoons she'd smelled before?

Then the animal woofed. Not a loud woof, but one that said he wasn't sure of himself. A wolf woof, not a dog's.

Owen immediately barked at him, and the young wolf came out of the brush. The juvenile wolf looked a little older than when she'd seen him two years ago—she figured it was like Owen had said, juveniles didn't grow up as fast because of their human halves—but she would swear it was Corey, the wolf pup who had bitten her. And then she realized she recognized his scent. Not when he had first bitten her, but later, when she was a wolf and cataloging all the scents around the campsite.

A howl rent the air, and Owen immediately howled back. She assumed the wolf who had howled was Corey's momma or daddy. Then the wolf appeared among the trees, just as big as Owen, just as white and majestic. He stared at Candice a moment, then sniffed the air. She was trying not to be too obvious about it as she sampled the air too. It was amazing how quickly humans turned into part-time wolves picked up the wolves' habits. It was impossible not to.

She walked over to greet Corey, to let him know she wasn't upset with him. He looked back at his dad, who just bowed his head a little as if to say it was okay to greet her back.

Corey poked his nose out at her, and they touched noses. She smiled. Despite all that had happened to her, she couldn't help but love the little fella. If she'd been a wolf pup when she was young, she could imagine the trouble she would have gotten into.

After she greeted Corey, Cameron came over and greeted her, and then he took his son away and Owen walked with Candice the rest of the way home. From the woods, the house looked magical, all lit up in its small clearing. She paused to take in the beauty of it, and Owen smiled at her, appearing pleased that she seemed so appreciative.

Once they'd gone inside and retreated to their respective rooms, they shifted, dressed—him in jeans and his lumberjack shirt, her in her soft flannel pajamas—and rejoined each other in the kitchen.

"That was Corey and his dad, if you hadn't guessed."

"I assumed as much. I actually recall Corey's scent from when he came into camp after I had been turned."

"I suspect he came over to see you tonight, unable to wait until tomorrow. Of their three children, he's the real alpha. Angie and Nick would rather watch and see what happens to him than venture into the unknown."

"I can imagine. He's as cute as the last time I saw him, just a little bigger. But if I fed him again when he was running as a wolf, I'd toss him the treat. Are you ready to call it a night?"

"Yeah." But Owen pulled her into his arms. He wanted to kiss her. It meant the world to him that she liked Corey and had treated him like a friend when he needed the encouragement. He was certain Corey, and even Candice, would sleep better tonight, having met each other again and made amends.

Owen decided that while Candice was here, he'd start writing his book. And maybe with her encouragement, he could really stick to one and finish it this time. Maybe if he got really good at it, he could write a book with her. Maybe this would make her consider him as more than a friend and help cement their relationship.

He lowered his head and kissed her, holding nothing back, and wondered if she'd write about this in a scene—the way her body warmed his, the press of their mouths together, the softness and sweetness, and hardness and spiciness. The way his arousal was growing by the millisecond, the labor of their breaths, the ragged beat of their hearts all had him wanting to tell her in no uncertain terms that he intended to court her as a wolf.

Her tongue sought entrance, and he quickly let her in, not believing how wondrous it was to kiss a woman who was a wolf, feeling a blaze of desire building between them. He didn't want to let go of this beginning if she felt half as intrigued with him as he did with her. He thought so, given the way she reacted to his kisses and rubbed her body lightly against him, the seductive minx.

She finally pulled her mouth away from his, smiled, and said, "Wow."

"Incredible," he said. "Just incredible."

"Is it you and me together, or the wolf in us?"

"Both," he said with certainty, but he didn't know for sure. What if she kissed the other guys and felt the same way about them, just because they were all wolves?

He wanted to sequester her away from them so he and Candice could get to know each other a whole hell of a lot better before his friends returned and met her.

"I know this is sudden, but…" He hesitated. He didn't want to sound like a desperate wolf, but he was. "…I'd like to court you."

"Court?" She looked a little surprised, then smiled. She patted him on the chest. "That means no dating your single wolf friends, right?"

He'd felt hope until she spoke the words. Yeah, it sounded way too controlling. But hell, he wasn't going to skirt the issue with her. "Hell yeah."

She laughed. "'Night, Owen. I had a lovely time. And thanks for everything." Then she slipped off to her guest room.

He wondered if he'd made a big mistake in pushing the issue. "You just need to think on it tonight, right?"

She laughed again and shut her door.

"Hell." He went straight to his computer, turned it on, pulled up a clean document and began writing:

> *In Love with the She-Wolf*
> *by Owen Nottingham*
>
> *Chapter One*
> *Lucky Ryder had taken a run with his Arctic wolf pack…*

Okay, so he was supposed to write a romantic mystery. But he should write about what he knew, like she was doing.

> *...and had been separated from the others when he spied the most beautiful wolf staring at him across the river. What were the odds that he would ever find an Arctic werewolf to mate in the land of ten thousand lakes?*
>
> *He knew then that he was in love, and he had to learn who she was, even if crossing the raging river killed him.*

Maybe a little over the top? He deleted and revised. Wrote some more. Stood up, looked at the time—midnight—sat down, wrote some more, finally left the computer and started to write by hand in a notebook on the couch, and promptly fell asleep.

Chapter 7

Candice got up in the middle of the night to pour herself a glass of milk to help her sleep and saw Owen's master bedroom door wide open. She peered in, but he wasn't there. What was he doing? Was he having trouble sleeping like she was? Thinking about their kiss? Worried she was upset with him about wanting to court her exclusively?

He was hot and sexy and lovable. But she didn't know enough about this business with male wolves and relationships. She definitely wanted to know the pack a little better. What if she really liked one of the other guys even more than she liked Owen? She couldn't imagine it. Still, she had to know: Would another male wolf spin her world around like Owen's touches did?

She saw the light on in the living room, and when she peered over the couch, she saw Owen sleeping soundly. She hadn't heard the TV and wondered if he fell asleep there regularly. Walking around the couch, she saw a notebook lying open. She wondered if he journaled like she did. She knew she shouldn't read what he'd written, but if he wanted to court her, he should be an open book, right? She was curious about what he might have said about her, so she leaned over gently, picking up the notebook.

She read—*In Love with the She-Wolf*—and stifled a laugh.

He was so cute. She got caught up in the beginning of his story, had to read until he ended it on a cliff-hanger, and nearly groaned out loud. He was searching for the wolf at the campsite but couldn't reach her because of the humans with her.

Candice smiled, set the notebook back on the couch—belatedly realizing he'd know she'd read it because her scent was all over the pages—and went to grab her milk, then returned to bed.

And dreamed about the wolf watching her from across the river and not being able to meet up with him like two star-crossed lovers.

Owen couldn't believe he'd fallen asleep on the couch last night while writing his first book. He immediately smelled Candice's scent on his notebook—and every page that he'd written—and smiled. Then frowned. He hoped she thought he had some talent. Though he'd started the book on the computer, he'd begun a whole new different version in the notebook. Well, similar, but different.

After he took a shower and dressed, he saw her pouring herself a glass of orange juice in the kitchen.

"Couldn't sleep last night?" she asked, smiling.

He smiled back. "Did you get in a little late-night reading?"

"About that—"

"I can take it. Bad, huh?"

"I hope you're going to write what happened next, pronto."

He laughed. "You're kidding, right?"

"Nope. Great start. But now you've got to finish it."

With her encouragement, he could do anything. "But first, we'll take a run this morning, right?"

"Yeah, so you'll have more scene material for your story."

He chuckled. "I'm glad you liked it."

"I've been meaning to ask you a question ever since you introduced yourself."

"Sure, ask away." Owen started blueberry waffles and sausage links while she made toast and poured him coffee and hot water for her tea.

"Is it true about the Sheriff of Nottingham?"

He laughed. "Okay, to set the story straight, the office of high sheriff was created by the Normans who conquered England. It's the oldest secular office created by the Crown. The High Sheriff of Nottinghamshire, Derbyshire, and the Royal Forests was one of these. Some centuries later, separate appointments were made and my distant relation became the High Sheriff of Nottinghamshire."

"You're pulling my leg."

"Nope. Sir Robert Clifton of Clifton Hall in Nottingham was supposed to be one of our forefathers. A branch of the family later called themselves Nottingham. They were far removed from Sir Robert Clifton, and Nottingham was their birthplace, so they became Nottinghams. Of course, that meant putting up with all the ribbing about being related to the villainous Sheriff of Nottingham. We retold the story as such: Robin of the Hood was a thief and scoundrel. Wanting to get concessions from the king, he stole Lady Marion, the king's cousin, and the sheriff was ordered to rescue her. By then, Maid Marion had fallen in love with the rake, but the sheriff was still under orders by the king's authority and had to return her home. Thus, the sheriff became the villain."

Candice laughed. "You, Sir Nottingham, are a storyteller at heart."

Owen smiled at her and dished up the waffles and sausage. They decided to sit in the sunroom to eat. He loved it there at any time of day or night, but especially sitting there with Candice.

"This is lovely," she said, motioning to the Christmas lights reflecting on the lake, "and great food. I haven't had a break from cooking in practically two years."

"I'm glad you enjoyed it." And he would happily do all the cooking if that encouraged her to stay here with him.

After eating, Owen was loading the dishwasher and Candice had begun to proof her book when someone knocked at the front door. He couldn't imagine who would be there at this early hour. If it had been an emergency, Cameron or Faith would have just called him.

When he looked through the speakeasy window, he couldn't believe David Davis was standing on his porch, grinning away, his shaggy brown hair neatly combed. Then again, if David had brought home a she-wolf, Owen would have been there to make sure he greeted her as soon as possible.

Owen wanted to pretend David was a salesman and tell him he didn't want any. But he knew David wouldn't go away. After Elizabeth, the white wolf who had freed them from the pack in Maine, had returned to her pack in the Arctic, David was just as available as the rest of the bachelor males. Owen had thought Elizabeth and

David would become mated wolves, but she'd learned her grandmother needed her, and that was the end.

Owen let out his breath and opened the door, only to see Gavin pull his truck up right behind David's. Hell, now he had to deal with both of them vying for Candice's attention.

"I thought you both had jobs," Owen said, trying to keep from sounding annoyed. Especially when he saw the flowers both of his friends had brought with them. Owen highly suspected they weren't for him. Though he'd made the comment anyway.

They just laughed. "We wanted to welcome the she-wolf to the pack," Gavin said.

"She's not joining just yet," Owen warned. He hadn't wanted everyone to scare her off. "You better not have messed up your jobs. We need all the good referrals and reviews we can get."

"No, they were quick jobs," David said.

"Made quicker," Gavin added, grinning. "And fully resolved to everyone's liking, which means we're available to help *you* with *your* job."

They both smiled at Candice and she smiled back, shaking her head. "Thanks for the welcome and the flowers. Maybe you could help us with something though."

Owen caught himself before he growled out loud. These guys didn't need any encouragement.

She described what she and Owen were doing to provide a reasonable explanation for why she couldn't see to her inheritance right away.

"I can work on the Photoshopped pictures," David said.

"I can schedule a ton of Twitter announcements," Gavin said.

"Good. We started on it last night, but with all four of us working on it, we can let my Uncle Strom know Owen located me overseas today. We were just going to go for a wolf run. Would you like to join us?"

Owen jumped in to nip that notion in the bud, hoping his partners would get a clue to get lost for a while. "I'm sure since they just got home, they want to unpack. Especially if they need to begin working on the blogs and all."

"We'll need to do it from here to ensure we are all on the same page. I'd love to go for a run," Gavin said.

"Yeah, we always have our running gear on us." David handed her the vase of flowers.

She took both vases and set them on the kitchen bar. "They're lovely. Thank you so much for the warm welcome."

Owen gave them each a look that said that was as warm as the welcome needed to be.

She motioned to the hallway. "I'll just be out in a minute if we're ready to run."

"Yeah," Owen said. "We'll meet you outside in our wolf coats."

As soon as she left, the men started stripping, smiling. Owen assumed they had already seen her photo and knew she was a real looker, though her hair color, hairstyle, and eye color were very different from in the photo.

"I can't believe you got the first job at the office, and you pick up an Arctic she-wolf." David dropped his sweater on the back of the couch.

Gavin ditched his boots. "Yeah, we weren't going in until later, figuring we wouldn't receive any bites that early in the morning. Goes to show the early bird catches the—" He paused when he saw Candice in her wolf form coming down the hall. "Uh, yeah. The really good job."

She woofed at them and headed out the back wolf door.

"Man, she's fast." David hurried to strip out of the rest of his clothes.

Owen knew she was fast, and so was he. He yanked off his boxers, shifted, and ran off to join her.

He found her checking out the woods nearby, smelling all the new smells after last night's run. After getting over his initial surprise—and annoyance—he really didn't mind that the guys were here. They had to meet her sometime. And he was glad they were going to help create her book tour to give her an alibi. He kept reminding himself he wanted the best for her. If she became interested in one of the other bachelor males, he was all right with it. Because no matter what, he wanted her to stay with the pack.

Yet when David and Gavin ran out to join them, Owen was having second thoughts. They greeted her like any of their wolf pack would, but he was having a time tamping down his need to claim her for his own. In theory, he wanted to be a nice guy. He didn't want her to think he was an overbearing, possessive man. In reality, he was a wolf. And that trumped everything else.

He wanted to show her his favorite haunts, and thankfully, the guys ran along with them, exploring like wolves would, and let him take the lead. His favorite place to visit was the waterfalls. Every season brought spectacular new sights. Fall colors in oranges, yellows, purples, and reds. The blue falls frozen as they cascaded over the rocky cliffs in late winter. The spring greens and wildflowers of summer.

But then Gavin led her to *his* favorite place. The lighthouse. Owen hadn't thought of that, but it was a lovely scenic spot he loved too. David took her to the lake where their cabins were situated and they could watch the sun rising, the oranges and yellows and pinks reflecting off the water.

Then they headed back to Owen's cabin. They had a few hours before lunch with Cameron and Faith and the kids. Owen wondered if the other guys would join them. As soon as they got back, shifted, and dressed, they all sat down to begin creating Candice's book-signing tour.

By the time they had it all figured out, it was time to eat lunch. Owen asked if Gavin and David wanted to go with them to Cameron and Faith's place.

They both bowed out. "We're going to continue to work on Candice's cover story. We'll do all we can, and then she can approve all of it when you arrive home," Gavin said. "We'll just stay here and keep working on it, if you don't mind."

"Yeah, we'll grab a bite at the hamburger joint," David added.

"Sounds good. Thanks," Owen said.

"We'll leave some of the gingerbread cookies Owen made for you. We'll take the rest to the others."

David smiled at Owen.

"He burned my cookies," she explained.

The other guys laughed.

Owen was glad they were helping and not crowding in while Candice got to meet the rest of the pack. The kids could be overwhelming for someone who wasn't used to them. "Oh, and the kids know there's no wolf Santa now, but everyone plays along with the game anyway."

"Wolf Santa?" she said smiling.

"Yeah. An Arctic wolf Santa. You know, because Arctic wolves are from the North Pole."

She laughed. "I forget what it was like back then, believing in Santa Claus and the like."

Owen hoped everyone made her feel completely welcome.

When they arrived at Faith and Cameron's place for lunch, the air was filled with the aromas of chicken and acorn squash roasting in the oven, and fresh baked bread sitting on the counter. The house looked just as much like Christmas here, with the cheery fire glowing in the fireplace, lights everywhere.

The tree was seven feet tall and decorated with bows and ribbons, balls and lights, and everything else Christmassy. It made her tree look like a diminutive, practically barren version. Though she hadn't needed anything bigger for just herself.

Faith greeted Candice with a hug and welcome to the pack, her blue eyes sparkling with cheer, her blond hair coiled up on top of her head. She was dressed in jeans and a Christmas sweater, sparkly and festive.

Cameron was handsome and just as blond and blue-eyed, though Candice liked the darker-haired guys herself. But they made a cute couple. He was wearing a matching blue sweater.

The three kids, all blonds, acted shy at first, standing back. The little girl wore pigtails with red-and-green bows, a red sweater, and jeans. She reminded Candice of when she was little and wore pigtails too.

"This is Angie, the youngest," Faith said, patting her daughter on the shoulder. "This is Nick, middle child of the triplets." She squeezed his hand. "And you've met Corey, though I guess only when he was a wolf pup." She ruffled Corey's hair. Then she said to Corey, "Did you have something to tell Candice?"

Even though Candice had met him as a wolf yesterday, Corey was eyeing her like he was afraid *she* might bite *him*. Then she smiled. "Well, do you still like beef jerky?"

He looked up at his mother as if that subject was taboo. "Tell her," Faith urged.

He nodded.

"I don't think I've ever seen Corey so subdued," Owen said.

Everyone laughed.

But their shyness didn't last past Candice asking the kids what their favorite games were. They grasped her hands to lead her into their bedrooms to show her. She glanced back at Owen, and for a minute, he wondered if she needed his rescue. He figured it would be good for her to be with the kids for a few minutes to show they could all be friends.

Cameron raised his brows at Owen in silent question: How was it going with the she-wolf?

Well, Owen thought. He told them about the book-signing tour. And he mentioned Gavin and David had unexpectedly dropped by to help him.

Cameron laughed. "You would have too, had you been the one on a different job. I'm not surprised at all."

"Well, I was."

Faith smiled as she began to serve the meal. "Owen,

do you want to rescue Candice from the kids and tell them lunch is served?"

"Yeah." He quickly headed for the bedrooms, hoping she was having fun and wasn't thinking that she was getting herself into a real mess.

When he walked into Corey and Nick's bedroom, what he saw was heartwarming. Both bunk beds were covered in stuffed animals. Angie was sitting on Candice's lap while she sat on a big, blue beanbag chair. Corey was reading a story to them, and Nick was sitting on the other side of Candice, listening with rapt attention.

Candice looked like she fit right in with the wolf pack. Owen hated interrupting them, but he cleared his throat. "Your mom said lunch is ready."

That had all the kids dashing out of the room. You'd think they'd been starved for hours. He offered Candice a hand up. "So what do you think?"

"They're cute. But the triplets make me wonder—do all shifters have multiple child births?"

Candice swore Owen looked nearly panic-stricken when she asked about multiple births. She was just curious. She couldn't imagine having a couple of kids at once, let alone three or more. How would she ever have time to write?

"Not always."

"But more than normal, right?"

"Well, Leidolf, the red wolf I was telling you about, has twins."

She nodded and took Owen's hand as they walked back down the hall to the dining room to let him know it was okay. She wasn't in panic mode or anything. Why would she be? She didn't have a mate and had no intention of having kids for the next several years at least, not until she could get this shifting under control. She couldn't even envision how hard that had to have been for Faith. Though Faith had the whole pack to help her out. That would make a big difference.

At lunch, they talked about a million different things, the kids adding discussion about what they liked to do at the lake—swimming, fishing, running. As long as one of the adults was always with them. And Faith said she'd started to read Candice's books and loved them.

Candice beamed. "Thank you." She'd never expected to end up with a fan from this visit. Then again, Owen was listening to her books too. "Owen's started writing his own," Candice said, proud of him.

Faith's jaw hung a little. "Really?"

"As long as they're not star-crossed lovers..." Candice said.

"Romances have happily ever afters. I know something about it," Owen said.

Smiling, Cameron just shook his head.

"I think it's a great idea." Faith began to clear the dishes off the table and Candice hurried to help her.

"I agree. He's got real talent. He even left the story on a cliff-hanger, making me want to read more." Candice suddenly got a call, so she washed and dried her hands, then fished her phone out of her pocket. She didn't recognize the caller's number, so she figured it was spam and let it go to voicemail. The caller identified himself as Rowdy Sanderson, the homicide detective from Montana who must have learned who owned the house where the wolf tracks had led.

Chapter 8

Owen had seen Candice pale as soon as she looked at her phone, and he wondered what was wrong. But he didn't want to broach the subject if she didn't want to discuss it in front of Cameron and Faith. She ignored the call and stuck the phone back in her pocket.

Maybe it was just a spam caller. But he didn't think so—she looked too worried. As soon as they left the MacPhersons' home and started walking back to his place, he would ask who had called.

Faith served the gingerbread cookies, coffee, and tea in the living room, and they talked about the case Cameron had been working on. "I got a little help from the police," he said. "They were arresting a man on drug charges and asked to speak with the father, whom I needed to serve. When he came outside, I handed him the papers, and then they hauled the son off and I was finished my job."

"So far, we've done pretty well with our new office and the jobs we're getting," Owen said. He couldn't have had better luck on his first case.

Candice said, "You know, I think I need to have a PI for one of my heroes, and I can obtain information for the story from all of you."

Owen hoped that meant she was seriously considering staying with the pack. "We've certainly got a ton of stories to share." At least she seemed to be fine now that she'd gotten over the phone call, and he was glad for that.

When the phone rang again in her pocket, she pulled it out, checked the ID, and then turned off her phone.

He was certain now that the caller was some kind of trouble. Not just a spam caller. Faith and Cameron tried to act like it was no big deal, but he knew from their concerned expressions that they thought the same as him. Something was wrong.

When they were finished visiting, Owen and Candice said their goodbyes and headed out to walk through the woods to his place. "Is someone bothering you?" he asked.

"Yeah. Our stalker. I listened to his voicemail. I can't believe it. It's Rowdy Sanderson and he must have learned who owned my home and then discovered my unlisted phone number."

"Because he's a homicide detective and would easily be able to learn all there was to know about you."

"Well, at least we drove here, so he wouldn't have any idea where I went."

"Unless he saw my license plate and recorded it when he was snooping around your place. Maybe yours too, to learn who was staying there."

"Great. Then he could know where you live."

"I doubt he'd come all the way here to look for you. Why would he? To learn if you have a couple of rescue wolves? Not only is it not his jurisdiction, but it's also not his field of expertise."

"So then why is he calling me?"

"Probably to ask about the wolves, just out of curiosity. I can't imagine why else he'd be so interested."

"Well, I'm not going to talk to him. I'm afraid I might slip up. I haven't murdered anyone or witnessed a murder, so I'm not required to answer any of his questions."

"I agree." Though if Rowdy had been calling Owen, he'd probably talk to the detective himself, just to learn what was up with the guy.

When they reached Owen's house, he and Candice talked to David and Gavin about everything they had put together. Candice approved everything, and then she figured out where she was supposed to be on her world tour so she could pretend to be calling her uncle from there. She was in Edinburgh, Scotland, and it was six hours later there. It would be nine at night now.

Owen hoped like hell that this worked. Lies could snowball in a hurry, but he couldn't think of a better cover story to explain why she didn't have the time to claim her inheritance.

"Okay, how do you want to do this?" she asked.

"I'll call Strom, tell him I found you, and give him your cell phone number. I'll just let him know which city you are in at the moment. I'll explain that you can't get out of the tour, but you said that you'd be back right after Christmas..." Owen looked up his moon phase calendar. "Well, make that around New Year's. You still have the waning gibbous during Christmas, but the new moon will be upon us over New Year's. You'd probably have a good chance of controlling the shifting anywhere between December 29 and January 7. And then you'll see him and the judge and sign the documents you need to."

Christmas. Despite everything being decorated for Christmas and loving the spirit of the holidays, Candice had never really given any thought to how she would celebrate. She suspected the pack had Christmas dinner together. She hadn't had anyone to give gifts to since her parents died. That was something she hadn't considered about staying with Owen and the pack over the holidays. Normally for her, it was just a day to write like any other. Speaking of which, she needed to proof her manuscript and send it in.

And New Year's? She didn't celebrate that at all. It was just the day to take down all her Christmas decorations, clean her house, and begin writing a new book, or finish the one she'd already started.

Owen and the other men were watching her, waiting for her to agree or disagree, and she realized she'd zoned out.

"Uh, yeah, okay, that sounds good. I'll make it the earliest possible date, allowing for driving time. I'll call him after you do, pretending you had just gotten word to me."

"Right."

They discussed the details some more, and then she waited with trepidation for Owen to make the call.

"Hello, Mr. Hart? I have good news. I've located your niece. She's changed to her pen name, Candice Mayfair. She's a romance author, on a worldwide book tour. I've got her phone number to share with you. She said she'll call you in about forty minutes or so." Owen gave Strom Candice's phone number, then paused. "Yeah, I'm positive Candice is your niece… Thanks, and good luck to both of you. Goodbye." Owen ended the call. "He didn't say anything but thanks, to send him my bill, and he'll pay me after he confirms you are Clara."

"Was he glad? Upset?" she asked.

"Neutral, I'd say."

"Okay, so I'm pretending to be driving back from

dinner. I have reached the hotel. I am going through the lobby and up in the elevator. Now to the room." She waited forty minutes to call. "Hi, Uncle Strom. This is Clara, though I've changed my name to Candice Mayfair, since I go by that for my writing."

"And because my brother disowned you?" He didn't sound like he was judging her. Just neutral, as Owen had said her uncle was with him.

"I loved my parents." She hated to have to explain that to him, feeling as though he wouldn't believe her no matter what she said.

"Which is why you refused to come home when they needed you the most." Strom's voice was hard, and she hated that everyone saw her that way—as an uncaring daughter, when she'd been anything but.

"I came home for a whole week every month to be with them. I constantly called, or wrote, or sent them packages. I was with them as much as I could be. I didn't expect any inheritance. Like you said, I thought Dad had disowned me." She hadn't meant to become upset about this. But damn it, she couldn't help what she was.

"Apparently, he had a change of heart. Did the private investigator say that you need to return right away and settle this?"

"No. He said I have a month. I've got this tour through the twenty-eighth. I can be there by the twenty-ninth or thirtieth."

"I would have thought if my brother or his wife couldn't convince you to come home for them, you would have at least have come home for the money."

She ground her teeth and noticed the men were all watching her, staying quiet. "I had real issues I was dealing with." If it wouldn't be a disaster telling him what those issues were, she'd explain. She was dying to clear the air with him, but she knew she couldn't do it.

"Drugs?"

"No. And not alcohol either."

"Okay, give me a date you'll be here, and I'll arrange to have us meet with the judge in his chambers. Send me a picture of yourself. I only found the one your dad had taken of you before you went on that camping trip."

"I didn't think you and Dad ever talked."

"We had issues, but yeah, we talked."

They set the date and then Candice said goodbye, feeling the hurt and loss all over again.

"You can't help what you are, or the difficulties you've had to overcome," Owen said, taking her in his arms as she set the phone on the counter. "If you could have told them, if they could have accepted you for what you are, everything would have ended differently. But you couldn't."

"You've lived with this five years longer than me. Do you ever feel you'll become used to it?"

Owen rubbed her back in a sweet, unassuming way, reassuring her she had nothing to be ashamed of. "We have one another. Sharing a common set of traits like this makes all the difference in the world to us. We accept one another and what we've become. We don't need to ask for anyone else's acceptance."

"Yeah," David said. "It makes all the difference in the world. We were like babes in the woods for quite a while. Misery loves company as the old saying goes."

"Hell yeah," Gavin added. "At least one of us was always able to retain his or her human form at any one time, and that helped to protect us."

"Have you ever considered joining a gray wolf pack somewhere else so there are even more of you...of us to have as friends?" she asked.

"We're Arctic wolves," Gavin reminded her. "It's harder for us to blend in with our surroundings except when we have snow. We would endanger another wolf pack if we joined them in an area that doesn't have as much snow. Especially since we're not royals."

"Royals?"

"The ones who were born *lupus garous* and have their human roots so diluted that they can control their shifting at all times. They are the ones who can shift during the new moon and not shift at any other time, if they choose," Owen said.

"That's what you meant when you said I could have a wolf at a signing with me."

"Right."

"What do we do now?" David asked.

"Just procure more PI jobs. In the meantime, I'll show Candice around the area and—"

"I have a book to proof. And another book to start," she reminded him. She needed to go back to work, not treat this as a vacation.

"Need any help with proofing?" Gavin quickly asked.

"She's got me," Owen said. "In fact, we need to work on that, like she said."

"Okay. We can take a hint. Call us if you need any help with anything." David slapped Owen on the back as he headed for the door.

Gavin echoed the sentiment and then followed David out, shutting the door behind him.

"I'll be just a moment." Owen hurried after his friends.

Candice turned her computer on, serious about proofing her book while Owen saw the men outside.

When he returned, Owen said, "I guess you don't need me for a while."

"Not until tomorrow, and then you can begin reading it." She didn't want him to feel he had to keep her company. She wasn't a guest who needed to be entertained.

"Okay. I'll chop some firewood, and I need to run into town for some groceries. If you want to make a list, I'll pick up whatever you need. Unless you want to go with me."

"No, that's okay. I'll make a list. I really need to get going on this." She wrote down several items she liked to have for meals, including lavender, jasmine, and mint teas, if the store had them.

"If you need anything while I'm gone, anything you forgot, just give me a call. And here's a list of everyone's phone numbers in case you have any kind of trouble. Not that you'd have any trouble, but just for reference."

"Thanks, Owen." Candice added the numbers in her cell's list of contacts. She was going to give him some money for the groceries, but he shook his head.

"I've got it." Then he left, and she decided to work on her laptop in the big sunroom with a view of the lake instead. She settled on the chair in front of a café table and looked across the lake at the cloud reflections drifting across its surface and watched a hawk flying high overhead—just beautiful.

Then she turned on her laptop and got busy.

Two hours later, Owen returned with groceries. She'd made some real progress proofing her manuscript, so she'd gone outside to take in the fresh air for a moment.

She was glad he came outside and checked on her. "How are you doing?"

"Great. You'll be able to read this soon." She headed into the living room with him, wanting to visit with him now that he was home.

"I look forward to it. Does fish and shrimp, wine, and rice pilaf sound good?" Owen asked.

"Love it." She put her laptop on the bar and helped him put away the groceries. "You were gone a long time. Is it that far to the grocery store?"

"I had to run into the office first. We had a couple of cases, but Gavin and Cameron are taking care of them."

"Sounds like business is picking up."

"We always have cases, just online mostly. But yeah, now that we have an office, it seems to be getting some attention." He pulled her into his arms and held her tight. "You're cold. Your nose is red."

"I am, but I was enjoying the outdoors and the view of the lake for a few minutes." Though she'd stayed out longer than she intended. This felt wonderful, being warmed up in Owen's arms, not just turning the heat on high or sitting beside a crackling fire.

Candice realized how much she'd missed anyone's intimate touches. Yet there was more than that with Owen. There was a sense of real belonging.

She hugged him tighter. "It was too nice to come in any earlier. But I admit this feels pretty good too." She thought about how it would be to always warm up like this on cold winter days. If she needed something when she couldn't control the shifting, she realized any of the pack members who had more control could take care of the issue for her.

He kissed her then, and Candice knew she should put

on the brakes a bit. She was just warming up to the idea of joining their pack, of moving here. She wasn't ready to mate a wolf for life.

Yet she kissed him like she was claiming him as her mate and telling herself she had to be sure they were right for each other in every way. He started to pull off her jacket, and she hoped she hadn't given him the wrong idea. He dropped it on the barstool, pulled off her hat, and gathered her in his arms again, holding her tight. Just holding her.

"Who's winning the competition?" she asked, snuggling up to him, glad his hard body was so warm.

"Which one?" He rubbed her back and kissed her cold nose.

"The Christmas decorating contest. What other would there be?"

He smiled. "You."

Candice sighed and pulled away, helping to put away the rest of the groceries, even though she had to open lots of cabinet doors to find where things went.

He started cooking the seasoned tilapia in hot olive oil.

"If I moved here—"

Owen glanced at her, looking so hopeful that she hated to give him the idea she wanted to mate him. She needed to get to know him first. They may not be compatible in the long run. He had to feel the same way about this, deep down.

"If I did...where would I stay?"

"With me. There's plenty of room. I'll have jobs and won't be home all that much. You can write to your heart's content. And if you're sitting outside and grow cold, I'll warm you right up when I arrive home."

"What if I…fell in love with one of your buddies?" She thought they both were really nice, cute, intriguing. Not like Owen though. She'd already started to build memories with him. She would never forget saving the snowmobilers while Owen dug at the snow just as vigorously beside her. Or how, with a sprained ankle, he went out to chase off the intruder and then later came looking for both the man and her to make sure they were fine.

"Well, I just have to ensure that doesn't happen, don't I?" He leaned down to kiss her thoroughly, and she felt light-headed when he let her up for air, her body thrumming with expectation.

Candice loved how he wanted to convince her to stay—with him. He didn't seem desperate either, which she was glad for. That would have been a sure-fire way to push her away.

"But if that happened, I would be thrilled to have you join the pack no matter what. Faith would love to have another woman to talk to. And the rest of us would help you move. We own enough property here that we could even build you your own house, if none of the guys appealed as a mate."

"What would everyone else think of that?"

"They're all in agreement." Owen turned and dished out the fish. "We've been best friends forever. As soon as they knew Corey had changed you, that you were an Arctic she-wolf, it went without saying."

"What if I'd been a guy?"

"I won't deny that bringing another male wolf into the pack could be troublesome. But if we thought he could work well with us, we would certainly have given it a shot."

Candice served the shrimp and cocktail sauce, while Owen brought over the rice pilaf and fish. She had thought another male wolf might cause problems. She was glad Owen was being honest with her.

"Just so you know, now that we are aware of your existence, we would worry about you being in South Dakota all by yourself. We wouldn't be able to see you all the time, but we'd be checking to make sure you weren't having trouble with anyone looking for the Arctic wolves supposedly living there. We wouldn't feel that it was an obligation, but more of a concern over a fellow wolf."

"A she-wolf, you mean."

He smiled. "Yeah, what can I say?"

"That homicide detective couldn't hang around for very long. The sheriff said he works in Montana. I love the location where I'm living—"

They took their seats at the table. "But…?"

"I have to admit that being with a pack has appeal. But what if it didn't work out? Still, I can't really see going back to the way things were. Completely isolated. No one to talk to about these issues. And I don't mean to do it just online either. Though that would be better than nothing."

"No matter what, we're willing to make this work. Just give us a chance."

"You don't feel desperate or anything, right?" She had to ask. She still couldn't quit thinking of it as being like she was the last woman on earth, and no matter how incompatible they might be, he would still want her as his mate.

"Does the desperation show? Too much?"

She laughed. She really did like him.

"So…you'll stay with us?" He looked like he was trying to act nonchalant about it.

"I just got here. What if in a couple of weeks, you decided you couldn't tolerate living with me?"

"Then I'd be certifiable, and believe me, Gavin and David would be knocking down my door to offer their hospitality. In fact, when I went to see them off, that's exactly what the two of them said."

"You told my uncle you know I am Clara. How did you verify it?"

"I didn't. I just intended to ask you, and then there was the wolf of my dreams standing at the door. You don't know how many times I went to that camping area to see if you ever returned. As if by some miracle you would. I had the idiot notion when I saw you across the river that you might be the one for me, though we've never crossed paths with an Arctic wolf since we were bitten in Maine and left there. I more than fantasized about you. I searched for you, but I came up with nothing. Then when I saw you at your door, I just knew it had to be fate. I was the only one who had seen you. Twice now. If I hadn't gotten the job, one of the other guys would have been there instead."

"Ha! I assumed I was hallucinating when I saw you at the river that time. Later, I thought your son had bitten me. At least, that's what I believed. No way would I have ever returned. I definitely wasn't thinking of how much I wanted to meet you again. I was thinking about what an alien world this whole situation had turned out to be."

"Are you sure? I thought when you saw me as a wolf you were wearing an intrigued look."

She smiled. "It was more of a curious and a little worried look. I mean, what would I have done if you had crossed the river and come to see me?" She would have been afraid of him, afraid he wouldn't want her in his pack's territory. And, if the little one was his, afraid she might be a danger to the pup.

"I would have greeted you and tried to convince you to see the pack then, not knowing you had been newly turned. You really never thought about me after that?"

"Oh, all right. Yes. But I reminded myself you had a litter of pups and probably a vicious mate."

He laughed. "Well, I didn't, on either count."

She saluted him with her wine. "Do you want to take the canoe out? I want to see the lake."

His cell phone rang, and she waited for him to answer it. But when he looked at the caller ID and then looked at her, she wondered if her uncle had somehow learned the truth. She wasn't on a book tour anywhere.

Chapter 9

"Hello?" Owen saw that the caller was from Montana, probably Rowdy Sanderson. He was surprised the homicide detective would call him after Candice wouldn't take his call. The detective sure was persistent. Owen figured Candice was right and Rowdy must have taken down his license plate number when he came snooping around Candice's place.

"Hello, I'm Rowdy Sanderson, a homicide detective with the police department in Bigfork, Montana. I don't want to alarm you, no murders committed or anything, but I was in South Dakota when two wolves rescued a couple of snowmobilers."

"Wolves? You can't be right about that. They're wild animals. No one could train them to do something like that. Even if that really happened, I don't know what I have to do with it."

Candice sat down on the barstool, frowning. Owen moved closer to her and swept his hand down her back.

"You were at Candice Mayfair's place when this happened. And she lives close enough as the wolf runs to reach the injured men and return to the house."

Now Owen was frowning. "You were the one trespassing on her land?" He figured it was time to turn the tables. Put the detective on the defensive.

"I was just tracking the wolves. I wanted to talk to Ms. Mayfair and offer my help in any way that I can."

"Help with what?" Before Sanderson could answer, Owen said, "Okay, listen. If this isn't a case of homicide that involves me…or her, then I have nothing further to say to you. I don't own wolves, and neither does she. But I've got business to take care of. Have a great day." Owen cut Sanderson off, ending the call before the detective could respond.

"He did see your license," Candice said.

"Yeah, but he's not going to come all the way out here to see me. And he won't know you're here."

"Except that you left, and I'm gone too." Candice got off the barstool and put on her coat. "That's if he put two and two together, and he seems to be really good at following up on leads."

Owen grabbed his jacket and slipped it on. "When we were eating breakfast that morning, he told the sheriff that he was on vacation. I doubt he'd use all his vacation time trying to track down a couple of wolves."

Once they were all bundled up, they headed outside.

"What if he does come here?"

"What would he do? Tell us he knew we had wolves when we don't? Then what?"

"Okay, but I keep thinking of that story you told me about the werewolf hunters."

Hell, Owen hadn't thought that this Rowdy might believe in werewolves like those other nut jobs who'd tried to kill them. "I'm sure if he were a werewolf hunter, he'd have some buddies, not be doing this on his own. And that's the only time we ever ran into anyone like that. I'm sure it's a fluke. The guys were chasing down Bigfoot."

Owen smiled at her and took her gloved hand, squeezing it. He was thrilled to take Candice out in the canoe, so he was annoyed with the detective for worrying her over this. Once they got back in, he'd call Cameron to let him know what was going on with this detective, and Cameron would tell everyone else.

He'd love to take Candice out for a sail too in the summer. Anything that would convince her she'd love to live here. With him. Was he desperate? Yeah, just a little.

After they got into the canoe and paddled out, he guided them near the bank to see the Christmas lights on Cameron and Faith's house, his own, and David's reflecting off the water. The homes were separated by a lot of forest acreage to give them each enough privacy, yet close enough that the pack members could run as wolves or hike on the trails as humans to one another's homes. Gavin was always forgetting to turn his outdoor lights on. But the Christmas lights decorating the tree inside were on and visible through his big lakeside windows.

"Beautiful. I never would have imagined something so magical." Candice was sitting up front, paddling like a pro.

Owen recalled that she and her hiking companions had taken canoes at one point and he had lost her trail completely. "I'd love to take you sailing when it's warmer in the spring."

"Okay, it's a deal. There's only one problem."

He couldn't imagine what could be a problem, though he detected a hint of a smile.

"Who's going to use the lake as a setting for his or her werewolf romance?"

He chuckled. "For you, I would give up anything. But I imagine the way I'd describe it could be much different from the way you would. Different voices, right?"

She smiled. "Yeah. I just wanted to make sure it was okay if I used it. It's just so romantic. Uh, one other thing."

Now she looked serious. "Yeah?"

"About Christmas..."

"Low key. No worries." He hadn't given it a lot of thought. Not when he wanted to do everything he possibly could to make her feel welcome. And get this business with the inheritance over so she could be settled here safely.

"Right. So exactly what happens?" Candice didn't sound like she thought Christmas would be low key.

It really was just a relaxed, family-filled gathering of the wolves. "Christmas dinner with Cameron and his family. One of the guys always has Christmas Eve dinner. Usually two of us prepare most of the dishes, though everyone pitches in with something. I did it with David last year. We have snowman contests, if we have fresh snow. Play board games."

"I've never made a snowman. Not a lot of snow in Houston, you know. Sure, South Dakota has snow, but it wasn't something I'd go out and do by myself. But with a bunch of us creating them, that really sounds like fun."

"It is. The cocoa and baked goods to warm us up afterward are great too. We have to do a lot of extra running to wear it all off, but it's worth it. The guys and I get a little fishing in. Now that the kids are growing older, they'll probably do some too. They did before, but they got too cold."

"I hadn't really considered I'd be staying over Christmas while I was here."

"It's low key. Really. Nobody expects you to buy them anything."

"And no one will be picking up anything for me. Right?"

"Are you kidding? If Gavin and David think it might make a difference in winning your affection, they'll be getting you something. The MacPhersons too, because they'll want you to feel welcome and stay with us."

"But you're not, right?"

"Hell yeah. I want you to feel welcome most of all."

Candice sighed. "Okay, so when we return to the house, you can tell me what everyone would like and I'll order them gifts online. They should arrive in time."

"You don't have—"

"Yeah, I do. I want to. It'll be fun. I haven't done Christmas in a couple of years. No gift giving, no celebration. I always decorate, but I just continue to work on books as if it's any other day of the year."

Owen had suspected that might be the case. He was glad she was here to celebrate the holidays with them, and that she fully intended to participate. "I can't tell you how excited everyone is that you're here. You've made the holidays truly special for all of us. But especially for me. A couple of days ago, I would never have imagined boating on the lake with a beautiful she-wolf."

Candice took a deep breath and dipped her paddle into the water. "I never imagined doing this with the beautiful wolf from across the river. Never in a million years."

The sun was beginning to set, the pinks and oranges reflecting off wisps of clouds, turning them pink, and coloring the water pink and orange in places as the sun's rays filtered through the trees bordering the lake. A snowy owl hooted in a dying tree near the shore.

"In the summer, you'll hear the mournful call of the loon to its mate, and she'll call back to let him know she's nearby."

"More story material."

He laughed. "Does everything go in a book?"

"Only what I can remember."

A wolf howled, and then another. She turned to look in the direction of the howls. She probably hadn't heard a chorus of wolves howling before.

"The first one was David; second one, Gavin," Owen said.

Then the wolves began running out of the woods and along the opposite bank as Owen and Candice paddled home. She waved at them. Then another howl sounded and several others deeper in the woods.

"Cameron was the first. Then Faith and the little ones in a jumble next."

"Now that's something I've never heard before. A whole wolf pack with pups. It's beautiful."

"It is. Makes us remember who we are and lets everyone know we're all safe."

"But they won't hear you howling."

"They'll assume..." He saw movement on the opposite beach. "They're all here, running along the beach, checking on us."

Candice laughed, loving that the pack was so close-knit. "This is lovely."

They were still quite a way from the dock when she saw two moose, one in the water and the other standing on the beach near the dock. They were stunning, huge, and she wished she had her camera. "They can be dangerous, can't they?"

"Yeah. We were up in Alaska one year, looking for a missing husband. We had clues that he had gone up there to get away from family obligations—namely, paying child support for four kids. We were told to wear bear repellent spray, but that the moose were more dangerous to hikers than the bears."

"Did you have any run-ins with bears?" She could imagine being frozen to the spot if she saw one close by.

"No, never saw a one."

"What do we do?" She couldn't even envision what it would be like to tangle with a moose. She'd always wanted to see one, but now she wasn't so sure. She was growing so cold. She figured she needed warmer gear to go canoeing in the winter if she was going to stay out this long.

"The wind is against us. It's carrying our scent to the moose. The trouble is, they'll smell our wolf halves."

"That should make them run away, right? I mean, most animals run away when they smell us coming."

"Not moose. They've been known to charge after dogs, and humans too. If they feel cornered, or if you are within fifty yards of them and in their space, they can grow riled."

"Do they attack with their antlers?"

"They can. But they'll kick out with their hooves and can be dangerous that way too."

"What do you do if you encounter one? Running would just make it follow, right?"

"Unlike how you would avoid bears—making noise to alert them you're in the area—you are better off running from an attacking moose. If you move out of the moose's space, they usually won't feel threatened any longer. But they can run up to thirty miles per hour. Another way is to climb a tree, or hide behind one to protect yourself. Most bears can climb trees, so that's not a guaranteed way to escape from one. But those are some ways to safely avoid a moose. They've chased us when we've been riding snowmobiles too. One charged David's, and he jumped off to avoid the moose's antlers. It kept coming after him, and he finally had to run for it."

"You didn't go back for him and save him?" She couldn't believe all those hunky male wolves would run and leave David behind to fend for himself.

"Hell no." Owen smiled at her. "He aggravated the moose, not us. We watched from a distance, in case he needed us to come to his rescue. We didn't want to irritate the moose any more than he was already. David ended up climbing a tree. The moose observed him for a while and then finally sauntered off. Moose aren't on any kind of schedule. They do what they want when they want. But as a matter of preservation, they can be aggressive if they smell we're wolves."

"Okay, so what do we do about it this time? I'm growing cold."

"Oh, I'm sorry, Candice. Let's go to David's place. It's closer. And we can leave the canoe there."

"Wait, the moose is moving off."

"Are you sure you can wait that long?"

"Yeah. We still have a distance to go, and maybe he'll move far enough away from the house by the time we reach the dock."

The moose on the shore sauntered off, and the other one left the water, dripping wet. He shook, then began to follow the other. They weren't in any hurry to move.

Since Candice was sitting up front in the canoe, she was growing closer to where the moose was, but she continued to dip her paddle into the water, matching Owen's strokes, bringing the canoe closer to the dock with every pull. The sun had nearly set, but the lights on the house and the deck and the dock provided plenty of light for their enhanced wolf's night vision.

The moose were maybe one hundred yards away when Candice and Owen reached the dock. Owen took hold of one of the dock posts and steadied the canoe so Candice could climb out. She should have been watching her footing, but she couldn't help observing the moose that continued to monitor her. She was as wary of them as they were of her.

"We'll be pulling the dock out of the water tomorrow before the ice really sets in," he said. Just as Candice set her boot on the dock, she felt her foot slipping out from under her as she stepped on a fresh sheen of light ice, and she gasped.

As soon as she had tried to leave the canoe, she'd pushed it away from the dock, and now she was falling into the water, her back hitting the edge of the canoe. As padded as she was with all the layers of clothing she was wearing, she didn't think she'd hurt herself. She fell into the water with a splash. She'd been mortified as soon as she began to fall, worried she might tip the canoe and force Owen into the water too.

She didn't see what Owen was doing as she was trying to rush out of the frigid water—cold, cold, cold. The layers of wet clothes, icy water, and big boots were impeding her movement as she waded to shore through the waist-deep water. Then she saw Owen shove the canoe onto the shore and hurry into the water to pull her out the rest of the way.

"You didn't have to come help me and end up all cold and wet too."

"Like hell I didn't. No more using the dock until spring. I need to dry you off and warm you up at once."

Candice glanced at the moose that were eyeing her right back. Owen practically hauled her up the steps to the deck, and that took some muscle, as wet as she was. She must have weighed an extra fifty pounds. She didn't want to leave a trail of water in the house, but he didn't seem to care. He just continued hauling her inside, then shut the door. Before she could react, he was pulling off her gloves and hat, unfastening her jacket, and then moving her to the fire.

"Your pants and boots are wet," she said, wanting him to take care of himself too.

"You first. It'll only take a moment for me to pull off my boots and drop my pants."

Shivering, she smiled at him while fumbling to pull off her sweater. Her hands were already numb from the cold, though the fire was helping some. She wished the heat could wrap around her and not just warm her front. He quickly pulled off her sweater and began unbuttoning her shirt.

Once he'd removed that, he took hold of her belt. "Here, let me help you out of your pants, and then I'll grab some towels and blankets for you."

She thought of taking a hot shower, but she liked that he was babying her. She hadn't had anyone do that to her since she was a child.

He'd stripped her of everything and wrapped her in

the blue throw on the sofa. He pulled her into a hug, held her tight for a moment, then kissed her forehead. "Curl up on the couch, and I'll be right back."

He was back before she knew it, with towels for her hair and body, warm blankets, and a heating pad. She laughed. "Now I know only to fall into frigid water when you're around."

"Hopefully, I won't put you in a situation where you're liable to fall into the water again."

"It wasn't your fault. I was worried about the moose and wasn't paying close enough attention to where I was stepping."

"Do you want me to bring you your warm pajamas?"

"Sure." She was dry and bundled up in the blanket on the couch, her hair wrapped in a towel, and was feeling perfectly comfortable. "It's in the middle drawer of the bachelor chest. Thanks."

As soon as he brought her the pajamas, he said, "Hot cocoa?"

She laughed. "Sure, that would be nice. Thanks. But you need to take off your wet pants first."

"If anyone else suggested that, I wouldn't think anything of it." He gave her a sexy smile.

Smiling, she shook her head.

"Need the heating pad?"

"No, I'm good, thanks." She really wanted *him* to change into something dry.

"All right. Be back with the cocoa in a few."

Reluctantly, Candice unwrapped herself from the blanket and pulled the towel off her hair to slip into her flannel pajamas. She put the damp towel on the glass top of the coffee table, dressed, then wrapped a dry towel around her hair. But her feet were cold. She headed to the guest room, not wanting Owen to think he had to go fetch her warm socks and booties too.

Owen had always loved boating and seeing the sunset on a crisp, cold night. Being with Candice would have made it perfect—if she hadn't fallen into the lake. He'd seen it happening but had been powerless to stop her fall. He knew he shouldn't blame himself—it was just an accident and could have happened to anyone—but he couldn't help it. He kept thinking about what he should have done differently to prevent it from occurring.

He was glad the moose didn't bother them when he was struggling to rush her to the house. In fact, he'd even forgotten about them for a moment.

Once he and Candice were inside, all he had wanted to do was pull off her wet clothes, dry her, and wrap her in blankets by the fire. It was impossible to forget the way she looked as he pulled off her clothes—her curly red hair and creamy skin, the freckles on her cheeks, her red curly hair at the apex of her thighs. She was just beautiful. But he'd tried to keep his mind on taking care of her.

When he had changed and was wearing a pair of slippers, thinking he needed to bring her socks and her slipper boots, he found her curled up on the couch, her laptop on her lap, and typing away. "I thought I'd work on proofing."

"Great idea. I'll just grab some socks for you and—"

"I got them, booties too." She stuck a foot out from underneath the blanket.

He smiled. "Okay. I'll join you in a minute." After a few minutes, he brought over the cocoa, then sat near her on the sofa, pulled out his notebook, and began to write his story.

"Thanks for the cocoa," she said, finally looking up.

"My pleasure."

She eyed his notebook. "Working on your story?"

"You bet. I always finish what I start. Always. Well, maybe not my writing, though I aim to this time. But everything else?"

She smiled at him.

"Always." He wondered if she got his meaning. He had every intention of wooing the wolf until she could do nothing but agree to be his.

Three days later, Candice had sent in her finished book and started working on her next one, while taking breaks running as a wolf with him and sometimes with several of the other pack members. They'd pulled the dock and the dock bubbler out of the water for the winter and hadn't seen any more signs of the moose. Though she'd told him enough times how much she'd love seeing them, despite what had happened to her. She wished she'd had her camera with her… Well, if she hadn't fallen in the water. That would have been the end of her camera too.

She couldn't help but want to sail across the lake with Owen. And add that to her stories. She was really enjoying the time she spent with him and the pack. She was already thinking about spending spring and summer here, and all the fun she could have.

Candice had even finished Christmas shopping for everyone. And baked more cookies with Owen, who had taken up the challenge and found a recipe for Fudge Crinkles. She decided that should be a Christmas cookie tradition from now on, as much as everyone loved them. She was beginning to think of this as her home now. That she wasn't returning to South Dakota for good.

She couldn't believe how much at home she felt with Owen and the pack already. She knew she couldn't go back to the way she'd lived before. Not now. Not when she had found others who were just like her. She loved everyone.

They didn't treat her as though they knew she was leaving. They acted as though she was staying here forever. That eventually she would be Owen's mate. She had to admit that the longer she got to know him, the more the idea had real appeal. He was working on his own book, not in a way that said he was doing it just to be on her good side, but because he really wanted to. Some nights while she continued to work on her book, he carved ornaments he planned to give to each of the pack members, though if he was carving one for her, he wasn't sharing. Every time he worked on another, she asked who it was for, and it was always someone different.

"They're so beautiful, Owen. What made you start carving wood?"

"My dad, and my grandfather before that. It was just something passed down from generation to generation. Somewhere I have a photo of four generations of carvers. I was ten when I started. Mom was having fits, but my dad said he was five when he began, and I was nearly an old man when I took it up."

Candice laughed. She wished she had the talent to create something as beautiful for everyone. Instead, she was working on a children's book about an Arctic wolf pup who made a friend and renewed their friendship years later at Christmastime. And how he brought his sister and brother to meet her too. She couldn't draw anything, but she had fun Photoshopping a bunch of pictures and creating a chapter book for the kids. Of course, then she realized she'd have to make one for each of the pups. When she wasn't writing and having fun with everything else, she was creating the kids' books. A printer in town said he would print them for her in time for Christmas.

They'd had another lovely canoe trip tonight, watched the sunset, and then returned for a nightcap. They'd found a delicious recipe for hot cocoa with peppermint schnapps and a candy cane crushed on top of it. A hot drink after the cold boat trip and time to unwind.

"These are going to be addictive," Candice said, licking her lips. When she saw a chip of candy cane and whipped cream on his lip, she pulled Owen in close to take care of it.

That led to kissing and hugging and rousing their pheromones, which made her want more. She'd never been driven to have sex with a guy, not like she was when she kissed and hugged Owen. But still, she was cautious because of the finality of it. Was this really what she wanted for the rest of her life? Was he someone she couldn't live without?

When she was kissing him, that was a big yes.

He pulled his mouth away from hers and held her close as if he was trying to get his raging need for her under control. She was glad he wasn't pressuring her about wanting more, though he constantly did everything he could to make her feel at home here. He didn't treat her as though she was just another fixture, but someone truly special.

She found it was getting harder to say good night to each other, and she really thought they might be taking this further sooner rather than later. Though she thought the other guys were cute and fun and likeable, Owen made her heartbeat quicken whenever he was near. When he was at work on a case, she missed his presence.

"Remember, I've got to leave first thing in the morning. I'll probably be away for a couple of days, trying to track down a missing husband in another state. Are you sure you're going to be all right?"

"Absolutely. I've got work to do on my new book, and I won't have any distractions then."

He smiled. "I'm a distraction now, am I?"

"A welcome distraction." She sighed. "Okay, you get some sleep, and I'll see you off in the morning." She thought it was a way to firm up how she was feeling about him. If she didn't miss him, wouldn't that be an indication?

When she retired to bed that night, she still worked on her story. She wondered what he did late at night. Carved an ornament for her? Would she find wood shavings in his bed?

The next morning, Owen had to leave early, and this was the first time he'd be away from Candice overnight. He hated leaving her. Not because he felt she couldn't manage on her own. She had for two years. But simply because he didn't want to leave her. He kissed her and reminded her to call Faith if she had any trouble, since all the guys were out on jobs.

"I'll be fine, Owen. Quit worrying. You'll be home before you know it."

"I'll miss you," he said quite honestly.

She smiled. "I'll miss you too. You're a great cook. You rescue me from cold lakes, and you make a great cup of hot chocolate."

He hoped she missed him enough to know she needed him in her life permanently. As far as he was concerned, after they took care of this business with the will, he wanted to convince her she couldn't live without him. Or at least the pack. But mostly him.

He hugged her soundly one last time, gave her a parting kiss that promised much more, and left. He swore he had never felt so disconcerted in his life. He listened to another of her books while he was on the road, which made him miss her even more. He kept picturing her in the scenario, now that he knew she used so many of her life experiences in the books. He could envision how much she had longed to have her life back, then resolved to make the most of it by finding a wolf mate to love—at least in her fantasy books.

And he was that wolf mate, as far as he was concerned. As he was crossing the state line, he figured she was working on her book. Despite the early-morning hour, he knew she wouldn't have gone back to sleep. She'd work on the book until he returned.

He thought about calling her, just to take his mind off the drive, to reassure himself she was missing him like he already missed her, but he fought the urge. She needed some space, and he needed the time to think about his case. Which is why he listened to her book and thought again about her in those scenes with him as her Arctic wolf lover—and smiled.

Candice walked to Faith's home to have lunch with her. She felt good about finally having a female friend who understood what she was going through.

The kids had already eaten and were in one of their rooms playing a game when Faith and Candice took seats at the dining room table to eat chicken pot pies.

"Owen told me how David and he were turned. How he accidentally bit Gavin, and how that came about. How Cameron was bitten, but Owen only said Cameron accidentally turned you."

Faith smiled. "I wasn't happy with him over that. He knew he was a wolf shifter, and he'd been wounded in a fight with a wolf while trying to protect me. I came into his tent to tend to his wounds, thinking he was human at that point. In the dark tent, I reached out to wake him, and I touched fur and nearly had a heart attack. He growled and bit me. I accidentally knocked the tent pole down, and it collapsed on top of us. I tried to scramble out of the tent, afraid he was going to attack. I finally found an opening in the tent, and there he was, his fluorescent amber eyes glowing in the dark tent as he stopped me from leaving. I didn't know if I'd be just like him, but I suspected so.

"Anyway, we really had the hots for each other before that, loved each other during all the trials we were going through, and then had to deal with the wolf business too. But not just us...Cameron's partners too. We were one big Arctic wolf pack family. We fumbled around in the dark trying to learn how to cope, and we've finally managed to get our lives back on track."

Candice thought being bitten by an adult male wolf might have been scarier than how she was turned. But the fact that they already loved each other would have made a difference.

"I can't tell you enough how sorry I am that our son bit you and turned you, but I have to say I'm glad you're here with us, that you and Owen are so good for each other, and"—Faith wiped away trails of tears—"I finally have a female friend to talk to. The guys have been wonderful, don't get me wrong. But they have one another when they're dealing with male issues. I haven't had anybody to commiserate with, both with having the children and raising them. And just..." She shrugged. "Girl talk."

Glad to be there for another woman in the same boat as herself, Candice reached across the table and squeezed Faith's hand, feeling just as emotional about finally having a girlfriend that she could talk to. "I would have been scared to pieces if I'd experienced that with a full-grown wolf. Corey was so cute, and with him being a pup, I knew he hadn't bitten me on purpose. My concern was that he might have rabies. That he could turn me into a werewolf?" She shook her head. "I'm glad I'm here, that we can be friends, and that I'm no longer alone."

"If you ever have any questions or just need to talk to me about anything, I'm here for you. It's like being an alien in a human world. We just learn as we go along."

"Thank you. And the same goes for me, if you ever need to talk," Candice said.

By two in the afternoon, Owen had to call Candice. She'd said she was going to have lunch with Faith at eleven, so he figured she'd be home by now. "Hey, it's me," he said as if they were already a couple.

"Hey, you. Miss me?"

"Hell, if I didn't have your book to listen to, yeah. I've been lost in the story, missed two of my exits, and keep thinking of you in those scenes. With me. You know, we can do all that for real."

She laughed.

"No, I'm serious."

"I know you are. I miss you. I thought about making some more Fudge Crinkles."

"Not without me, you don't. That's our special dessert."

"Which is why I've been craving them so badly."

Which he wanted to believe meant she was really craving being with him. "We'll make a batch when I arrive home."

"How are the roads?"

"Good. I'm almost to the hotel, and I'll start searching the town to see if I can locate the perp. He's supposed to have a job here. I need to find his home address. How's your writing coming along?"

"Great. I came up with this new scene. Heroine tries to leave canoe and tips the boat, knocking them both in the water. Moose charges them, and for a few minutes, they're under the dock while they wait the moose out."

"They'd grow awfully cold."

"They're shivering and hugging each other. As soon as they feel it's safe, they make a slow dash and reach the house. Inside, they begin stripping off their wet clothes, and the next thing you know, they're taking a hot shower, kissing, and declaring their love for each other, and then they're mated."

"Wait, I missed the mating part."

"You'll have to read the book."

He laughed. "Okay, so that means I did it all wrong."

"Did what wrong?"

He sighed dramatically. "I was supposed to fall into the water and hide with you underneath the dock."

"No, you did everything just right. This is fantasy."

"I could use a little more fantasy in my life."

She laughed. "I have to admit my stay here has really jump-started my writing."

"I will do anything you need to help you write the rest of your books. Oh, here's the hotel. I'll call you back in a little bit."

"Okay, bye, Owen. Be careful. Talk soon."

"Same here," Owen said and ended the call. He fully intended to be back before the other guys.

But after two days of trying to track the guy down, Owen worried that, at this rate, one of the other men in his pack would have to take Candice to Houston when the time was right.

It was as if someone had tipped off Kendall Malt and he'd gone into hiding. His workplace said he'd quit his job at the fish-packing plant without a really good reason, and Owen wasn't able to determine where he lived. Until he discovered Kendall had a girlfriend who worked in receiving at the plant.

"What's it to you?" she asked, twirling long, dark strands of hair around her finger, green eyes rounded.

"He's owed some money," Owen said. The promise of money got them every time.

"How much?"

"I can only discuss it with him."

"He's staying with me."

"Why did he quit his job?"

"He didn't get along with the manager. But he's got another job already."

"How can I reach him?"

She gave Owen her home address and Kendall's new place of employment.

"Thanks. He'll thank you for this. Good day." Owen was certain she'd call Kendall right away with the good news, but Owen was already feeding the information to the local police department to pick Kendall up for failure to pay child support. The mom was struggling with two jobs to make ends meet for her and her two kids, living at her mom's house while Grandmom took care of the kids. If Kendall had the money, he needed to do what was right.

Owen wanted to call Candice right away with the good news, but he quashed the inclination until he was certain the police had arrested Kendall.

Once that was done, Owen called her right away as he headed home.

"Oh, that's great, Owen. Don't kill yourself trying to rush home or anything."

"Why would I do that?"

"Because you're craving those Fudge Crinkles as much as I am."

He chuckled. "You bet." And a hell of a lot more. Even just sitting on the couch, his arms wrapped around her while they watched a show, totally appealed right now. They talked for about an hour, and then they ended the call and all he could think of was how he couldn't wait to be with her soon.

Candice hoped she'd sounded low key about being eager to have Owen home right away. She'd meant what she'd said about him not rushing home, not with the winter weather conditions the way they were. She wanted him home in one piece.

She could hardly wait to see him. She cleaned house, did their laundry, and sat out on the deck, watching the lake and imagining another couple of canoe trips before it was too late to go boating. And she was already thinking of other ways to occupy themselves. Like building a snowman as soon as they had another good snowfall, for one thing.

Then she saw two moose near the lake some distance off and ran inside to grab her camera. She took some shots of them, perfect for describing them in her book. Owen wouldn't be home until tomorrow at the soonest.

He called her every once in a while with progress reports, and she told him she'd captured pictures of the moose.

"You didn't get close to them, did you?"

"Only with a zoom lens. They were a long way off. And I was on the deck, an easy dash to the back door if they'd miraculously flown through the air like Santa's reindeer to come and get me." She appreciated his concern and loved even having anyone to talk to like this about what she was doing. And she loved hearing about his experiences.

"All right."

"Believe me, I'm not getting near moose unless you're here to protect me."

"Under the dock."

"That might be a little too cold."

He chuckled. She loved that he had a sense of humor.

"I've missed you," he said.

"You've been so busy chasing down the deadbeat father. How could you have?"

"I miss hearing your voice, smelling your scent, sharing meals and other pursuits."

"We'll have to run as wolves when you arrive home."

"Are...you having trouble with shifting?"

"Some. I mean, not any trouble with shifting as long as I don't plan to go anywhere, which I don't. Staying at home is no problem. What about you?"

"I'm okay for now."

Still, she worried. If he'd said he never lost control of his shifting, she would have felt better.

Then they signed off, and the next evening, she couldn't sit still. He'd called several times on the drive home, but when he was near the lake, he gave her another call. "Did you fix us anything to eat?"

"I'd tease you and tell you that you need to bring home takeout, but knowing you, you'd do it. Yeah, I fixed you something. See you in a few minutes."

She'd baked him a small welcome-home chocolate fudge cake and made his favorite spareribs, grilled asparagus, and sweet potatoes for dinner. She greeted him on the porch, unable to hide how she was feeling. Not only was she glad he was home, but she appreciated everything he'd done for her.

Instead of waiting for him to join her, she hurried to stand beside the SUV while he cut off the engine. As soon as he left the vehicle, she threw her arms around him, kissing and hugging him with enthusiasm.

He kissed her back, his arms wrapped snuggly around her. "Wow, you can't imagine how I've envisioned coming home to see you. I thought you would be sitting on the couch, lost in your manuscript, a mug of cold tea at hand, or sitting on the back deck taking pictures of moose or writing in your book. But you couldn't have made my coming home any more welcome than this."

"No way would I have my nose in my book when the hero of said book needs a hero's welcome."

"Just so you can write the scene correctly?"

She smiled. "You got it." She dragged him in the house before he could grab his bag. She was starving, and she didn't want the food to grow cold.

"You really know how to make a hero feel like a king."

"Right, to ensure the story is told just right."

He laughed.

When they had nearly finished supper, Owen's phone rang. He wiped his greasy fingers on his paper napkin and looked at the caller ID. "Your uncle. I need to take this. Hello, sir, this is Owen Nottingham." Owen's jaw dropped slightly. He covered the mouthpiece and said to Candice, "You'll want to hear this. Putting it on speaker."

Candice knew at once something wasn't right. She was afraid her uncle had somehow learned her book-signing tour hadn't happened at all.

Chapter 10

"I'M EXTREMELY DISAPPOINTED IN WHAT YOU'VE PULLED. I hired a new PI to look into this matter. Mr. Felix Underwood has proven the woman you say is my niece is really a fraud. In the meantime, he found Clara Hart for me," Strom Hart told Owen. "When I learned you had found Clara under an assumed name—"

"Pen name, sir. Candice Mayfair is an established author." Owen reached over and took hold of Candice's cold hand and squeezed.

"And when she wouldn't return home to collect a billion and a half in assets, I was certain it was some kind of scam."

Owen couldn't have been any more surprised to hear that. Candice was worth over a billion dollars?

"Mr. Underwood has investigated you and discovered you and your associates closed your practice after abandoning it in Seattle under suspicious circumstances. And you haven't had a legitimate office for seven years, just a fly-by-night online PI service. Then you finally opened up an office after all these years. He wasn't sure if any of the work you're doing was legitimate."

"If he says he found the right woman, he's lying, or the woman is. Or they're both in on the scam to collect the money."

"Figured you would say that. He said the same thing about you and your Candice Mayfair. Isn't she selling enough books? Wants a little extra money to help her pay her living expenses? I'll take her down too. Don't think I can't. I'll go straight to her publisher and tell them what kind of a fraud she's perpetuating, and that she'll be brought up on charges. I'll be back in the country in five days, which is when I'm meeting with Clara and the judge and will settle this matter. For your information, she's eager to see me and finish this, like anyone who has nothing to hide."

"Candice, your real niece, doesn't have anything to hide. The woman who claims to be her would be eager to finish this before you learn the truth and put a stop to it." Owen was angry, but he was trying to stay professional, even if the man was threatening to ruin him and Candice and their friends.

"Oh, and by the way, I had halfway believed you until I was in Edinburgh. I saw no sign of a Candice Mayfair autographing books anywhere, nor had she signed any books in the city. Nice try. My investigator has checked all the locations where Candice is supposed to have been and is supposed to go to. No autographed books anywhere. No signings listed for the places she's supposed to be staying. I'm working to have your PI licenses revoked and your office shut down. If you hadn't told me she had delayed seeing me for so long, I would have believed she was Clara. Which was why I hired the other investigator, and he found her right away. You can talk to my lawyer if you have anything further to say." Then Strom hung up on him.

"Hell." Owen paced across the floor, furious that Strom probably had the means to shut them down and ruin Candice's career if they couldn't convince him that she was his real niece.

"Why didn't he just call me?"

"Because I'm the one in charge of the fraudulent plan, he thinks. If he hadn't come to me first, I wouldn't have found a fake Clara Hart."

"I have to go there before that impostor signs for the money. You know, the money never mattered to me. I never believed I'd see any of it, and I accepted that. But I'd rather Uncle Strom receive it—not that he needs the money—rather than some woman, and probably the investigator, who are trying to scam my parents' estate. Maybe if I'm a wolf part of the day or night and then shift and go over to the judge's office, I can manage."

"Do you have that much control during the full moon?"

"No. But maybe I will this time. We have to risk it."

"If you shift in front of lawyers and a judge, and your uncle, it could be a real disaster," Owen said.

"I'm going. My mind's made up. I'll do this and return home, stopping the fraudster from getting her hands on the money. The investigator probably has a big stake in this too. How else would he have found a replacement Clara so easily?"

"I agree. I'm going with you. We'll need to learn everything we can about this PI. Anything dirty we can find on him," Owen said. "I wonder if he's been really looking into us. Digging deep."

"You mean like learning about your wolf halves?" Candice asked, wide-eyed.

"I would hope not, but I don't want to take any chances. Everyone will need to be on their guard more than usual. And we need to let Cameron and his family know what's going on. Also, how can you prove you're the Harts' adopted daughter?" Owen asked Candice, not believing the bizarre turn of events.

"I am her. Don't tell me you don't believe me now."

"It's not that. I'm not the one you have to convince."

"I'm sorry for all of the trouble this is causing you and wish you weren't involved. I don't want you to lose your licenses."

"Or have your contract with your publisher thrown out either. We need to ensure Strom knows you are his niece and the other woman is a fraud. You said you published before the change. Your parents must have known that you were writing under a pen name...but then Strom would also have known."

"Are you kidding? My parents would have died if they'd known I was writing hot romantic suspense. And then werewolf romance? Just the same, I didn't change my name on anything until after they died. I thought they had disowned me. They were gone. I decided to just be Candice Mayfair."

"But documents must show when you changed your name from Clara Hart to Candice Mayfair."

"I haven't lied about who I am. You really don't believe me, do you? How did you find me? I wasn't looking for a meal ticket. As far as I knew, my parents hadn't left me anything. I sure wasn't looking for an inheritance."

"Lyn Rose, your coworker, said you were the file clerk in their office. She said one of the incidents you wrote about was eerily like a situation that happened at her office. And she put two and two together and realized you were Clara, except you had a pen name. She remembered you writing on your lunch breaks. It all fit."

"You know how people read a story and recognize some of it as something that happened to them, even though it's not really about them? I mean, you could have been in a boating accident and I describe one, and you believe it's about you because it's so similar."

"You're saying you didn't use the story that happened at the office?"

"I'm saying just because I write a scene in a book, that doesn't mean I am writing about something I've really witnessed. Sometimes, yes. Forget it. I'm Clara, okay? Or was. I'm Candice now. But you know what? I had a different identity before that."

Owen frowned at her.

"My real birth parents, all right? Another name? Jeesh."

"I know. Okay, listen. You must have some recollection of things you did with your parents—"

"Lots of them. But Uncle Strom wasn't part of our lives. He was off making billions on his own. I don't know anything about his life except he was always off making money and too busy to see his brother and his family."

"Did your dad or mother ever mention anything about him that only they would know?"

"No. If they talked to each other about him, they did so in private."

"Your dad said nothing about his childhood with his brother? Their parents? Squabbles? Fun vacations? Anything?"

"No. Like I said, my parents were older when they brought me home. In their early fifties. Dad was still working for the oil industry and making a mint. Mom met him in college and helped further his career as the perfect social butterfly. But she felt she was missing something in her life and desperately wanted a baby. She couldn't have one at her age, so I was it. They doted on me. I had a happy life. They were great parents. But Uncle Strom wouldn't know about any of that. Not unless they talked to him about it. And I'm sure he wouldn't have cared. He wouldn't know I was sixteen when I wrecked my first car the first time I drove it on my own on the highway. Or that when I was ten I threw up on my dad's slippers when I had the flu. Or that I dyed my hair green for Saint Patrick's Day when I was twelve and got sent home from school. Or that I took in six stray cats until we learned Dad was deathly allergic to them. I doubt Uncle Strom would know about any of these things."

"Did your parents have any birthmarks or mannerisms, habits that you know of? Particularly your dad. Something maybe his brother would know but that wouldn't be common knowledge."

Candice shook her head. "I do have a safe-deposit box at the bank in Houston. I probably have my old social security card with my original name on it, and pictures of me with my parents earlier on. First thing in the morning, we'll go," she said. "And thanks for helping me with this. I'm sorry if I'm all growly about it. Everything would have been perfect if I could have gone down there when I had planned. I never, ever expected someone to try to steal my inheritance or that I'd have to prove who I was to my uncle. I just figured it would be a given."

"The truth is, I could have done what this Felix Underwood has managed to do, so without your uncle really knowing you better, you'd have to prove you're his niece no matter what," Owen said. "We just need to make sure we do that before Strom causes trouble for all of us. The things you have in your safe-deposit box could help."

"Right. But the other PI has to have that information."

"Okay, listen. We need to prove this other PI is corrupt and working on a scam. That the woman he found is the impostor."

"What do you need me to do?"

"We still have the problem with the moon phases. The woman intends to claim her—your—inheritance and not wait, which makes it appear she has a legitimate claim. If you did, why would you make up this story about the world book tour? Why not just go and say the inheritance is yours?"

"We all made that up."

"I know. Which is why all of our careers are on the line. I'm just saying they're going to have a hard time believing you because you haven't just gone down there and claimed it. That's one hell of a lot of money."

She paced across the floor. "I told you I'm going. And if I shift, I'll just bite everyone who sees me do it."

"We all need to learn everything we can about this PI. Everything dirty. We need to go after the woman he's claiming is Clara too. Learn who she really is. In the meantime, the two of us will go down early and stay somewhere out of the city so we can have some privacy. Since you are from there, you can obtain the documents to prove who you are. But we need to go now while you have more control over your shifting."

Candice couldn't believe anyone would claim to be her, but then again, the price was right. Why couldn't all of this have happened during the new moon? Then she could have just run down there with no threat of turning and taken care of this once and for all.

Owen called his partners and let them know what was going on. They agreed to look into the PI's and the woman's backgrounds right away. Candice knew that despite what that PI had said about them, Owen and his friends would be good at exposing these people for the frauds they were.

All the pack members had been in the same bind as her, turned without a choice and having to deal with the fallout the best they could, so they knew how difficult and important this situation was for her.

"Are you okay?" Owen asked her.

"No. I'm so afraid I will turn at the wrong time. Then what will I do?"

"We'll deal with it then. We can't worry about what may or may not happen. When was the last time you tried and couldn't control the full moon's calls to you to shift?"

She quit pacing and folded her arms. "Last month. Which was why I was adamant about not going until the waning crescent or the new moon was upon us."

"This will make it harder to deal with, but we'll do it."

"And if everything goes to hell?"

He pulled her into his arms. "Candice, we'll handle it. One way or another."

"You mean turning people?"

"That could be a disaster. We can feign you're suddenly ill or something. We'll figure it out. We might not have any problems at all." He rubbed her back, but she couldn't let go of the worry.

When someone knocked on the door, Owen glanced at it and frowned.

"One of the guys?"

"Maybe Cameron coming to talk to us in person."

She followed Owen to the door, and he peeked out. "Aw, hell," he said under his breath.

"What?"

"We have a new problem. That homicide detective, Rowdy Sanderson." Owen opened the door and said, "We don't allow salesman to solicit around here."

"I'm not selling anything. May I speak with Candice Mayfair? I'm Homicide Detective Rowdy Sanderson. I spoke with you earlier and tried to call Ms. Mayfair, but she's not answering her phone." Rowdy flashed his badge. "I know something about the Arctic wolves that rescued two snowmobilers in South Dakota a few days ago. I also am well aware that Miss Mayfair is an author of Arctic wolf romances, and I've read all of her books. You see, in my business, I'm called when the victim is deceased. I like a happily ever after. I love the paranormal. Do you mind if I come in and talk with her?"

Candice couldn't believe he'd follow her here. Or that he'd been reading her books! She wasn't sure if he suspected the rescue wolves had been werewolves, except for his reference to her writing. Still, that would be a really far reach. He probably assumed she used her Arctic wolf pets' antics to write more realistic Arctic werewolf stories.

"You're trespassing. Your badge says you're from Montana. No dead bodies around here, and you're out of your jurisdiction anyway," Owen said.

"I know what I know. I find the world an incredibly fascinating place. Just open your eyes and your mind a bit, and it's amazing what you'll see. I'm on your side. Really, I'm friends with a couple of divers out of Montana who are just like you. Or almost."

"I don't know what you think you know, but we don't own any wolves."

Rowdy cleared his throat. "I'm well aware that what Candice writes about isn't fantasy."

"Hold up a minute. You're saying these people you know in Montana are werewolves? And what? That Candice knows werewolves, and that's why she's writing about them?" Owen asked, sounding convincingly like he thought Rowdy had a screw loose.

She thought Owen would just shut the door in Rowdy's face, but he didn't, probably as curious as she was about the people Rowdy had mentioned. And what he knew about them. Were they really werewolves?

"Paul Cunningham and his wife and their friends Allan Rappaport and his wife. The two men were SEALs, and they're with the sheriff's dive team. So is Allan's wife. Here's my card. If you don't know them, here's Allan's number." Rowdy wrote it on the back of the card. "He can verify that we're good friends and that I want to help you in any way I can if you run into any trouble because you rescued the snowmobilers."

"Thanks. We don't need any help. But I appreciate the offer." Owen closed the door, and he and Candice watched out the window until the detective left.

"That isn't good news," Owen said.

"I'm going to call them, unless you know them already."

"I don't." Owen gave her the card, and they sat in the living room while she called Allan with the phone on speaker. "Hi, I'm Candice Mayfair. I just got a visit from a Montana homicide detective who says he's a friend of yours. A Rowdy—"

"Sanderson? Yeah, I know him. Why did he give you my number?"

"He's trying to track down two Arctic wolves that rescued a couple of snowmobilers in South Dakota. You might have seen it on the news."

Silence.

"He thinks I had something to do with it because the wolves left a trail to my cabin."

"Did you? Have something to do with it?"

"Believe me, I'd like to say I had everything to do with it."

"So…you're in South Dakota. You wouldn't happen to know anything about a little Arctic wolf pup that ended up in Texas and was returned to a family in Minnesota, would you?"

"Corey? Yeah, I had a close encounter with him in Minnesota on a camping trip. And I'm visiting with his family and friends now here."

"Well, hell," Allan said.

"What's the deal with this guy?" Owen asked. "Should we be worried?"

"And you are…?"

"Owen Nottingham. I'm with the group here in Minnesota. A PI like the other men. Cameron's a good friend, and Corey is his son."

Candice couldn't believe the homicide detective actually knew about werewolves, but she found the conversation with another wolf fascinating. No one was willing to admit they were members of wolf packs until the dots were well connected.

"He suspects there's more to us than meets the eye. But he's covered for us so far, so we still consider him one of the good guys," Allan said.

"And you haven't turned him or killed him yet?" Owen asked, sounding amazed.

"That could cause real problems for us. He has no family to speak of, but if a homicide detective is killed, it would create an ongoing investigation into the matter. If he's turned, then he'll have a hell of a time working his job. All we need is another newly turned wolf to have to take care of. As long as he doesn't cause trouble for us, we leave things the way they are. But I don't like hearing that he's been chasing Arctic wolves all over. I know he went to see a cousin in South Dakota. I saw about the wolves rescuing the men and figured they were some of our kind. But I had no idea Rowdy would stick his nose into it."

"Okay, thanks. We just needed to make sure we weren't going to have to do something drastic with this guy." Owen gave his phone number to Allan in case they ever needed to get in touch.

Candice thanked Allan and then ended the call.

"I wonder if a homicide detective could look into this Houston PI and his newfound Clara...and learn some things we're not able to," Owen said.

"You have a good point. Though I'm still nervous about flat-out admitting we're wolves to anyone who isn't one of us. Rowdy might be able to help us when we go to Houston to lay claim to the inheritance. He might be willing to serve as an official detective to put a stop to whoever the impostor is and the PI who 'found' her," Candice said.

"We'll have to discuss this with the rest of the pack though. We never do anything that would impact the rest of us without talking it over with everyone." Owen called Cameron with the news and said to Candice, "All of them should be over in a few minutes."

Chapter 11

THE PACK GOT TOGETHER, THE KIDS PLAYING COMPUTER games while everyone else sat down to discuss the issue with Rowdy and Candice's problem controlling the shift. Even Owen and the rest of them could have trouble at this time of month.

"I don't want to share our secrets with some stranger," Cameron said.

"I agree, but he already seems to know them." Owen brought cups of coffee over for everyone.

"And if other wolves seem to think he's all right and if he could help us with this, I'm inclined to think we could use his assistance." Candice thanked Owen for the coffee and sipped from the snowman mug.

"Like Count Dracula? And his minion, Renfield?" Faith asked, smiling.

They all laughed.

"I'm sure he would love hearing that's what we would think of him." But Candice thought it was so true. "Okay, so I'll call him...and tell him what? That I have an inheritance that is at stake?"

"Maybe he can use his own resources to find dirt on the PI and the girl. He doesn't have to meet with us. We don't have to tell him about the problem with your shifting. Or mine either. Just tell him we're doing all we can to investigate this case of fraud, and if he could help, that would be great. If not, then no problem."

"Okay. Sounds good." Candice called Rowdy and put him on speaker as soon as he answered. "Hi, this is Candice Mayfair. I wasn't sure if you could really help us with this or not, but I do have a problem." She explained to him about how the PI agency was looking into this, but if Rowdy had other resources he could tap, they would be grateful.

Everyone was quiet while they listened to what she said. The kids had even turned down the sound on their laptops when their mom told them to.

"Okay, give me the name of the investigator, and I'll learn what I can. When are you going down there to sign the paperwork?"

"We're leaving tomorrow. The signing will be in a few days."

"Driving though, right? It's probably too close to the full moon to fly."

"We're driving. Do you ever worry that some people might feel threatened by what you think you know?" Candice really didn't understand this guy. She wasn't sure what she would have done, had she known werewolves existed, but she didn't think she would have been contacting them to tell them she knew about them.

"Truthfully? That's a hazard of my job. The perpetrator usually doesn't want to be apprehended. That means I'm often facing a lethal foe. I've had a number of near-death experiences on the job. I'm good at what I do, having one of the highest success rates in bringing in murderers and procuring their convictions. But what if I had superpowers like all of you have? I could be even better, both in apprehending the criminal and in ensuring I have the right man, and probably in less time than it would normally take. Which can be years sometimes."

"Superpowers?"

"Yeah, sure. What else would you call your enhanced abilities? Okay, look. Allan's wife would have died—well, she did, twice—and she would have been permanently dead if Allan and his friends hadn't stepped in to help out. Allan loves her. He did from the beginning, I believe. I didn't stand a chance against him in the romance department."

"Do you think you'll have enhanced sexual powers too?" Candice asked, getting a kick out of him. Though she realized that was somewhat true because of how the pheromones deepened the experience. At least for her with Owen.

All the adults were smiling.

"Your books say they do. Whether it's true or not, I'd be willing to test the theory myself. But back to Allan's wife. If I got shot on the job, I'd stand a lot better chance at recovery. Right?"

"And could be discovered for your faster healing genetics. Plus, you'd more than likely take more risks, thinking you were invincible," Candice warned.

"Which could help me solve more cases and faster. Witness identifications aren't that reliable. But what if I could smell the scents of those who were at the scene of the crime?"

"And how would you explain how you knew it was the real perp? Tell them you smelled him there? Even if you could identify the murderer by scent, you'd have a hell of a time proving it," Owen said.

"Yeah, but at least it would narrow our suspect list, and I could put all available resources on the correct guy."

"Let's say, for the sake of argument, you became a part-time wolf. You wouldn't be able to work your job until you had the shifting under control. What would you do?"

"I'd find a job I could work from home until I could return to the other job. Like you did. Like the private investigators do. Hell, maybe you could use an investigator like me who has prior Special Forces experience, is hard charging, and would never let you down."

"You don't even know us."

"You're some of the good guys. I know, because I've dealt with a lot of bad guys over the years."

"We'll think about it," Candice said as the other adults shook their heads no. They probably figured they already had enough issues—with being turned seven years ago and then adding a pack member more newly turned—without taking a brand-new wolf into the fold. "But if you can help us look into this case of fraud, we'd be grateful."

"I'd be happy to. And we can meet in Houston. I'll keep you informed about what I learn."

"Thanks. We'll talk later." She was hopeful someone on the outside with other resources might be a help. Or were they just creating more trouble for themselves by taking him into their confidence?

At four the next morning, Candice and Owen got up and began loading the car. They took a couple of suitcases and emergency weather gear—blankets, thermal and regular, plus food and water—in case they had any trouble along the way, and both of them brought their laptops.

After a quick breakfast of ham and eggs, Candice climbed into the passenger seat. "I can drive too, possibly today. Just let me know when you need a break." She opened her laptop to work on her new book—set in Minnesota, of course. She just loved the new setting and had been writing away with her new muse helping her.

A little while later, Owen finally reached more of a highway and started the long drive to Houston. "When you have to shift, do you feel it coming on beforehand so you have a bit of a warning?" he asked, sounding a little concerned.

She didn't blame him for worrying about whether she could manage the shift okay. She'd learned early on that driving was out of the question while she was having a lot of trouble controlling the shifts. "Yeah, I can fight it for about a half hour, most of the time. Sometimes longer. Sometimes shorter. Then I have to give in."

"During the phase of the full moon, I can fight it for a couple of hours. But then I can't hold off any longer," Owen said. "I've tried to fight shifting completely, to see if I can learn to control it, but I can't. When the new moon phase is here, I can't shift, even if I wanted to. I've tried, just to see if I could force it. But it won't happen."

"Do you find you miss the ability during the new moon?" Candice asked.

"Yeah. It's like a habit. Or maybe a better word for it would be an ability. And then all of a sudden, you don't have it. Like you said, you run a couple of times a day, morning and night, great exercise, and it makes you feel good. I do too. I have a lot harder time getting motivated to exercise when I can't run as a wolf. You don't have to bundle up in the winter. You just strip and shift and run."

"I feel the same way. Though I do like to take walks in the woods as a human sometimes."

"Then we need to do that too when we return."

Candice pulled up her file on her laptop. "I'm going to work on my book for a while. Just let me know if you become tired of driving."

"Sounds good." Though if Candice was happily working on her book and didn't need to take a break from it, Owen would keep driving. He liked to go on long driving trips, which was a good thing since flying was out of the question when the full moon phase was drawing close.

While he was driving, Candice was typing away, pausing sometimes and then typing again. He drove for several hours, and she seemed to be really adding to her word count, so he was glad. He finally had to pull into a service station travel center where they could grab lunch.

"Do you want hamburgers or something else?" he asked.

"Hamburgers would be great. A cheeseburger. I'm going to run to the little girls' room."

"Okay, be inside in just a second."

David called as soon as Owen started to fill the tank. Owen hoped that meant his partner had good news.

Candice stretched and then headed for the building.

"The PI, Felix Underwood, is legitimate," David said. "As much as I could discover so far. He's a lone investigator and has had a Houston office since 2000. He's been doing this for a while. No brushes with the law that I could find. He owns a car and home, no mortgages. Lives in a nice home out in the country with some acreage, so he has a bit of a commute to his office in downtown Houston. He has a secretary. No dirt on her either."

"And the woman calling herself Clara Hart that he so fortuitously found?"

"Cameron is trying to run her down. Rowdy said he's digging deeper on the PI. This guy might be perfectly legit, but the temptation to find a fake Clara was just too enticing not to make an attempt. Not when Strom had gotten suspicious about Candice and confirmed she had a fraudulent book tour. The opportunity to find the real Clara would have been hard to pass up, particularly when there is no other real Clara. And the deadline is quickly approaching. He might believe you're really a fraud with a great scheme, and he's copycatting you."

"You're saying he's never done anything wrong in the past, and he wouldn't have this time if he hadn't had such a lucrative deal dumped in his lap."

"On the surface, it looks like it. Of course, he might have done illegal stuff and never gotten caught. Think of it. A multibillionaire tells you he thinks the woman who claims to be Clara is a fraud. Maybe the PI looks a little but can't find the real one. Then what does he do? He can either fail to find the right woman—and Strom obtains all the money—or he can find someone who fits the bill and take a cut of the proceeds. Maybe retire and leave the area permanently afterward, in case the real Clara ever shows up."

"Okay, sounds viable." Owen finished filling the tank and closed up the cap on his car.

"How are things going for you two?" David asked.

Owen knew he didn't mean the drive, but the issue of shifting. "Good, so far. We just stopped for gas, and we're going to grab a couple of cheeseburgers." He headed for the building. "Let me know if you learn anything else. We'll talk later."

"Sounds great. And good luck."

They signed off and Owen entered the travel center, the smell of cheeseburgers catching his attention. He didn't see Candice in the shopping area, so he went into the hamburger place, but she wasn't there either. He had to make a pit stop too, so he used the men's facilities and then went to order their food. After grabbing the tray of cheeseburgers, fries, soda for him and tea for her, he sat at one of the tables and waited.

He'd planned to let her drive for a while if she'd like, though he didn't mind driving the whole way there. The roads had been clear, so they were making good time.

After a few minutes when Candice still didn't show up, Owen began to really worry. What if she was feeling sick to her stomach? Worse-case scenario: What if she was stuck in the ladies' room as a wolf?

She hadn't indicated she needed to shift, and she'd said she could usually fight it for around half an hour. Or less. Nothing with the business of shifting was set in concrete. He grabbed their sack of food and drinks and left the restaurant, then walked over to the windows and looked out, in case she had returned to the car. But she wasn't there.

Owen was trying not to panic. He wasn't sure what to do. He returned to the restaurant and waited. But after another few minutes passed, he figured if she had turned into a wolf, she couldn't just shift back into her human form right away. It sometimes took a couple of hours or more. There was no figuring it exactly, as far as he could tell. Even if he managed to slip her out of the restroom without creating too much of a circus, he'd have to retrieve her clothes and purse from in there.

He returned to the short hallway where the men's and women's restrooms were located and waited. No one came in or out, and he couldn't hear running water or toilets flushing in either of them. Finally satisfied no one was in the women's room other than Candice, he opened the door a crack and said, "Candice?"

Chapter 12

Candice couldn't believe she was stuck in the women's room of a travel plaza, hoping Owen would finally realize she needed his help.

As soon as she'd gotten out of the car and stretched, she'd felt the urge coming, but she'd hoped it would wait until they'd eaten their cheeseburgers and were on their way again. Not that undressing in the car was all that easy, but it was a hell of a lot better than stripping in the ladies' room.

She really had to tamp down the urge to howl her frustration. She hated that she was taking up the handicapped stall, but she knew it would be better for maneuverability when she was trying to undress and shift.

She waited, paced, waited, wondering how long Owen would take before he realized she was not coming out. He'd been talking to someone on the phone when she'd left him, but she'd had to go to the bathroom, so she didn't wait to see who was calling. And he was filling his gas tank, so that would take a few minutes. Someone had used the men's room, so that might have been Owen. Then he would have gotten their cheeseburgers, waited for her, then maybe checked the car to see if she'd gone back out to it.

Then what? Waited in the restaurant for her? Ugh. She wished he'd just call out to her in the restroom. No one was in here, other than one annoyed wolf.

She was so relieved when she heard the door open and Owen call out to see if she was in there.

Candice woofed at Owen from the bowels of the ladies' restroom. His heart hitched. God, he loved her and he wanted to mate her, to take care of her in her time of need, and she could take care of him when he was in trouble too. It definitely was a two-way street.

"I've got our food." He was sure she'd wonder why that was important right now, but he had to delay rescuing her for a moment while he took the food out to the car. "I need to drop it off at the car, and I'll bring a bag back for your clothes. Return in a moment. Just wait for me." As if she was going anywhere.

He wanted to sprint through the store, but settled on a brisk walk. As soon as he'd set the sack of food and drinks in the car, he dumped a small backpack's contents on the backseat and grabbed a leash and collar—not that a *lupus garou* would need to be leashed, but to give the appearance that it was a dog or domesticated wolf dog in the event of an emergency like this. He locked the car and hurried back to the travel plaza.

The good thing was that most people wouldn't believe someone would be traveling with a wolf. They would assume it had to be a dog. Especially as well behaved as Candice would be.

Owen finally reached the bathroom again and waited to learn if anyone was inside. The hand dryer began running. He assumed Candice wasn't using it. Then he heard a mom and two little girls talking.

"I don't want cheese on my burger."

"I do."

The mom bustled them out of the restroom, and he

tried to look as though he was just waiting for his wife. As soon as the three of them left the short hallway, he opened the door a crack and said, "Candice? I've got a bag for you."

She woofed softly. Great. Owen realized she had locked the stall door, and he would have to crawl underneath it to retrieve her clothes. The door was low, and he wasn't small by any means, but at least he could crawl underneath it. He hurried into the restroom before anyone else came. He had to lie down on his back and wriggle underneath the door. He was still trying when Candice licked his face in greeting. He smiled up at her but continued to work his way into the stall. His boots were still sticking out when he heard a couple of women talking outside the room as they approached, and he'd just managed to pull himself the rest of the way under the stall door when the outer door opened.

With a modicum of relief, he began to gather up Candice's clothes and quickly shoved them in the bag while she sat beside him, looking woeful. He ran his hand over her head, smiling to let her know everything would be fine. He prayed they weren't caught. How would he explain being in a ladies' room stall with a wolf? He'd done a lot of crazy things in his life, but crawling under a stall door in a woman's restroom was totally new and something he hoped to never have to repeat.

They waited for the women to finish their business and then leave. But the trickle of women with kids kept coming in for another half hour.

When the last of them had left, Owen and Candice made a break for it. He unlocked the stall door and they ran across the floor, Candice bumping up against him as if to say he wasn't leaving her behind. He'd forgotten to put the leash and collar on her, which would make her look more like a service dog.

He had to slip Candice out of the women's room, hopefully without being seen. When they exited, a man and a woman and their son and daughter just stared at them.

"Wrong room," Owen mumbled. "Service dog in training." He quickly put the collar on Candice and attached the leash, then rushed out of the building with her. "You know, that's something we could do in an emergency like this. We could buy service dog vests. Then we could go anywhere."

Candice woofed at him as if in agreement, dragging him over to the pet area while he was trying to take her to the car. He guessed the shift had occurred before she could use the women's facilities. She squatted on the grass, glanced at him as he watched, and barked as if to tell him to give her some privacy.

"Sorry." He looked away. "That was a close call, though I guess you didn't have much warning."

She shook her head and pulled on the leash, yanking him to the car. "You're a service dog. Well, in training," he reminded her.

She nipped at his jeans.

"Okay, so just started training." He smiled down at her, then opened the door so she could climb in the passenger's seat. He unwrapped her cheeseburger so she could eat it on the wrapper on top of the console. Then he removed her collar and leash.

Owen ate his cheeseburger before they got back on the road again. He called Cameron with an update. "Okay, we had our first trouble with Candice shifting.

Can anyone check and see if we can order service dog vests for the pack? Then we can use them on whichever of us is in trouble anywhere we need to. I'd check pet stores on the way to Houston, but I think it's going to be too much trouble if Candice is a wolf or worried she might shift again while shopping."

"That's a brilliant idea. Why didn't any of us think of it before?" Cameron said.

"Because for two years after we were turned, we never went anywhere we didn't have to. Candice and I are good for now though. We're in the car and on the road again."

"At least you didn't have any real trouble, did you?"

"No."

"Okay, I'm looking up the requirements," Faith said. "According to this site, misrepresenting a pet as a service dog is against federal and state law, and violators are subject to prosecution."

"Well, we'll obtain certification. Then we'll be covered."

"Sounds good, as long as no one believes we're wolves. They say that you can procure Service Dog ADA information cards to let people know the rules and regulations in case someone doesn't know the law and won't let you go into a building with the dog," Faith said.

"We'll look into certification procedures. We might only need to certify a couple of us—a male and female. That way, we could just use the identity for outings like this. People buy fake registrations, and we could create our own official-looking ones, but it would be easy enough to legitimately go through the process," Cameron added.

"Okay, well, we're continuing our adventure and will

let you know when we stop for the night. For now, I need to locate a pet hotel."

Candice growled.

"A hotel that allows pets, I mean." Owen smiled at her. Then he signed off with Cameron and Faith.

Four hours later, Owen pulled into a service station to fill up on gas and check for a hotel in the area that allowed pets. He found one, made reservations, and climbed back in the car. "Okay, I got a room, but they only had one king-size bed. We can order room service if you still haven't changed back."

Candice nodded.

"I'll probably have to take you in the side door after I register for the room. Better than parading you through the lobby, since I don't have the proper ID to show you're a service dog, in case anyone believes you're a wolf and won't let you stay." He pulled out of the service station and back onto the road. "Having a pet really narrows down the availability of a hotel we can stay at."

She let out her breath.

"I know. It's a pain, but at least we both didn't shift. What a disaster that would be." Twenty minutes later, he located the hotel and pulled into a parking area with trees and grass away from the front of the hotel. Three people were walking their dogs—a German shepherd, a schnauzer, and a poodle mix of some sort. Owen rolled down the window for Candice so she would have some fresh air while he was inside checking in. "Okay, I'll be right back."

He hurried off to obtain their room key, hoping she didn't shift in the middle of moving from the car to the hotel room. As soon as he went inside, he saw a number of guests standing in line to check in and a couple of families with small dogs in carriers. When he finally made it out of the hotel with the key card in hand, he walked around to the side of the building and saw several guests taking pictures of Candice as she watched for him out the window. He wished now he'd told her to lie down, though he was sure that wouldn't have gone over big with her.

"Will they let you take your wolf dog in the hotel?" a man asked, pausing with his cell phone in hand.

"She's a Samoyed," Owen said.

"She looks like an Arctic wolf. Or wolf dog, I should say."

Owen had to grab Candice's collar and leash, and he wished he'd thought about it before he had an audience. He put her collar on while she waited patiently, like a good service dog would. Then he attached the leash. He thought she'd just jump off the seat onto the asphalt, but she waited for him to give her a command. He smiled.

"Come, Candice."

She leaped out of the car, and everyone took a quick couple of steps back, the cameras still snapping away. She ignored them, and Owen reached in to grab their laptops, locked the car, and proceeded to the side entrance.

"Can we pet her?" asked one of the older kids, who was about ten.

Now Owen was in a predicament. He wanted it to be Candice's choice. After all, she wasn't a pet. She stepped forward and licked the boy.

Owen smiled. Okay, good PR work. If it had been him, he probably would have been annoyed. The kids began petting her, and she was licking their cheeks, being a loving wolf.

"What percentage wolf is she?" the same man asked.

"She's a Samoyed. I'm not sure what other breed she has mixed in, maybe a German shepherd that made her legs a little longer than a Samoyed? I don't know. We didn't have her tested, but the person that was trying to find a home for her said she was pure. You know, so they could charge a higher price. But I suspect she has a taller dog in her background. Maybe a white German shepherd? She's mostly Samoyed."

"Really." The man sounded skeptical. "She looks closer to, hmm, maybe fifty percent wolf."

Owen swore Candice smiled at the man.

Owen started to walk her toward the hotel. "I've got to get settled. Thanks for making her feel welcome."

"Can we buy one like her?" one of the kids asked a woman as Owen headed for the side door.

Even though Candice was "safe" to be around people, he didn't want to have to worry guests who might be using the elevator and thought she looked like a wolf, so he took her up the stairs. "Sorry, we're six flights up." He unhooked the leash so she could move at her own pace.

When he reached the sixth floor, she was standing there waiting for him. He took a chance not attaching the leash, opened the door, and saw the hall was clear. "I'll grab our other bags as soon as you're settled." Thankfully, no one was around, and they made it to their room without any trouble.

When they reached the room, he unlocked the door and let her in.

Candice leaped onto the bed. Owen was thinking she'd leave white wolf hairs on the comforter, but he would just sweep them off. He knew she had to be aggravated about having to shift at such inconvenient times, and he didn't want to make her feel any less comfortable. "I'll order room service as soon as I return."

Using the elevator, he went back down and headed out to the car where an employee was milling around outside. Owen wouldn't have suspected anything was wrong if the guy hadn't been eyeballing him so much. Owen had left his license plate number at the front desk, so they could easily look him up anyway, which meant no hiding who he was. But he suspected someone had mentioned to the staff at the front desk that he had a wolf dog.

The guy approached him and said, "Sir, one of our guests said you have a really tame wolf dog. Our policy for accepting pets is strictly dogs only. Nothing wild or partially wild."

"She's a Samoyed, extremely well behaved and obedience trained, and she has served as a service dog. But I need to recertify her. They wouldn't allow a wolf dog to be a certified service dog, would they? I'm sure she's a mix with something taller, but the breeder claimed she was full Samoyed."

"My manager wants to see her."

"Sure." Hell, he had to warn Candice to leave the bed before the manager arrived, but he had no way of doing it. He grabbed their bags and locked the car door.

The employee held the door for him at the side entrance, and this time, Owen took the elevator while the employee called his manager.

As soon as Owen left the elevator, he sprinted for their room, which was around the bend and near the end of the hall. When he reached the door, he unlocked it and carried the bags in.

He shut the door and set their suitcases in the closet. Candice's head lifted, her ears twitching back and forth.

"Got to stay off the bed for a little bit," he said, coming over to rub her head. "Some yahoo told the staff you were a wolf dog, and the manager is coming to check you out. They won't allow us to stay here if you don't act enough like a dog. I said you were a service dog but that your certification had expired. You're a Samoyed, maybe part white German shepherd."

She jumped off the bed and sat on the floor.

"I said you were obedience trained and extremely lovable. If we have to do a show, are you okay with it?"

She nodded.

Owen was glad they could work together so well. He certainly would do anything she asked if the roles had been reversed and he had to suddenly shift.

Someone knocked on the door, and he said to Candice, "I'll order room service for us as soon as the manager leaves." Though he hoped she could eat her food in her human form soon.

She nodded. He was glad she wasn't woofing. Best not to disturb any other guests.

He answered the door, and the manager identified herself, peering around Owen at the Samoyed.

Then she said, "Can I see her?"

"Absolutely." He let the manager in and shut the door. "Down, Candice."

She lay down on her belly.

"Over."

She rolled over on her back and wagged her tail like a happy puppy. He hoped she didn't pay him back for this later.

"Sit."

She quickly sat.

"Come."

She rose and trotted over, showing she wasn't reluctant in the least to obey commands. She circled around him and sat down at his side.

"Shake hands."

She lifted a paw, and Owen motioned for the manager to shake it.

"Wow," she said and took Candice's paw and shook it. "If only I could teach my dog to do half of what yours does."

Good. No mention of a wolf. Wolves had a mind of their own. Even wolf dogs wouldn't have done so many commands.

"High five!" He held out his hands, and Candice jumped up to give him a high five, slapping her paws on his hands. "Circle."

She went around in a circle, then sat, looking up at him with eagerness for her next trick.

He figured he was pushing his luck to do much more and said, "Good dog. I love you." And he meant it.

She was panting, but she closed her mouth to hear his declaration, her ears perked, maybe wondering if he meant it. He did. He just hadn't meant to tell her that when she was a wolf.

"She's beautiful. Thanks so much for letting me see her. Have a good night."

"Thanks." Owen let the manager leave on her own, then once the door was shut, he locked it and grabbed the menu. Showtime over, Candice jumped on the bed.

He started calling off the menu items, figuring she'd

let him know what appealed. When she got to the steak, she nodded vigorously and wagged her tail.

"Okay, steak it is. Do you need to go to the bathroom? I should have asked when we were outside."

She shook her head.

"I'll take you out when it grows darker. Unless you have to go sooner. Maybe we'll have fewer people to deal with. Sorry about the dog tricks. You're a great sport."

He wished she would shift back. He wanted to talk to her about staying with him, permanently, not just because they could help each other out, but he couldn't imagine coming home from his job and not having her to talk with, to share meals with, to run and go boating with. To be a wolf with him. And he was having a blast writing his book and brainstorming on his book and hers. But he wanted more than that. He wanted to love her as a mate would.

Chapter 13

Candice sniffed the air, her ears perking up when she heard a squeaky cart and thought the waiter might be bringing their food. The steaks sure smelled good. She hoped it was their food and not somebody else's. She felt hungry enough to make the waiter give her the food if it wasn't theirs. Because she was a wolf. So much for her being a highly trained obedience dog.

Before the waiter reached the door, Candice suddenly had the urge to shift and jumped off the bed. As soon as she landed on the floor, her whole wolf form blurred into a human's.

"Talk about perfect timing," she said, turning to get her bag. "You know you didn't have to make me do *that* many tricks to prove I was a good little doggie." She wasn't annoyed with him, just harassing him. She grabbed her bag and headed for the bathroom. "She got the point after a couple of them. Were you trying to prove how good you were with training your dog? Just be prepared if the roles are reversed one of these days." She smiled.

Owen took hold of her hand and pulled her into his arms for a warm embrace, not about to miss the opportunity to show how much he cared about her. "I would do anything you commanded. Though in my defense, I have to say I wanted to make sure, beyond a shadow of a doubt, that she believed you were a dog."

"I'm sorry for dragging you into this mess. I'm sure you were glad to get your own shifting more under control, and the prospect of dealing with someone like me who has more trouble isn't what you had in mind when you came to find me."

"Are you kidding?" He kissed her lips and ignored the fact the cart was nearly to their door, as if it didn't matter that she was naked in his arms. "I meant what I said about loving you. I want you for my mate. My mind's made up."

She laughed. "That wouldn't have anything to do with me being an heiress, would it?"

He laughed. "No. Truthfully, we already have quite a fortune between us. Which is why we were able to buy so much land and build our homes. With the sale of our homes in the Seattle suburbs, the sale of our business, the money we had saved, and the inheritances some of us had, we're set."

"Room service," a man said, tapping at their door.

"Coming," Owen said.

"Did you say there were two of us and a dog?" Candice asked as she slipped out of his arms and into the bathroom.

"Yeah." Owen waited for her to shut the bathroom door, then opened the door to their room. She heard the waiter carry in the trays of food and set them on the table.

After Owen paid him a tip, the waiter left and Owen locked the door. "All clear," he said to Candice.

She was just glad she could eat her meal as a human, enjoying the steaks and the rest of the meal, rather than wolfing the food down off a plate on the floor.

She wasn't entirely surprised Owen told her that he

loved her. Everything he did showed how considerate and concerned he was. How he desperately wanted her to be part of the pack, but was trying hard not to show his desperation.

From the moment she met him—once she was certain he wasn't a daddy wolf with a mate—Candice had known he was someone to trust and rely on. But it was more than that. He was her inspiration—the hot wolf she needed in her life to make the hot wolf scenes even more real in her books. When people asked her where she got her inspiration, she would be able to point to him. He could be hers right now, and she didn't have any reason to doubt he was the one for her.

Would she have felt any differently if she hadn't been turned? She didn't believe so. She was still worried about eating before she shifted again, so she'd let him know how she felt *after* they ate.

"This looks delicious." She sat down across from him. "I was so afraid you were going to have to eat as a wolf."

"Believe me, so was I. I don't know. Suddenly I smelled the steaks, and it was like that triggered the shift, though food never has done that before. It might have just been that I'd been a wolf long enough. I have to say you were amazing when you rescued me today."

"Hell." Owen cut into his steak. "That's something I've never had to do before. I envisioned my big feet still sticking out from underneath the stall door as the women came inside. Believe me, I was relieved I made it in time."

Candice laughed.

"What happened? I thought you could control it for about a half hour."

"You must know how it goes. I can sometimes. But when I'm feeling stressed, that's another story. I don't think I'll be able to safely help you drive to Houston."

"No problem. I love driving, so I'll be fine all the way there and back."

"About that." She cut off another piece of tender steak. "After I sign all the paperwork, it's going to be really close to the night of the fullest full moon. What if you can't control your shifting any more than I can? Then what are we going to do?"

"We'll play it by ear. We can get a hotel where they allow pets and sit it out if we need to. We could just put up the Do Not Disturb sign and put out the card that says no room service. Then no one would bother us. After that, we could settle in for a long wolf's winter nap. Together."

"Okay, sounds like a good plan for now."

When they'd finished their dinner, Owen set the trays outside their room and bolted the door again. "I was serious concerning how I feel about you." He pulled her into his arms and held her close, his blue eyes beautiful as he gazed down at her.

Smiling, she shook her head. "You told me when I was pretending to be a dog." She slipped her arms around his waist. "I can't go back to the way it was before. All I'd think of was you and wanting to be with you if I returned home to stay. Since the change, I haven't felt this happy in a long time. I haven't felt like I was part of a family. I've just been drifting along, doing what I needed to for work and taking quiet runs by myself as a wolf when I could. You changed all that for me. I can't imagine not waking up to smell the coffee already on, or hearing you talking to your characters when you're trying to work out a scene in your head. Except it's not exactly in your head."

He laughed. "Sorry about that."

She smiled at him. "It's okay. I might steal some of your ideas."

"I'll have to be quieter then."

"By all means, talk away. You were right there to rescue me when I shifted so unexpectedly. I mean, how many guys would crawl under a woman's stall door to rescue her and risk getting caught?"

He nuzzled her cheek. "I'm serious, Candice. I would do anything for you."

"I have to warn you," she said, running her hand up his back. "You're going to be in all my books."

"As long as I'm not the villain, I'll do whatever I can to give you new experiences you can write about."

"Ohmigod, yes! Let's get started."

Owen's jaw dropped. "Wait, you mean it? You want to mate me?"

"Did you ever doubt I would want to? That you couldn't convince me you were the only one for me?" She smiled up at him, loving him.

"You're the best thing that's happened to me in the last seven years, and I'm not exaggerating."

"You don't think it's too impulsive of us? Are you sure I won't be too much trouble?"

"Hell no. I couldn't live without you, no matter the trouble we get into. I loved you from the moment I saw you standing across the river. I just never had any hope I'd find you again."

"The other guys—"

"Will love that you're in our pack and treat you as protectively as any of us will."

"Like I'll protect them back." She took a deep breath and placed her hands on either side of his face and pulled him down for a kiss. "I love you." And that was all the talking she was going to do.

He kissed her right back, and she started tugging at his sweatshirt. He was trying to unfasten her jeans when his phone rang, and he growled.

"Better make sure it's not important news," she said, as much as she didn't want to be interrupted.

"Yeah, Gavin, did you get anything?"

"No, we just wanted to make sure Candice is okay."

"She shifted back, and we just had dinner. We're kind of busy. Let's talk later unless you've got really important news."

"Ah, hell. Man. She agreed to mate you? You were supposed to bring her home so we could have more of a chance to prove one of us is the one for her."

Owen laughed. "Not this time, buddy. We'll talk later."

"Congratulations. Hell, now I've got to be the one to tell David. We'll only call you if it's really an emergency."

"Thanks. We appreciate it." Owen hung up and set his phone on the desk, then turned to help Candice out of her clothes, but she was way ahead of him.

Owen jerked off his shirt, and Candice slid her hands up his bare chest. He paused to cup her face and kiss her, their mouths fusing before he gained entrance, plundering her mouth and deepening the kiss. He inhaled her scent—sweetness and light, desperate need, sexy and compelling.

She slid her hands down his hips to his pants and tugged to unfasten the belt. He kissed her cheek and nibbled on her ear as she undressed him. Then she unfastened his zipper and ran her hand over his boxer briefs, her warm fingers caressing in a tantalizing way, his erection jerking under her touch.

He quickly kicked off his boots and tugged down his jeans, tossing them aside. He yanked off his boxer briefs and removed his socks before he placed his hands over her silky, red bra. Her nipples pressed against his palms. He captured her mouth in another searing kiss, not believing they would soon be mated.

Owen reached behind her and unfastened her bra, throwing it on the floor. His cock, hard and throbbing with need, pressed against her as he straddled her on the bed. "Condom," he said belatedly, thinking he needed to fish one out of his bag. It was way too soon to try to have little ones. They needed to get to know each other inside and out as a couple first, and he needed to give her more time to adjust to being a wolf.

"Got it covered." Then she frowned. "It does work for shifters, doesn't it?"

"Yeah. Faith and Cameron already have triplets so they use birth control. I only know because David was asking why they weren't having another litter of pups." Owen assumed she was using birth control, not knowing how rare it was to have a shifter baby with a human and wanting to be prepared.

"I use them to regulate my periods," she said, smiling, as if she knew just what he was thinking.

He smiled at her, then they were kissing again, and he was rubbing himself against her glorious body, loving the silky, warm, soft feel of her. Loving her. Ready to make a whole new life for himself, wrapped in her love.

Candice never thought of herself as impulsive, and she usually thought things out more than she had this time. Yet every part of her being believed Owen was the right one for her as he kissed her senseless and began to sweep his hand down her belly toward the center of her. He stroked her hard, then soft, sending sparks of desire shooting through her.

She hadn't realized what she had been missing for the last two years, but it wasn't the same as being with anyone else. The raw, primal passion she felt for Owen as she raked her nails gently down his back, his familiar masculine scent, spicy and musky, made her feel at home with him. The way he set her world on fire with his strokes only helped to confirm how much she needed him in her life.

His blue eyes were darkened with lust as he devoured her mouth again, as if he couldn't get enough of her. She clasped his face with her hands and kissed him back just as hard, before they were frantically licking and tonguing each other again. And then she felt heaven and earth collide in a shattering orgasm like she'd never experienced before, the headiness leaving her thrumming with pleasure.

"Ohmigod," she said. "Owen. I. Love. You."

He smiled at her and then centered himself between her legs. "I love you too, more than I can say. Are you sure you're ready?"

"Yeah, we're mating and you're not getting out of it."

He chuckled, leaned down, and took her nipple in his mouth. He teased the tip with his tongue, enjoying the sweet taste of her, the heat of her body warming him on the cold night. "Wouldn't think of it." And then he pushed inside her until he was all the way in and began to thrust, his muscles tensing. He felt her wet heat surrounding him, her inner muscles just as tense until he began kissing her again.

Then Candice relaxed and the driving need to take, to consume, filled him with an overwhelming necessity to finish this, knowing full well it was only the beginning.

Releasing his seed inside her, he felt relief and joy—that she was his, and he didn't have to fight any longer to win her over. Not that he wouldn't do everything he could to make her happy for the rest of their mated lives, but at least the pressure was off to prove he was the best-suited wolf for her. He couldn't love her any more than he did.

Owen rolled onto his back, pulled her into his arms, yanked the covers over them, and snuggled with her. He suspected she had not had sex with anyone in the last couple of years due to the trouble with shifting and the possible complications of a relationship with a human. He was so glad she was with him and all his.

"How do you feel?" he asked.

"Hopeful that you haven't made a mistake in me."

He snorted. "Why? Because you're the wolf of my dreams, and I might think differently when I wake in the morning? Not on your life." He rubbed her arm and kissed the top of her head.

"What if I turn into a wolf in the middle of the night?"

"I'll love you just the same. What if I shift in the middle of the night?" he asked.

"No animals allowed in bed."

He laughed. “We’ll see about that.”

She might push him out of bed if he was kicking in his sleep as a wolf, chasing after rabbits in his dreams, and that was all right with him. If she shifted, he was pulling her close and hugging her. He couldn’t be more pleased to have her in his bed or in his life, no matter what form she was.

They made love two more times that night before he woke to find her kicking him in bed as a wolf. He was going to prove he loved her just as much in that form. Half asleep, she woofed while he petted her head until she woke enough from her dream to sit, as if she hadn’t realized she’d shifted.

“Come on. Lie down with me.”

She licked his cheek first, snuggling between his legs, her head on his crotch. He’d never last like this.

Chapter 14

The next morning on the drive to Houston, Owen felt uneasy. He'd had the urge to shift twice last night and he'd fought it. He'd wanted to cuddle with his mate as a human, not crowd her in bed as a wolf. Though he hadn't minded that she had been a wolf for a while last night. How would she have felt if he had all of a sudden been a wolf in bed with her? But he was having second thoughts about fighting the shift all night long.

Maybe if he'd shifted last night and been in his wolf form for a while, he wouldn't be feeling so edgy. Maybe he wouldn't be experiencing this growing urge to turn into his wolf. Most of all, he was worried about handing the driving over to Candice if she had trouble with shifting today. He glanced at her. She was sound asleep, her head resting against a pillow next to the door, tuckered out from all their lovemaking.

"Hey, Candice," he said, hating to wake her. "I'm having trouble with needing to shift. I've been fighting this for a while, like I always do, trying to stretch the limits. Do you think you can drive for a bit?"

She quickly sat up. "Yeah, sure. Just pull over, and I'll drive."

"How are you feeling?"

"Fine for now."

"We're not close to anything much right now." He pulled the SUV over onto the shoulder of the country road.

"Where are we?"

"I took a detour a while back so we wouldn't be on the main highway. It's slower, but in case of shifting emergencies, I didn't want to be so exposed on the highway. If we get desperate, we could stop early and get a hotel room."

"We'll never make it before that impostor claims my inheritance if we keep stopping."

"I agree, but we won't make it either if both of us have shifted into wolves in the middle of civilization while we're driving."

"What if I have to shift?"

"Just pull off the road somewhere that we can sit for a while without the vehicle being too noticeable."

He got out of the vehicle, and they switched places. He hated that he didn't have more control over his shifting. None of them worried about it back home because they always had one another's backs. Living out in the country with the woods and lakes all around them, they felt relatively safe. Out here on their own? That was a whole other story.

"It's okay, Owen. We'll be fine. Just take a nap for a while."

He appreciated that she was trying to sound like she wasn't worried. But he knew better. He could hear the concern in her voice, no matter how much she tried to pretend everything was fine.

"Are you certain? We could just stop out here for a while. Maybe I can shift back after a bit."

"An hour? Two?"

"Possibly three or four. Maybe more. Or a whole lot less. I never really know."

"We need to cover more distance today." Then she started driving on the two-lane country road, passing acres of plowed fields, a few scattered homes surrounded by trees, a few cattle ranches, and that was it.

Twenty minutes later, Owen couldn't hold off any longer. "Gotta shift."

"Okay, just take a nap. I'm sure you need to rest too."

"Yeah, for tonight." He winked at her, and she smiled at him.

He began stripping and shifted. He woofed at her and then jumped into the backseat so he could stretch out and sleep for a while. He hoped he could shift back in a couple of hours at most and that Candice would be fine until then.

Candice tried not to show the panic she'd felt when Owen told her he had to shift. He was her lifeline and she had to be his, but how long could she hold on? She had driven for about an hour and half—and was glad she had gotten that far at least—when she felt the craving to shift. At home, she was used to it. She'd just quit writing, save her manuscript, and either take a nap as a wolf, or run if it was later at night.

But out here like this, she felt vulnerable, and she was putting them both at risk.

She pulled off onto a farm road, not sure what else to do. She was glad Owen had taken them off the main highway though. If they'd parked on the side of the highway for hours, a cop might have stopped and checked out the car—and found two wolves inside. Then what? Call animal control? She could envision being tranquilized and taken to a facility somewhere far away. She was pretty certain a regular facility would be afraid to handle dogs that looked like pure wolves. She could imagine the media sensation surrounding that. Two Arctic wolves in two separate news stories—wouldn't that cause some speculation?

She could envision Rowdy hearing about it and maybe coming to their rescue. But how could he intercede? Yeah, he knows the family who owns the wolf-like dogs, and he'll take them in?

Now she almost wished they'd asked him to drive them down to Houston.

She pulled onto a dirt trail where farm equipment could be off-loaded to plow the fields. With winter in full force, no one was doing anything with the land right now. Should they leave the car and run for a bit? She'd rather stay with the car and protect it. But what if someone found two wolves sleeping in it and called the sheriff?

They might pack them off, thinking the owner was neglecting them. Of course, if they were running loose, someone might try to shoot wild wolves that would surely kill their livestock.

She glanced over the seat and saw that Owen was fast asleep. "Owen, I've got to shift."

Owen quickly sat up and looked at their surroundings. He woofed at her.

"We'll have to stay with the car. I'm afraid we might be shot if we run around as wolves. In the unlikely event someone tried to steal from the car—our laptops, wallets, or even the car itself—they'd change their minds in a hurry. I'll join you in a moment." She opened the windows a bit so they'd have fresh air, but not enough to encourage potential thieves to check out the car for easy pickings. She figured if anyone came near, they could make a ruckus, and whoever it was more than likely would leave the car alone.

Hopefully, if it happened, whoever came to check out the SUV wouldn't call the sheriff.

Then she began to shift. There were houses around, but mostly set way back off the road and hundreds of acres apart, the homes surrounded by trees. No one should see them, unless they happened to be driving by.

She hadn't encountered more than two cars in all the time she'd been driving, so she hoped if anyone passed them, he wouldn't care that an SUV was parked off to the side.

As soon as she tossed the last of her clothes onto the passenger seat, she shifted, then leaped over the seat. She hoped Owen would be able to shift back, but he didn't. She snuggled with him, and he licked her cheek. She licked his nose back, wishing they were somewhere safe and not out here like this.

As soon as Candice had calmly warned Owen she had to shift, he'd come fully awake and started trying to shift back again. Try as he might, he just wasn't able to. Soon, hopefully. He'd given the situation a lot of thought before he'd shifted and come to the same conclusion. It was best to stay with the car. If they made it to Dallas and were still having issues, maybe they could contact the jaguars they knew there to take them the remaining three and half hours to Houston.

He'd slept enough already, but he didn't want to sit up and watch out the window for trouble. Best to just rest with Candice. And he did end up falling asleep anyway, all curled up with her.

At some point, he became aware that a pickup truck was approaching them on the road. He lifted his head, though no one could see him in the car unless he sat up. He didn't want to make anyone aware he was there in case the driver worried about the animal's health and welfare.

Owen summoned the urge to shift over and over in a silent mantra to himself, hoping that whatever shifter god was up there would listen to him and grant his wish.

The truck slowed down as it grew nearer to where Candice had pulled off to park. Owen really didn't like the sound of it. Candice had lifted her head like he was doing, not sitting up, trying to keep out of sight.

The truck pulled onto the dirt trail and parked behind their vehicle. A door opened, and then another. Suddenly, Owen was shifting as if his prayers had belatedly been answered.

Hell, now he was a naked guy in the backseat with a wolf. He leaned over the console and grabbed some of his clothes, mixed in with Candice's things—bra and panties the most problematic. Why would a lone guy have a woman's clothes all over his passenger seat and no sign of the woman?

He hurried to yank on his sweatshirt and struggled to get into his boxer briefs in the confines of the backseat as the men's boots crunched on the soil with their approach.

Candice sat up now in defensive mode, her hackles raised.

"We're good," Owen said, yanking on his jeans and

then his socks as the men placed their faces against the glass and peered in.

Candice growled and barked, and both men jumped away from the car.

Owen hurried to shove his feet in his boots, then climbed into the front seat, since the doors in back were locked. He opened the front door, stepped out of the car, and reached his hand out to shake the two men's hands. The dark-bearded older man extended his hand. "This is private property."

"Yes, sir." Owen shook the younger man's hand. He had the same small eyes, long chin, and prominent nose that the older man had, probably a son. "I've been driving from northern Minnesota and got so sleepy that I had to pull over and sleep or fall asleep at the wheel. I thought I could last, but I just couldn't."

"Where you headed?" the older man asked.

"Houston."

"That's a fer piece. You'd better get some sleep at the next town."

"I aim to. Thanks. Sorry for bothering you."

"No problem. We don't get too many people out here on the back roads that don't belong, so we just had to check it out." The man glanced at Candice. "Wolf?"

"Nah. Pure dog. But she looks so much like a wolf, I often get that. She definitely doesn't howl." He smiled at her, reached back, and petted her head. "She's a good dog, but she sure keeps anyone at bay who thinks to break into my place."

The men smiled then. "I can see why. Take it easy and get some real sleep."

"Will do. Thanks."

The men returned to their truck, and Owen waved at them, smiling like they were the best of friends, then climbed into the driver's seat. "Hell, that was close."

Candice woofed.

"I'm calling Everett and Demetria, the jaguar shifters living in Dallas who brought Corey home to Cameron and Faith. They said if we ever needed their help, we could call on them. Even though that's a long way from here, we could still get in touch with them to help us out, just in case."

Candice woofed, then climbed into the front passenger seat.

"If I knew of any wolf packs along the way that had royals, I'd give them a call, but other than Leidolf's red pack in Portland and the few I've heard of in Colorado, I don't know any close by."

He called Demetria and Everett. "Hey, this is Owen Nottingham. I'm with the Arctic wolf pack that you brought Corey home to. I've located a woman who was turned a couple of years ago, so she and I have been having trouble with the full moon's approach and involuntary shifting, but we have to go to Houston because she needs to sign off on her inheritance in a few days. Is there anyone who could maybe help us with this?"

"Hell yeah," Everett said. "Demetria's giving some classes to jaguar and wolf shifter parents to help them teach their children diversity and tolerance, but I'll sure do it. You're coming from up around Ely, Minnesota?"

"Yeah, and we've nearly made it to Topeka, Kansas. We don't know how long it will take us to get to Dallas—I'm guessing about seven hours unless we have more problems. If you could take us from there to Houston and maybe help us out a bit if we shift while we're down there, you would be a real lifesaver."

"We're coming to get you. I'll bring Howard with me. He works with me on this new job. That way, one of us can drive your car. Plan to meet us about a half hour south of Tulsa. That will make it three and half hours for each of us, and hopefully we'll connect about the same time. Just give us an update when you can. Demetria's calling Howard now to let him know we have a mission to go on. If you have more trouble, just sit it out somewhere, and we'll come to you. And good luck. We'll see you in a bit."

"Okay, we can't thank you enough."

Half an hour later, Candice leaped over the backseat, and Owen figured she was shifting. She did and began pulling on her clothes. "I'm so glad you called the jaguar shifters. But what if it was all for nothing? What if we don't shift again except when we're okay to do so? Then we've bothered them for no reason."

"Then we'll be lucky we didn't shift, and we'll be able to visit with them. After all, they went through a lot to bring Corey home. They even came to visit us—before I found you—to celebrate Corey's and his brother's and sister's birthday like they had done back at Everett's mother's day care. They're good people. And at least they don't have any trouble with shifting based on the phases of the moon. I'm not sure about newly turned jaguars. Demetria and Everett were born that way. They started the United Shifter Force to help deal with shifter issues between the species. This isn't like one of their usual missions, but it's a way to promote goodwill between the wolves and jaguars. Besides, we're already friends."

"That's great. Do any jaguars live in Houston?"

"I'm not sure. We were so glad to get Corey back, and so surprised jaguars shifters even existed, that we weren't thinking about much else. Except that Christmas was approaching that time too."

Candice climbed back into the passenger seat. "Christmas. We might not make it back in time to celebrate with the others."

"We'll have an after-Christmas celebration when we're able to return. All that matters is that we gather the pack together and have fun. It doesn't have to be a particular day."

"Any regrets about being with me? I mean, wishing you had a wolf who was less of a detriment and more of a help on a trip like this? One who was born as a wolf?"

"I wouldn't want you any other way. You're perfect for me. This is what I call an adventure. So now, how were you going to portray me in your next book?"

She smiled and pulled her laptop onto her lap. "The heroine is tuckered out from a night of lovemaking with the hero and worried she's going to shift because of the full moon. Then her mate tells her he's got to shift too."

Owen laughed. "Okay, don't tell me. A farmer and his son chased them off their property and—"

"Nope. The farmer called the sheriff's department because both of the shifters were still in wolf form and the farmer knew they were wolves. The sheriff didn't believe anyone would have wolves in a car, so he called animal control. When the officers arrived, they were certain the two were wolves, so they tranquilized them and took them to a wolf reserve."

"You were worried that would happen, weren't you?"

"Yeah, I was. Weren't you?"

"I was. So, what happens?"

"Okay, so they're locked in a pen, no clothes, but the wolf reserve has a gift shop full of all kinds of wolf stuff—stuffed toys, sweatshirts, T-shirts, pictures, post cards, calendars, coffee mugs, you name it. It's night-time when they finally shift back. They move the platforms where the alpha wolves sat over to the side of the pen—which was a real job, believe me—and finally manage to climb over the fence. They can't worry about what anyone thinks of two wolves moving the platforms around, which probably will be attributed to humans anyway, but the lock will still be untouched, so they'll have an unsolvable puzzle to figure out."

"If homicide detective Rowdy was around, he'd probably guess."

"Yes. Especially since he knows where we're headed. Wait, this is my story, not about us."

Owen laughed. "It seems too real."

"Okay, so then they have to break into the gift shop—can't be helped—but it's too cold to run around... Wait, I'll make it summer. They can grab long T-shirts, and maybe the gift shop stocks shorts or something with wolves on them."

Candice loved brainstorming with Owen. She was glad she had mated with him and hoped he never regretted that she was more newly turned than him.

They talked for an hour or so about how to get the fictional wolves out of the trouble they were in. Then

Owen called to let Everett and Howard know they were still just fine, which he continued to do every hour on the hour.

Candice was still worried about the situation with her uncle. It was one thing to have one of the jaguar shifters drive them to Houston if either she or Owen, or both, turned. But actually meeting up with her uncle? And signing the paperwork? She could envision having to shift as she was holding the pen to sign the documents.

Still, she was relieved the jaguars would help them out. Naturally, neither of them had any trouble with shifter issues when they met with Everett and Howard at a travel center.

"Any trouble?" Everett asked, shaking their hands. He was tall, green-eyed, and brown-haired, and didn't look like he was anything other than a good-looking guy.

Candice tried to envision him as a jaguar, but except for his green eyes, she couldn't. Howard was black-haired and blue-eyed. She had the same difficulty imagining him as a jaguar. Wolves, maybe. They were both sturdy men and wore pleasant expressions, but they had an intensity that made her think if anyone gave them any trouble, they could deal with it.

Howard pulled Candice into a hug and smiled. "I didn't get to meet the whole family, just Corey, so I wanted to thank both of you for enriching our lives so."

"Corey impacted my life in a big way too," Candice said, although she had not previously believed that could ever be a good thing. "I wasn't around when he got lost."

"So, you mean Corey is up to his usual tricks," Everett said, smiling.

Owen explained how Candice had been camping

with her friends and had the misfortune to hand-feed Corey, who accidentally bit her.

"Fortunate for you though, right?" Howard said to Owen.

"Hell yeah. I saw this beautiful Arctic she-wolf across the river, but by the time I reached the other side, she had returned to a campsite and was in one of the tents. I followed them for some time as they hiked for several miles the next day, but I didn't want to get too far from home without letting everyone know what was going on with me. Returning home was the hardest thing for me to do. Once I was back, I let everyone know I was in pursuit of a white wolf I believed was a shifter. Naturally, Gavin and David wanted to come with me. I told them they should probably stay with the pack, but I couldn't deter them. Candice's group ended up using canoes and were gone. I never found her after that."

She smiled at him. "Until a few days ago. You know how it is. When you're looking for something, you can't find it. Quit looking for it and—"

Owen wrapped his arm around her shoulders. "I was still looking for you, but I had no idea you were the wolf of my dreams."

Howard folded his arms. "If only I could be that lucky. With a she-cat," he amended.

They all laughed, and then Everett said he'd drive them while Howard drove the other car back to Dallas.

"Demetria is thrilled about seeing you again, Owen, and meeting you, Candice. If there's anything we can do to help you with signing the paperwork, I'll be there for you," Everett said.

"We really appreciate it." Candice still wondered how

similar they were to wolves as far as shifting behavior was concerned. "Owen said you were born as jaguar shifters. How about if you had been turned? Would a newly turned shifter have the same trouble as we're experiencing?"

"Yes, we were born that way. Newly turned shifters do have trouble controlling the shift. We're not affected by the phases of the moon though."

"But that means you don't have a week free of shifting. Right? Like for us, we don't shift during the new moon. Which, if we desperately wanted to, we couldn't," Candice said.

"That's correct. Like with wolves, it can take years for the jaguar shifters to gain more control over shifting. I take it you had no choice about coming down at this time to sign the papers to claim your inheritance?"

Candice snorted. "No." She told him about the other PI and the woman he claimed was the real Clara Hart.

"What are you going to do?" Everett asked, sounding angry anyone would attempt to cheat her out of her inheritance.

"Prove she's a fraud. Do you know of any jaguar shifters in Houston?" she asked.

"Yeah, they actually have a jaguar club there. The Clawed and Dangerous Kitty Cat Club. It was called Jungle Fever Cat Club to begin with, but the franchise did a marketing survey of its patrons and they liked a wilder name for it."

"Do any wolves go there?" she asked.

"I don't know. I haven't been back in a while. So possibly there's a wolf pack there. We didn't learn of one when we were trying to find Owen's pack. You should have seen us trying to let on that we had a werewolf pup in our custody, and that we were wolves, not jaguars. None of the wolves would have believed us if we had told them over the phone we were jaguar shifters."

Candice smiled. She couldn't even visualize it. "The wolves don't have a registry of wolf packs. I imagine it was hard to find any of them."

"We got lucky. What can we do to help with proving this PI and the woman are frauds?"

"We have several people on it already, but if you want to help, we'd love all the aid you can offer." Candice was afraid the PI and the woman would slip through the cracks otherwise. Maybe with a ton of shifters looking into this, they could nail the two of them. She gave him the PI's name, Felix Underwood, but they only had the woman's name as Clara Hart.

Howard gave them a call when they reached Dallas, and they took it over Bluetooth. "Hey, heading home. Have a job to do in the morning."

"You sure you don't want to have dinner with us?" Everett asked.

"No, truth is, I have a date."

Everett smiled. "Okay, then have a nice date and we'll be in touch."

It was getting late when they got in, the house aglow with Christmas lights and the tree sitting in the window sparkling with lights too. A dark-haired woman—Everett's mate, Demetria—gave them a warm welcome. She hugged Candice first, then Owen, and finally her own husband. Demetria couldn't stop telling them how delighted she was to see them.

Candice loved the jaguars and how good they'd been to her and Owen already.

While Candice was visiting with Demetria, Owen walked out on the back porch with Everett and said, "I need you to be my cover story for a moment, like we're considering options for this business tomorrow. I really need to order something for Candice for Christmas."

Everett smiled. "Go right ahead." He got them a couple of beers, and they sat overlooking the lighted swimming pool while Owen called Cameron.

"Hey, we're in Dallas safe and sound. Everett's taking us to Houston, and he'll bring us back here when we're done. We might not make it back in time for Christmas, but I want to order something really special for Candice to welcome her to my home and the pack. I'll need your help with it while I'm away."

"Okay, shoot."

"I want to buy a gazebo for Candice. But it would take too long to build one for Christmas. I picked out a prefabricated design and have the location in mind. Or a couple of ideas. Maybe sitting half over the lake to have it reflected in the water? I already have the deck out there, and it would fit perfectly on that. Or a garden setting?"

"A gazebo? As in something permanent? Faith is making motions for me to ask the big question. Does this mean Candice wants to stay with us? Or is this just something you're doing in the hopes you can convince her to stay?"

Owen laughed. Faith clearly wanted to know if he'd mated with her. "Yes, she's staying with us. We haven't discussed selling her house yet. But yes. Which is why I want to pick up something really special for her."

"You mated her?" Cameron sounded surprised, but Owen didn't think he should have been.

Owen smiled. "Yes. The other guys will just have to look elsewhere."

"Hot damn. They figured they didn't have a chance, so no problem there. Everyone will be thrilled."

"I already told them."

"And they didn't tell us? Okay, so back to the question of where you want to put the gazebo. Does she garden?"

"I don't know. But I know she loves the water. Still, about the garden, her yard was under a couple of feet of snow, so she might have one buried back at her place."

"Maybe you should ask her."

"Nah. I want it to be a surprise. I can have a different kind built in a garden for her for next spring, if she likes to garden. Maybe for her birthday."

"When's her birthday?"

"June 4, two days after mine."

"That would be a great time for it then. Screened in, right?"

"Yeah, and we'll need to run electricity to it for lights and outlets for plugging in phone chargers and laptops. Okay, then if you're all right with it, I'm sending you the link for the picture of the premade gazebo they have at the local hardware store. If you can make all the arrangements, I'll be forever grateful."

"I'll get right on it first thing tomorrow. Though I can see Faith and the kids wanting one too."

Owen smiled. "Did you learn anything about the impostor?" He put the phone on speaker. "Everett is listening and said he'd help us with this."

"Thanks, Everett. We appreciate all you have done for us. Rowdy is in Houston already. He drove most of the night, stopped for a few hours, and hit the road again. He wanted to make sure he stopped this scam. He doesn't have much time left before he has to return to his job."

"I can't believe he's willing to help us like this." Owen explained to Everett about Rowdy and the SEAL wolves he worked with in Montana, then seeing the news report in South Dakota about the snowmobilers.

"Hell, that was the two of you?" Everett asked. "We just assumed it was another Arctic wolf pack up there. We should have known it was some of you."

"Yeah, it was us. I guess the news went all around the world and back," Owen said.

"I'll say," Cameron said. "Rowdy said being in Houston is the only way for him to pick up the fake Clara Hart's trail to learn who she is. If he can discover what she's driving, he can run her plates."

"And?" Owen asked.

"He hasn't seen her yet. He's been following the PI around, but he's had no luck seeing a woman who would fit the description. Like the rest of us, he assumes the woman will have her hair styled like the picture of Clara, or Candice, from a couple of years back."

"Does Rowdy think she's lying low until she can go in and sign the paperwork and claim the inheritance?"

"Maybe. Or Rowdy said she might just be doing whatever she normally does, while the PI is busy with his job. In any event, Rowdy's keeping close tabs on Felix Underwood in case a woman matching Candice's former description visits the PI."

"Has the PI seen Strom further?"

"No. I doubt Underwood needs to until he wants payment for his services. Even then, Strom might not actually see him and just have the money sent to him. What is your plan for tomorrow?"

"We're going to Houston first thing in the morning to take some of Candice's papers out of her safe-deposit box to prove who she is."

"Okay. We'll keep you informed if we learn anything further, and we'll get started on the Christmas project tomorrow. Congratulations again."

"Thanks, Cameron. I'm grateful for the way things turned out."

"Hell, I bet. I'm glad about it too. So is Faith."

They ended the call, and Everett and Owen made tentative plans for tomorrow, hoping both Owen and Candice could keep the shifting under control for the next couple of days. After the signing, they might have to stay with Everett and his wife for the holidays instead of going home right away.

Despite saying it wouldn't make any difference to him or the others, Owen knew it would to Candice.

Chapter 15

THAT NIGHT WHILE CANDICE WAS TAKING A SHOWER IN the upstairs bathroom, she was glad Demetria and Everett had a nice-sized, two-story brick home located way outside the suburbs of Dallas. The upstairs had three bedrooms and a game room where the jaguar couple had their computers set next to each other so they could play together. Candice thought it would be fun for her and Owen too, if he liked playing computer games. Or just to set up their computers side by side while they wrote. She was really loving the arrangement the jaguars had, and she couldn't wait to sell her place and move. Then she worried. Could she fit some of her stuff in his home? She'd never even considered that. This had all been so sudden that they hadn't really discussed her selling and moving, or anything.

Yet she really shouldn't have cared. All that mattered was that she was with someone she loved and he loved her back. That she no longer had to be alone. She had a whole pack to love, the little ones too. She could even consider having kids of her own now, something she never thought she'd be able to do. She'd have all kinds of help raising them. She hadn't known what would happen if she had unprotected sex with a human. Would she have had a wolf kid? Or not? She didn't even know the answer to that.

She rinsed the soap out of her hair and turned off the

shower. Grabbing a towel, she began drying herself off. Owen was still downstairs talking to Everett. Demetria had retired to their master bedroom.

There were so many things Candice didn't know about the wolves, and now she could safely learn. The idea she could be with the wolves for Christmas had real appeal, making it more of a special holiday than it would have been for her alone, even if they didn't make it home for Christmas Day because of the shifting issue. But having another woman to talk to, like Faith, who was just like her—fairly newly changed—was going to be wonderful. If Candice had children of her own, Faith would be a lifesaver. Candice couldn't even imagine having to go through that all on her own with only a bunch of males surrounding her who were as clueless as those with Faith had to have been.

Candice tugged on her warm, purple polka-dot flannel pajamas. As she left the bathroom, she saw Owen looking out the game room window. She padded down the hallway to the large open area to join him. He turned and smiled at her. "What are you watching?" she asked.

Owen pulled her into his arms and kissed her, hugging her, warming her. "Two jaguars playing in the water and looking like they're having a wild time of it."

A small pine tree was decorated in Christmas lights and reflected off the water, adding to the cheeriness of the scene before them.

Owen held her in his arms as they watched the two jaguars swimming and playing and dunking each other, the smaller one leaving the pool and leaping back in, while the bigger male waited and tackled her. The lights were on in the pool, the water aqua, a mist rising from the warm water to mix with the cold air—just magical.

Candice laughed. "They are so cute."

"Wait until we go swimming next summer in the lake."

Her back was now to Owen's front, and he was holding her close while they watched the jaguars play.

"I can't believe they're really jaguar shifters."

"Just like they couldn't believe we were wolves. They were dumbfounded when Corey shifted at the jaguar day care."

"I can't imagine how that would have been to witness firsthand."

"They were so good to him."

"Like we would be with one of theirs."

He nuzzled her neck. "Want to go for a swim?"

"*Brrr.*"

"It could be fun. As a wolf."

"I've been one way too many times today. I'll pass. Do you ever worry you'll turn and get stuck that way?"

"Early on, yes."

She grabbed his hand and hauled him to the guest bedroom. "We can have just as much fun in here. And it would be lots warmer. But we need to hurry, just in case," Candice warned. She hated worrying about getting the urge to shift when it was inconvenient at any time, but especially when she and Owen wanted to make love. Not that it had happened yet, but just the same, she worried about it.

"In that case..." Owen swept her up in his arms and she cried out, not expecting him to pull her off her feet. He cradled her as he quickened his pace to the guest bedroom.

She smiled up at him, loving him.

He entered the blue-and-white guest bedroom and shut the door with his knee. A little blue-and-white-decorated tree sparkled on top of the dresser. As soon as he deposited her on the bed, he began yanking off his clothes and tossing them on a chair, all but his boots. He dumped those on the floor while she watched him, smiling.

"My, oh, my." She unbuttoned one of her pajama buttons. "Someone sure is ready for some action."

"You bet." Naked, beautiful, and all hers, he leaned over and tugged off her pajama bottoms. Then he unbuttoned her top and helped her out of it.

He joined her in bed and sealed her mouth with his, kissing her fiercely as she caressed his whiskery jaw. She gave him the same ardent response—nips on his mouth, her tongue tantalizing his, their kisses deepening. Leaving her breathless and wanting more.

She drank in every bit of him: the feel of his hot thigh pressed against hers, the sweet and spicy lime shampoo and body wash he'd showered with, the champagne on his lips he'd had to celebrate seeing Everett and Demetria again, the sound of his rapid heartbeat, and the delicious way he massaged her breast, making her nipple tingle with responsiveness.

He coaxed his fingers through her hair, then suckled a breast before sweeping his hand down her belly to the place between her thighs. She was needy and aching for his touch. She loved his hot mouth against her breast. Her hands swept down his sides, wanting to touch him as much as he was touching her, making her feel needed and desirable. His passion infused her, made her arch to his touches and grip his waist, trying to hold on to the sensations building deep inside her.

Their kisses were more insistent, hungrier, hotter, until she felt she was on fire. She let go and cried out with release. She was filled with joy that she had agreed to be his mate and eager to have him deep inside her so he could fulfill his needs too.

Owen loved watching Candice come, listening to her rapid heartbeat, and seeing her face flushed with ardor. "You're beautiful," he said breathlessly, his fingers touching her soft hair before he moved in between her legs, unable to wait any longer. And she was his.

He pushed inside where she welcomed him with her tight, silky heat, and he began to thrust.

She wrapped her arms and legs around him, her heels high on the back of his thighs, which allowed him deeper access. He slowed his thrusts, wanting to extend the pleasure, wanting to bring her to climax again, kissing her throat, her neck, her jaw. But he was losing control and began to thrust hard, consumed by her heat and eagerness, pushing home until he couldn't hold on any longer and released. She groaned out his name with her own climax and smiled up at him.

He continued to thrust until he was completely spent and settled on top of her, burying her in his heat and pinning her to the mattress. He kissed her mouth again and thanked her for being his mate. She kept him in place, her hands and legs still wrapped around him as if she didn't want the connection between them broken just yet.

Then he lifted himself off her and settled next to her,

pulling the sheets and comforter over them. He wrapped her in his arms and caressed her back with a light touch. "I think I just found heaven."

She kissed his chest. "I think I did too."

He'd wanted her from the first time he'd set eyes on her by the White River, but more as a lustful male wolf needs a mate. He'd never expected to feel this physical and emotional attraction to such an intense degree as he did with her. He was still reeling from the aftermath of what they'd shared. The connection they'd forged.

Then she groaned and he knew at once what the matter was.

"I will never make it at this rate."

"You need to shift again?"

She let out her breath and nodded against his chest, still not letting go of him, as if he could help her fight it. Which he wished he could. He kissed her mouth. "Do you usually have to shift this often?"

"Sometimes, mostly when I have a book deadline. I think some of the urge to shift at this phase of the moon is caused from stress."

He rubbed her back. "Let's talk about anything else then. Anything that will help you to relax." It worked as he rubbed her back and kissed her, but he got himself all worked up until he was ready to have sex again.

She smiled up at him. "Let's hurry."

"No stress, right?"

She chuckled, and they hurried to make love. Half an hour after they'd made love and were settled in each other's arms again, she sighed against his chest.

He knew she couldn't hold off this time. "I love you, my beautiful wolf."

"Just shove me out of bed if I bother you," she said, sounding serious.

"Are you kidding? I didn't think I'd ever be lucky enough to have a wolf companion whom I love as much as I do you. I'm thrilled to be able to share my bed with you in any form you take on."

"You don't know how much that means to me, Owen. But seriously, if I start kicking you, wake me and make me move. You won't hurt my feelings at all." She had barely spoken the words when she shifted, and he pulled her into his arms. She laid her head on his chest to get comfortable.

"I'm serious. You're the best thing that has ever happened to me in my life. I'll always cherish the day you said you'd be my mate," he said.

She lifted her chin and licked his jaw. He laughed. "'Night, honey. We'll get through tomorrow without a hitch."

At least he sure as hell hoped so.

The next morning, Candice woke wrapped around her mate as a human, thankfully. They got up early, had breakfast, and said goodbye to Demetria before she headed to work.

"She wishes she could come with us," Everett said.

"Hopefully, there won't be any...well, too much drama." Candice climbed into the backseat, ready to confront her impostor.

Neither Owen nor Candice shifted the whole way to Houston, and after getting a hotel for the night there, they ran over to the bank before they had any inclination to shift.

The bank clerk took them back to unlock the safe-deposit box, but when Candice tried to use her key, it didn't work. "Why isn't it working?" Candice asked the clerk.

"Did you find your old key? Is that it? The lock was changed yesterday. You came in a couple of days ago and said you'd lost your key, so we had to replace the lock. We took the money out of your checking for it, just like we automatically do with your safe-deposit monthly rental fee. You had us open the box after we changed it out." The bank clerk showed her the signature paper where "Clara" had signed in yesterday.

Candice felt sick about it and angry at the same time. "Well, that wasn't me."

"She had to have an ID just like you did. I have to admit, she looked more like your photo ID than you do." The gray-haired woman frowned a little at Candice, as if she wasn't sure she was the right Clara.

Which irritated Candice even more. Though she could understand why the woman would think she was the impostor and not the other woman. But why would Candice make a stink about it? She wouldn't, if she were the impostor.

She would have closed her account out right then and there, but it would be easier to transfer any money she might get from the inheritance to a local bank account and then transfer it again later.

Then she realized she would have another home to sell. She didn't intend to live anywhere near Houston in the future, even though there were still a lot of wooded areas around the outskirts. She'd much prefer the solitude and quiet of northern Minnesota.

"Well, I haven't had dyed hair in two years. She colored hers to match that photo. I want to cancel my box. She might have stolen all my papers, but I'm still the one paying for it!"

After more of a hassle, because she had to make a police statement stating that another woman had stolen her ID and the contents of her safe-deposit box, Candice canceled her box and they headed to the hotel for the night. After signing the paperwork tomorrow afternoon, they were driving back to Dallas with Everett.

Candice couldn't get over being furious with the woman. It was bad enough that she was trying to steal Candice's inheritance, but the pictures were priceless. And she'd put a pearl ring from her parents in there since she couldn't wear it any longer. Which was why she had kept them secure in the safe-deposit box in the first place!

"I'm so sorry about what happened," Owen said. "Unfortunately, there's no recourse. Contents of safe-deposit boxes are not insured by the FDIC. But maybe the police can shed some light on the impostor. And maybe we can get everything back from her once she's proven to be an impostor."

"The documents are all replaceable. The photos are not. And the ring my parents gave to me isn't either. I just hope that the woman doesn't get away with this." That's what Candice was still worried about. That the woman would manage to lie her way through this and end up with the inheritance. It could be a long, drawn-out process to straighten out the situation, and it would put Candice and Owen more at risk, because she knew he wasn't about to let her handle this all on her own.

As soon as they'd checked into adjoining rooms at the hotel and settled in them, Candice got a call from Rowdy, which she put on speaker.

"Hope the two of you made it to Houston all right," Rowdy said. "Cameron said you had some trouble earlier. You should have ridden with me."

"We have another friend helping out," Owen said.

Candice was sure he didn't want to tell the homicide detective that jaguar shifters existed, if he didn't already know it.

"What did you learn?" Candice asked, eager to know if he had any more news.

"Felix Underwood has no record of any violations of any laws. He's squeaky clean. The woman's name is Dora Emerson. She's Felix's sister. She went to see Felix at his downtown office, which is how I managed to learn who she is from her license plate. I have to say, she looks similar to you. Considering you were unable to see your uncle right away, that must have triggered Felix's scheme to pass his sister off as you. I have her address, but I don't want anyone going there to confront her."

Candice was shocked the PI would use his own sister to parade around as Clara Hart. Then again, they could keep all the money in the family. And if she fit the part, so much the better. "Sister. Felix Underwood knew exactly who she was and is a coconspirator in this."

"Correct. Looked like easy money, no sign of a real Clara Hart, so he must have figured since you were a fake, it would be easy to pass off a different one. She's been into some petty theft. Nothing big-time. She's been married and divorced, but she still goes by her married name."

Candice was furious with the PI and the woman. "She stole the documents and pictures from my safe-deposit box at the bank. I closed it out, but she has everything I'd kept in there, including a pearl ring from my parents. My birthstone ring for my birthday when I turned sixteen. I wore it constantly—until I couldn't and was afraid I'd lose it one of these times." If the impostor was wearing that ring…

"Okay, I'll see what I can do."

She ground her teeth. "But you're going to try to get my documents and the other items she stole?"

"I'll try. I've got a couple of friends in Houston who are cops. I've alerted them to the fraud, and I'll give them a call with the latest update concerning the safe-deposit theft. They already know who she really is, so they're not surprised she'd try something that could mean a huge amount of money if she and her brother could pull it off."

Candice still worried that these people would get away with the scam if they weren't stopped. "What if my uncle believes her?"

"I've already spoken with him. He said he was willing to hear what you have to say…in person. I know how much trouble that is for you, but he can't believe anyone with that much money coming to them would not want to sign for it right away."

Candice sighed with relief. "Rowdy, thanks so much for helping us." She still couldn't believe a human knew what they were and was all right with it. After all the trouble he had gone through, she thought it would only be polite to buy him a meal. But she thought they should meet him at the hotel restaurant so she or Owen could make a fast getaway to their room if they needed to. "We'd love to buy you lunch at the steak restaurant in the hotel where we're staying, if you haven't eaten."

"I'd love to. Meet you there in half an hour?"

"See you then." Candice ended the call. "That's all right with you guys, isn't it?"

"Yeah, sure." Owen rubbed her back and kissed her cheek. "I think it's a real nice gesture."

"Sounds good to me. Thanks for not telling Rowdy what I am. I'd prefer he didn't know about us. He probably just figures I'm a wolf helping you out. I still can't imagine he knows and no one has done anything about it though," Everett said.

"Neither could we, but killing him could get dicey because he's a homicide detective," Candice said.

Owen agreed. "And turning him would mean he'd have to quit his job for no good reason and hide what he was until he had enough control over the shifting. Maybe the Montana wolves feel that no one would believe him anyway. Still, the more of us who know of him and that he knows of, the greater the likelihood of him getting turned, I'd say."

"If I didn't think it sounded totally crazy, I'd almost believe he wanted to be turned," Candice said.

"Wouldn't he be surprised if a jaguar turned him and not a wolf?" Everett said.

"When he doesn't even know they exist?" Candice smiled. "Yep, he'd be shocked all right."

They all headed down to the Longhorn Bar and Grille to get a seat before Rowdy arrived. Decorated in a Western theme—with paintings of longhorn cattle standing among bluebonnets, cowboy boots tacked to the wall, old photos of Texas ranch hands, and canvas prints of the Lone Star flag—it gave Candice a twinge of homesickness.

But as an Arctic wolf, she loved the winters up north, the fall colors. She really was going to enjoy living in Minnesota, especially the company she would be keeping. She could imagine sitting out on the deck in the mornings and taking in nature as she began warming up to write—blogging, sharing pictures—oh, pictures. The photos she could take!

As soon as they got a table, Rowdy joined them. He greeted everyone with a friendly handshake, but with enough reserve to let them know he understood he wasn't one of them, an outsider, and had to be on his best behavior. Or someone might just...bite him.

Candice asked, "How did my uncle react to the news that the other woman was an impostor?"

"He didn't say a whole lot. I think he was surprised, if the way his eyes widened a bit was any indication, but he's good at schooling his emotions." Rowdy glanced at his menu, while everyone looked over theirs. "He's a businessman, and I imagine he's not happy someone else tried to take him for a fool. I did tell him about my arrangements with the police, so when we all meet over there, they can take the two fraudsters into custody. Your uncle began grinding his teeth a bit, and I got the impression he would have liked to handle it himself. But this is the best way for everyone concerned."

The waitress came and took their orders then. Rowdy wanted the deluxe Texas-sized steak. Everett and Owen got the same, and Candice ordered the petite filet mignon.

"I'm curious why, if you know so much about us,

you let any of us know you know. Don't you worry that some of us will feel you could be a threat?" Everett placed his napkin on his lap.

"Life is meant to be lived. If I go out with a bang, so be it."

"Or a bite?" Everett asked.

Rowdy smiled. "I could have the same concern when working my job."

"I think you want to be like us, but you're also afraid to be like us." Candice knew the feeling. If she'd been given a choice? Before she'd met Owen, no way. After meeting him? She would have had a hard time letting him go and not taking the jump into the world of the unknown.

"Not afraid, really. But it would be a challenge to do my job until I could control the shifting."

Candice gave a ladylike snort. That was an understatement, if she'd ever heard one.

After a nice meal with Rowdy and Everett, they said they'd meet tomorrow.

When Candice went to bed that night with Owen, they made love, which helped to take her mind off seeing her uncle. But as soon as she snuggled against her mate, all she could think of was meeting Uncle Strom, turning, and the possible disaster that could be.

Chapter 16

Owen knew Candice was feeling the strain of meeting her uncle the next day and keeping from shifting, which could prove disastrous. Actually, he was too. At least when he made love to her, she'd seemed focused on their lovemaking, and not on the events of the next day.

They had the morning to chill, so instead of joining Everett for breakfast, they had room service while Everett had breakfast in the hotel restaurant with Rowdy. Candice didn't need to leave the hotel for another five hours to meet with Strom and the judge, so for now, Owen wanted her to be relaxed and not worry about anything. They had made love in the shower, dressed, and had just finished having bowls of oatmeal and blueberries when he asked, "Do you want to watch something on TV?"

Maybe that would help get her mind off the meeting. "Sure, an on-the-edge-of-our-seats thriller."

"You got it."

They settled onto the bed together, pillows and spare pillows propped behind them as he wrapped his arm around her and found a good thriller—*Red Eye*.

They'd watched the movie and started another. They had barely gotten started when Candice's cell phone rang. She tensed as she pulled her phone out of her pocket and looked at the caller ID.

"Uncle Strom," she whispered, as if he could hear her words. "Now what?"

"Probably nothing." But Owen didn't think her uncle would bother her if it was nothing.

Candice loved Owen for trying his hardest to help her not to think about the signing. When Owen had been making love to her, she hadn't given the pending meeting a thought. She'd hoped the thriller would take her mind off it, and she figured they'd just watch movies until they had to leave. She felt bad that they weren't doing something with Everett since he'd brought them here, but the jaguar shifter had assured them he wanted Candice to be completely unstressed before they left for the meeting.

And then, right as she was snuggling with Owen, blanking out the business with her uncle and the judge, her phone rang. Sure enough, her uncle was calling, bringing the worry of what would happen next to the forefront again.

Owen muted the TV.

She answered the phone and put it on speaker. "Hello?"

"I want you to come over now," Uncle Strom said.

"But the—"

"The signing of the paperwork isn't until four this afternoon. I want to see you for a bit before then. I want to apologize for what I said to you and Owen in person."

This was so not good. She had really planned only to meet him, sign the paperwork, and that was it. She hadn't thought he would want to see any more of her than that. She was really surprised he wanted to spend some time with her. Unless he still didn't believe who she was and was pretending he meant to apologize to her. Then again, he was worth billions. So why would he play games with her? Wouldn't he be more professional than that?

"I insist."

She wasn't sure if he meant because he really didn't trust who she was or he really wanted to see her.

"Okay. We'll be there in an hour, as long as the traffic permits us."

"All right. Plan to have lunch with me at noon and dinner with me after the signing."

Could she last? Candice was so afraid she wouldn't be able to. What then? She would have to bite him. Make him one of their pack. He could build a billionaire mansion on the lake in Minnesota. He might raise their property taxes though. Was she crazy, thinking he would be all right with her biting him? She would though. Then he'd know why she made up the book-signing story and couldn't come home. He could be real family, now that she'd lost her parents. He could have family too, since he'd never married or had children of his own.

"I can have a car sent for you."

To make sure she really came? No way. She didn't want to have to bite his driver too, if she should have the urge to shift and couldn't control it. "No, that's okay. Our friend Everett, who lives in Dallas, brought us to Houston. He'll drive us there, if that's okay with you."

"Yeah, that's fine."

"Okay, we're headed out. See you in about an hour."

They ended the call, and Candice felt her skin crawling with unease.

"I'll let Rowdy and Everett know." Owen got right on the phone and called Everett first, putting it on speaker. "Strom Hart wants us to have lunch and dinner with him at his house. He wants us there now so he can apologize to Candice and me. He said it's fine for you to come with us."

"I'll meet you in the lobby."

"Okay, Everett, thanks." Owen called Rowdy next.

"I'll meet you at his house with the police officers to arrest the impostor and her accomplice, the PI. I've already made arrangements with Mr. Hart concerning the matter."

"Okay, good show." When Owen ended the call, he squeezed Candice's hand. "We can do this."

"And if it doesn't work out, I'm biting him."

Owen smiled and kissed her cheek.

She was a little surprised. She thought maybe he would say no to that, or try to talk her out of it or something. But nope. Owen either didn't believe she'd do it, or he also thought it was the only option.

When they met Everett in the lobby, he said to Candice, "I hope you don't have to turn your uncle, should the situation get out of hand."

"I agree. I just don't see any other way around it."

"If you have to shift and your uncle learns of it, just talk to him about it. Maybe he can accept us for what we are, like Rowdy does," Owen said.

"Do you think Rowdy has a hidden agenda?"

"I suspect anyone who's not one of us has an agenda, but in a different case, the man seems to be fine," Everett said as they reached his car in the parking tower.

Candice frowned. "There are more who know about us?"

"One other man we know of. He works for a zoo in Portland, Oregon. He's been quiet about it, so we're good. But we still worry when anyone knows anything about us."

"I feel the same way," Candice said. Owen agreed.

They climbed into the car, and Everett headed out to the country.

"Rowdy just texted me and asked if he should come earlier. I told him no. That if we have trouble, we'll have to deal with it the way we see fit." Owen settled into the backseat.

"Have you ever been out to your uncle's place?" Everett asked Candice.

"No. I'm really interested to see the kind of place he has. My parents' home was pretty extravagant, though much more modest when I was younger."

"I've never been to a mansion before," Owen said.

Everett shook his head. "Me neither. What's the deal with the impostor then? Is she coming at the same time? Or closer to the time of the signing?"

"I don't know. I thought from what Rowdy said, they planned to arrest them at the house. It sounds to me like they're not going to meet him at the signing. Or go there even," Owen said. "Which would be the best for all concerned."

"Sounds good. I would think it would confuse the issue if you both showed up to sign for the money and properties." Everett turned off the highway and headed onto another.

"I agree. And I think my uncle would prefer to keep this in the family, not make frontline news if he can help it. At least I would think so." Candice couldn't believe how nervous she was about seeing her uncle. It wasn't about proving who she was to him, but feeling guilty all over again about not being there for her mother and father when they needed her most. She wondered if her uncle had gone to see them when she couldn't.

Forty minutes later, they entered the gated property, started down the long drive, and finally saw the four-story home in the distance, a round tower on each corner making it look like a medieval manor. It was a palatial, ivory brick mansion, way out of the city and surrounded by forests. It was beautiful, and Candice thought that if it wasn't for her wolf shifting problems, she would have liked to have visited him here, just to see the estate, if nothing more.

She was already thinking of a billionaire wolf story set here as they drove up the long drive to the mansion. It had a large circle drive in front of it and a six-car unattached garage off the side—with the doors all shut, which made her wonder if he really had that many vehicles. A large pond sat off to one side of the property, with a rock waterfall built into a man-made hill and a fountain spouting water in the center. A gazebo was perched above, overlooking the picturesque pond where a couple of black swans were swimming. She wondered if koi were swimming in it too.

"Can we stop over there for a moment?" Candice asked, wanting to see for herself.

Everett parked the Suburban.

"Setting for a story," Owen said, guessing.

"My story. Not yours."

Everett laughed. "You're writing a book too?"

"New writer," Owen quickly said. "But yeah,

Candice thinks it has possibility. And she's more the expert than me."

"More than possibility. It's great. I think I'm the heroine in the story. No faults at all."

Everett laughed.

"Does she need to have faults? I can add some."

Smiling, Candice shook her head and pulled out her phone, capturing shots of the gazebo, the fountain, the colorful orange-and-gold koi, and the swans for future reference.

Once she was done, they got back into the car and headed the rest of the way to the house. She felt a little better, having taken the time to stop for a few minutes. She hoped the guys didn't think she was nuts for wanting to take pictures and see the fish. But it was more than that. She'd wanted to breathe in the fresh air for a second and fortify herself before she had to face what came next.

It wasn't that she was afraid of her uncle or what he might say or do, but about what might happen in the time they had to stay there if she or Owen—or horrors, both of them—had to shift.

The place was so big that she couldn't imagine her uncle living in the house all by himself. He probably had gala social events though. Maybe visiting guests a lot of the time. She hoped he didn't invite her and Owen and Everett to stay for any longer than this. They'd have to decline.

Everett parked the car next to the brick walkway that led to the front door of the mansion, two giant bronze lion statues guarding the entrance.

With her stomach flip-flopping all over the place,

Candice climbed out of the Suburban. She wondered if her uncle was watching them get out of the car.

She'd barely rung the doorbell when a man answered. He was blond-haired and green-eyed, wearing cargo pants, a sporty blue shirt, and cowboy boots. What she didn't expect was for him to look over her shoulder at Everett and say, "Son-of-a-gun, Everett Anderson..." But then he switched his attention back to Candice and Owen. "What the hell."

Which was just what she was thinking as she caught his scent. He smelled like a jaguar.

Chapter 17

Candice couldn't believe her uncle would have a jaguar shifter working for him. The man must have been born as one and had control over his shifting. "How do you hide what you are?" she whispered. "Don't you ever have the urge to shift?"

The man smiled. "Your uncle is also a jaguar. All the staff is. I'm Jim, by the way."

Her heart pounding, Candice felt as light-headed as when she'd learned Owen was a wolf. He must have sensed it because he quickly wrapped his arm around her to support her. Tears filled her eyes and spilled down her cheeks. She quickly brushed them away, feeling overwhelmed by the news.

A million thoughts were racing through her mind. Had her parents been jaguars all along too? Had she avoided them because of her shifting problems when they would have welcomed her home even if she wasn't a jaguar shifter, but a wolf shifter instead? She felt devastated all over again, even though she should be glad her uncle would understand now why she believed she couldn't see her parents.

"My...my mother and father too?" she choked out.

"Oh, no," Jim quickly assured her. "Come in. Just your uncle. He was turned years ago."

That made Candice glad she'd kept the secret from her parents, but she wished she'd known about her uncle once she'd been turned.

"I take it that's why you changed so much after your camping trip to White River."

She nodded as Owen helped her into the mansion.

Owen couldn't believe it when he realized that Jim Winchester, Strom's assistant, was a jaguar like Everett, and so was her uncle. He was damn glad to hear it, but he could understand how shaken up Candice was. First, he popped into her life as an Arctic wolf, and now her uncle and his staff had turned out to be jaguars. Owen continued to keep her close for physical and moral support, glad he was here for her.

Everett quickly filled them in on how he knew Jim. "Jim's a former JAG agent like me, Golden Claws, but he abandoned us with a smirk, saying he had some rich new boss who was paying him ten times what we earned with the Force. Hell, and here we all thought he was doing something super important. A butler for a billionaire?" Everett laughed.

Jim smiled at him. "That's one of the jobs. I'm actually his assistant and personal bodyguard in case he needs one. The only reason I would work for him is because he's a jaguar. Nice benefits. Lots of trips. First class everywhere." Jim eyed Candice. "Man, is he going to be torqued off that a wolf turned you." He glanced at Owen. "Better not have been you."

Owen raised his hands in a way that said not him.

"The little boy of one of his packmates did it. It was purely by accident," Candice said in protective mode.

"Hell. Come on in. I'm to usher you into the great room. He'll be down in a minute, but I've got to let him know what's happened. That's why you didn't come when you should have earlier. You're newly turned,"

Jim said, as if the whole situation was now crystal clear to him.

"Yes. The full moon is upon us. I've been having trouble the whole time."

"Not to worry. You're completely safe here." Jim led them into a grand room furnished with oil paintings of jungle scenes, rich and opulent leather chairs and couches, Turkish tapestries, and chandeliers. "Maggie will bring some refreshments. I'll be back in a minute."

Candice briefly wondered why her uncle didn't have bronze statues of jaguars out front instead of lions.

A few minutes later, a dark-haired woman came in to offer drinks. Candice surreptitiously took in a deep breath to smell if the woman was human or jaguar. She was a big-cat shifter too.

When Candice told her water would be fine, Maggie gave her a list of things they had, and Candice chose hot cherry-blossom tea. Everett and Owen asked for coffee, and then the woman left the room.

"I can't believe my uncle is a jaguar," Candice said.

"It's not something we can advertise." Everett looked out the french patio doors at the Olympic-size swimming pool and gardens. "This is big enough to run as a jaguar and never have any trouble. That pool sure looks inviting."

"It does," Candice said. Instead of envisioning her uncle exercising in it as a human, she could imagine him swimming as a jaguar.

"I can't believe it either. But I'm glad they're all shifters. Takes a bit of the stress off." Owen pulled Candice into his arms and hugged her tight. "Are you all right?"

"Better, knowing he's a shifter too. That everyone here is. Unless he's really angry with me that I'm a wolf."

"That's my job," Everett said. "To intervene and help resolve issues between the different shifters."

"I'm surprised you didn't know my uncle."

"We don't travel in the same circles. I'm certain he keeps his true shifter self secret from everyone else... the public, that is."

A few minutes later, Maggie brought their drinks, along with a vegetable-and-fruit tray, chips, and dip.

They all thanked her, and once she left, Jim returned. He shook his head, looking concerned. "Well, Mr. Hart is not happy. I will say he's glad to know why you were absent from your parents' lives when they needed you. Really glad. He'll be down in a little bit. He had some urgent business to take care of. Everett, do you want to take a walk with me and catch me up on what's going on?"

He and Everett walked outside, and Everett began telling Jim about his mate and forming a new branch of the Force.

Candice and Owen waited another twenty minutes to see her uncle, though she filled the time by taking pictures, trying to keep her mind off meeting him. She hadn't met him before, and now to learn he wasn't even human? She hoped he was as nice as Everett was, but if not, she'd just get done what she needed to do and maybe someday they could get to know each other better. Or not. She was only adopted, after all. He might not want to have anything to do with her beyond settling her parents' estate. That made her feel a little sad.

Owen was trying not to show his impatience and glad Candice was occupying her time and not fretting about seeing her uncle. He understood the man could be busy with important business, but since her uncle wanted Candice here earlier, Owen wished he'd come see her. He hoped Jim was only making a bigger deal of Candice being a wolf, and Strom didn't feel that negative about it. Then they heard footfalls and Owen moved in closer to Candice. It was an instinctive move, like a wolf protecting his mate. He didn't want her to feel he was being overprotective, but when she took his hand and smiled up at him, he knew he'd made the right move.

Strom entered the room—tall at six foot four or thereabout, his hair dark, his face clean-shaven. He was wearing a dark suit, his expression just as dark. He gave Candice a growly look, then shifted his hard look to Owen. "*You* turned her? You knew who and what she was when my assistant first contacted you? And she's been living with you all this time?"

"No, sir." Owen explained what had happened, though Candice broke in to tell more of the details and what had happened once she had returned home after the camping trip, unable to work any longer and needing to find a safe place to live, given what she had become.

"You were living in South Dakota?" Strom asked her.

"Yes. I needed to be someplace way out, but also where there's some snow in the winter to help hide the fact I'm running around as an Arctic wolf."

"You're an Arctic wolf?" He gave Owen another irritated look, as if he had anything to do with what she had become.

Owen should have realized the jaguar shifters wouldn't have guessed they were Arctic wolves, as opposed to regular gray wolves. He explained how that had come about with him and the rest of his pack—all about the wolf pack from north of the border visiting Maine and turning them.

"Well, hell, Candice," Strom said. "Not only are you at more of a risk because you're a white wolf with a pack of white wolves, but they're nearly as newly turned as you."

Owen suspected her uncle wouldn't want to hear they were mated either. Then again, maybe he would feel she'd be taken care of if she had a mate.

"Wait… I saw that news report of two Arctic wolves rescuing a couple of snowmobilers in South Dakota. Don't tell me that was the two of you."

"Yeah, that was us. We had to do something," Candice said.

"Hell. That was damn foolishness. What if you'd been shot? What if people had thought you were trying to eat those men?"

"The thought did occur to us," Owen said. "What would you have done in our place?"

Strom snorted.

"You would have rescued them. Or tried." Owen was certain he would have.

"And if they'd seen you running as wolves? You think they would have let you be? Or tried chasing you down?" Strom asked.

"We can't know the answer to that." Candice relaxed a little. "You can't imagine how awful it felt being cooped up in the house when I wanted to run free. How did you become a jaguar shifter?" Candice asked, getting the subject off them.

"I was turned nineteen years ago, so I know just what it felt like back then. I was lucky a few jaguars showed me the ropes. It taught me not to mess around with girls

I didn't know, even though it was too late to do anything about what I'd become. Cynthia Taylor was my first too. Both of us were sixteen. She'd invited me to a party one of her friends had at his parents' house while they were out of town. Several of her friends took her aside and said she shouldn't have brought me. I was popular with the kids at school, so I didn't need their approval. I told her I was ready to go, and she said not yet. That she was going to show me something really wild."

Candice shook her head.

"Boy, did she ever. I was feeling damn good…until she bit me and I woke to find a jaguar in the guest bed. I was terrified. Screaming. She quickly shifted into a naked girl. She'd bitten me by accident…so she said. I don't remember much after that except for a bunch of people crowding into the room and staring at me."

She couldn't imagine how horrified he must have felt. At least she hadn't been terrified by being bitten, only with what came next.

"It's not like with wolves, as far as I understand it. The other guys in the house said I could die, or I could keep my mouth shut and live. Neither of us were interested enough in each other to pursue anything permanent. We were way too young. And I was angry with Cynthia for wrecking my life. I ended up having to drop out of school and began taking private lessons from some of the other jaguar families. Her friends had become my friends, and no one was happy with what she had done to me. My parents weren't happy about me quitting school, but it all worked out in the end."

"Do you ever see her now?" Candice asked.

"No. She married a guy when she was eighteen and

moved away. At the time, my brother, your dad, was thirty-six, married, and working on his first billion. I was a late-in-life baby, so we didn't really have anything in common. After the change, we *really* didn't have anything in common."

"I can't believe you're a jaguar, Uncle Strom." Candice was shocked to learn it. After all the worry about shifting, he'd been a shifter too.

"I would never have guessed you were a wolf shifter. So how did you locate her then?" Strom asked Owen.

"I learned her new name through her old workplace, and I was intrigued she was writing Arctic werewolf romances. But I didn't know she was a wolf shifter until I went to see her in South Dakota."

"That's why you could only return home at certain times," Strom said.

"Yes. When I had to leave my life behind, I wanted to tell Mom and Dad why I only returned during the waxing or waning crescent or new moon, but I couldn't. I visited them for a week every month, allowing for travel there and home again, once I learned I either had more control over shifting or couldn't shift at all during those times. Every time they had major health issues, it was during the full moon or too close to it, as if that had triggered all the bad things in their life, like it had in mine. They weren't satisfied that I didn't come home when they needed me most. I couldn't blame them either."

"The fact you returned as much as you did had to have influenced John. He could be hardheaded, but he could be fair too, once he got over being annoyed about something. This explains everything. Why you made up that story about the world tour. Why you couldn't see me for another week. I just never imagined the timing coincided with the new moon and that was your reason for staying away. What would you have believed in my place?"

"That something wasn't right."

"Correct."

"Is that why you stayed away from Mom and Dad?"

"I never had anything in common with them. We had our own lifestyles. Our own business pursuits. I did take care of them when they became ill. They always asked for you, were worried about you. I can't tell you how angry I was that you didn't come home for them."

"I couldn't. I swear, every time they became ill, the waxing or waning gibbous or full moon was out."

"I completely understand. I want you to live with me. You have your own estates, but I'm here alone and would enjoy your company and getting to know you. You'd have full use of my facilities and cars, and the jet can take you wherever you want to go without the fear of shifting."

"I'm mated. To Owen. I'll be moving to Minnesota. Though I'll need to sell off the houses here and in South Dakota."

Strom narrowed his eyes at Owen. "Was this mutually agreed upon?"

"Of course it was. We love each other. We're happy together. We'd love to take you up on coming to visit. During the new moon, of course," Candice said, growling.

"Anytime. I'll just have my jet pick you up." Strom took a deep breath. "Any of your pack. The whole pack. I have plenty of room, as you can see."

"You believe me now? That I am who I said I was? I don't look much like my picture anymore." Candice was surprised her uncle didn't expect her to prove who she was. "The PI's sister got into my safe-deposit and stole my papers and family photos. I couldn't believe it. She called ahead and said she'd lost the keys, and they had to drill out the old lock and make new keys for it."

"She had an ID with your name on it, I take it?" Strom asked.

"Yep. I guess her brother made all the arrangements for her. Anyway, my baby pictures with my parents holding me, my high school diploma, paperwork on the house I bought and sold, the pearl ring my parents gave me when I turned sixteen, and all kinds of documents were in there. I hadn't moved everything to where I am now because there are no local banks with safe-deposit boxes close by. I planned to eventually move it all to the nearest big city."

"Robbing a bank's safe-deposit box should be a federal offense," Strom said.

"Yeah. I couldn't believe it. It was still in my old name. I just didn't think to change it over. I still have the old driver's license I kept for an ID in case I ever needed it. Did you want to see it?"

"No, that's okay. I have duplicates of all the pictures. Your hair was red back then, just like it is now. The other woman dyed her hair to match the picture I gave the PI and Owen, and you were wearing the violet contact lenses. But your workplace said that when you returned from the camping trip and packed up your things at the office when you quit, your hair was red, not dyed."

"Being a wolf knocked the color right out of my hair. You should have heard me telling everyone it was just temporary theater hair color, and I washed it all out in the river that night while everyone was sleeping."

Her uncle laughed. "I can imagine how that would have sounded."

"Yeah. Unbelievable. So how do you know it's really me?" She liked hearing him laugh. Her uncle sounded a lot like her father when he laughed.

"I've been to your parents' home several times. I'd know your scent anywhere. You didn't have to do anything to prove that you are who you are. Once I met the other woman, I would have known she was a fraud right away."

Candice took a relieved breath. "I was so worried about having to shift while I was here, but when we learned you were shifters too, I was thrilled."

"What about Felix Underwood, the other PI?" Owen asked.

"He's done some business for my firm. He was out of town when I needed a PI at first to locate Clara... Candice. But, Owen, I had thought you might get at the root of why Candice had changed so much after that camping trip. It seems you were the perfect one for the job." Strom said to Candice, "When Felix learned you were reluctant to come to claim your inheritance, he proved beyond a doubt you were not on a world book tour. He believed you were an impostor."

"He figured he could create his own impostor to pass off as me to gain the inheritance, especially since there was no way he was going to find someone else who was the real one," Candice said. "He couldn't have known I was a newly turned wolf and couldn't come to see you. He and the woman, his sister, would split the proceeds, and no one would be the wiser."

"They'll be here after lunch, which, from what I can smell, is about to be served, and then you can have fun with them. After that, the police will arrest them, and we'll go to see the judge."

"What if I have to turn while we're in the judge's chamber? Is he one of us?"

"No, he isn't. If you shift before we see him, I'll give him a call and we'll meet a little later and get this done. He owes me for all the money I've spent helping his political campaigns. But we still have time left."

"Good." She didn't know what she was going to say to the impostor, but she figured the woman had already cooked her goose. "You've talked with Felix and his sister?"

"On the phone, but not in person. And 'Clara' has been excited about seeing me, unlike you."

Candice rolled her eyes. "You never came by. You didn't speak with my parents, and they never talked about you. What do you expect?"

"That's what I really expected from a niece who was at odds with me. Not one who would be excited to see me. But she's nervous too. While you seem comfortable around me."

"Now that I know you're a shifter, yes. I was worried sick about this. Didn't sleep hardly at all last night. You can't know how concerned I was that I might shift. And still could while I'm here or on the way home."

Strom frowned. "At least stay for a while. Until the new moon. I'd really like you to stay for Christmas. You know you're my only living relative."

She couldn't believe it. "Could you come to see us?"

He laughed. "In the snow?" He shook his head.

Chapter 18

THEY WERE EATING CHICKEN AND BROCCOLI CREPES with Everett and her uncle when Jim came in and announced the police had arrived.

"Put them in my study, will you? We're almost done here," Strom said, his face darkly amused.

"Is Rowdy, the homicide detective, with them?" Candice asked.

"He is," Jim said.

"About that. How in the world did a homicide detective get involved in this when he's from Montana?" Strom asked.

Owen hadn't expected that question, though he should have considered it, as sharp as Strom was. When they both hesitated to say, Owen not wanting to tell one story and Candice another, Strom folded his arms and eyed them both. "*Okay*, the real story."

"He knows about us," Candice said.

Though Owen hadn't intended to tell Strom anything, he figured their only other choice would have been to lie to cover for Rowdy and probably be found out anyway. Besides, though Rowdy had helped Candice tremendously and had Owen's undying gratitude, he had been the one to reveal what he knew, so this was really on him.

"He was visiting family in South Dakota," Candice started, and then she explained the rest, beating Owen to it.

Jim shook his head. Strom was frowning.

"If it wasn't for him, Felix Underwood and the fake Clara could have gotten Candice's inheritance," Owen said.

"No. I would have smelled the deception once I met her." Strom ground his teeth. "What is anyone going to do about it?"

"We hadn't planned to do anything. It's up to the Montana pack to handle it." Owen suspected Rowdy would want to stay there and not live somewhere else.

"He doesn't know about us," Everett said. "Just about wolves. He most likely assumes I'm a wolf, though maybe he thinks I'm just like him. He hasn't asked, and I haven't offered any information about myself. He knows how worried Candice was about shifting and wanted to help her in any way he could, including identifying the impostor and involving the local police in apprehending the fraudsters."

"He seems like a decent man and not interested in exposing us. Just wanting to be friends and help out when he can," Owen said, but he didn't seem to be convincing Strom…or Jim.

Candice let out her breath in exasperation. "You can't kill him."

Her uncle shook his head. "I wouldn't think of it."

"It's like Owen said. The local wolf pack should handle it," she said.

"But they haven't. And from the sound of it, they aren't interested in turning him and making him one of their pack."

"You can't make him a jaguar shifter. He doesn't even know about you. What if he would rather be a wolf?"

Strom smiled, but his expression made Owen believe that's just what he planned to do. What would he do with Rowdy afterward? Strom would be stuck with a person who would have difficulty shifting for years. Owen didn't think Strom would be irresponsible enough to let Rowdy fend for himself.

Owen turned to Everett. "What would your organization say about that?"

"I'm not sure. I would think it would be handled on an individual basis. It's like with another man who knows of us."

Strom scowled. "Another? I can't believe you would let this go."

"In his case, he's known about wolves for years. He saved a jaguar shifter's life. He knew about both of us—wolves and jaguars—even before we knew about each other. All that time, he said nothing about it. Not even to his wife. I think if some non-shifters can tolerate us, even help us out when we're in a bind, they should be allowed to continue as before. He has a wife and step-kids he's raising.

"With Rowdy? No family to speak of, so there is that. If it were up to me, I'd give him a choice. Would he want to be turned? Maybe he does, but he can't get up the nerve to ask. If he does want to be turned, ask him which he'd rather be. If he doesn't say, then decide one way or another. I sincerely believe we'd be better off if humans who learn of us and are okay with it—and can keep their mouths shut—would be allowed to continue on as before," Everett said.

"If they can keep their mouths shut, I suppose so." Strom didn't sound like he really believed it. Then his phone played a jingle, and he pulled it out of his pocket and answered it. "Yeah, Brenner?"

"His lawyer," Jim told them. "He's meeting us at the judge's chambers."

"What?" Strom's face reddened. "Let me talk to Judge Watkins now." Strom rose abruptly from the table. "All right. We're coming over right this minute. I'll send the police over there right away. Whatever you do, don't allow that woman to sign the paperwork."

"I'll take care of it," Jim said. "And get your driver to bring the car around." He hurried out of the dining room as everyone got up to leave.

Candice felt sick to her stomach about this. What if the impostor had managed to see the judge somehow and pulled it off? The woman had Candice's documentation proving she was really Clara.

They left the house to find a black limousine parked out front, waiting for them. The driver, Denny, greeted them, dressed in a black suit, his long, black hair tied back in a tail. Everyone but Jim sat in the back as they headed into town to meet with the judge. The police and Rowdy had already left to intercept the woman and her accomplice brother at the courthouse.

Halfway to town, Candice's muscles tingled and warmed, warning her she was going to shift. She couldn't ignore the need to run wild and shed her human skin. To be the wolf. She hadn't even realized she had squeezed Owen's hand so hard until he glanced over at her and whispered, "Do you need to shift?"

She nodded, curbing the urge to swear. She was so stressed out and having a devil of a time getting her anxieties under control. Of all the times to have to do this! But she reminded herself it could be worse. She could be in the courthouse and needing to shift. She could just envision being in one of the ladies' restroom stalls, bringing back memories of her earlier catastrophe at the travel plaza.

"Hey," Owen said, "can we have the driver pull the car over and let everyone get out for a minute?"

Strom looked up from his cell phone and considered Candice. "Hell, you need to shift?"

Owen knew Candice felt bad enough without her uncle sounding like he was thoroughly annoyed with her.

"Yes," she said, glowering at her uncle.

"Okay." Strom pushed the intercom to speak with the driver. "Denny, I need you to pull the car as far onto the shoulder as you can as soon as it's safe to do so."

"That means I won't be able to sign the documents," Candice said. "I'm so sorry, Uncle Strom."

Hating that she felt so bad about this, Owen squeezed her hand with reassurance.

"Don't be. It's not your fault." Strom got on his phone again and called his lawyer. "Brenner, as soon as you're able to see the judge, tell him we've had some difficulties and it looks like Candice can't make it to sign the paperwork now. We'll have to meet with him another time… Yeah, shifter trouble. We're still on our way to the courthouse to make sure the judge knows not to sign over the estate to the other woman, but then we'll return home. As soon as Candice can shift back, we'll return to the courthouse."

Denny finally found a good spot to pull over and parked as far off the road as he could without ending up in the ditch. Owen was glad the windows were darkly tinted. He figured it would look odd for everyone to pile out of the limousine on the highway, but most would probably believe they were having car trouble. He had every intention of staying with Candice to lend moral support and help her out.

Everett and Strom, the driver and Jim all climbed out and moved to stand down in the culvert away from the highway.

"I can't believe this. I just can't believe this." Candice rushed to strip out of her clothes while Owen helped her undress.

"Your uncle has it all in hand. He'll get this done. Thank God he's a shifter too. And with the kind of money he has, he should have no problem convincing the judge to come out to the house, no matter what other plans he might have had."

She was naked now. Owen took her in his arms and hugged her tight. "We'll get through this, and before you know it, we'll be home for Christmas."

She nodded, and they kissed, but she didn't shift right away.

Was she just having a false alarm? He'd had a few of those over the years. Then she started to shift, and just as she did, they heard the screech of tires.

Owen looked back, saw a silver SUV heading straight for them, and grabbed hold of his wolf mate, just as the Suburban crashed into the limousine with a thunderous bang.

Chapter 19

As soon as the vehicle hit the limousine, the impact threw Owen against the glass dividing the driver and front passenger seat from the rest of the limousine, making him lose his hold on Candice before he fell to the floor. Thankfully, he was okay. He quickly picked himself up and checked on Candice, sprawled in her wolf form on the floor.

"Are you all right?" he asked, coming to her aid and giving her a hug.

She woofed, then growled, looking behind them through the window at the silver Suburban and the thirty-ish man leaving his vehicle.

He had hit them on one corner of the limousine, crumpling it. Owen looked out the side windows, but everyone was in the ditch, scrambling to climb up the incline to check on the driver of the SUV and Candice and Owen. He was damn glad no one by the side of the road had been hurt.

Strom yanked open the door to the limousine and poked his head in. "Everyone okay?"

"Yeah, we're good. The others?"

"All of us are fine. Jim and Everett are checking on the driver, no passengers. Damn people who can't watch their driving when a vehicle is off to the side of the road," Strom said.

Traffic was beginning to back up, so Strom called the

police officers who were supposed to arrest the impostor at the courthouse to let them know that he and his niece might be delayed a bit.

"Is anyone calling the police to make a report?" Owen asked, hoping the car was in good working order, and that the police didn't get involved and ask about the wolf in the car.

Jim was taking down the insurance details from the other driver and gave his for the limousine.

"No need to. Jim caught it all on video. He was a great agent with the JAG. That's why I enticed him over to the dark side to work for me."

Jim smiled back at Strom and told the driver, "All right. Well, thankfully, I captured the whole thing on video in case we have any trouble over the car insurance. Can you drive okay?"

"Yeah," said the other driver, who had been really nice, but didn't look too happy about the accident being caught on video.

"What about us, Mr. Hart?" Jim asked.

Strom glanced at the driver. "Denny?"

"The limousine is fine," Denny said. "I'll need to take her in for repairs, but in the meantime, she'll take us to the courthouse and back home again. That rear taillight's not going to be working for signals and brakes though."

"Okay, let's get on the road then. *If* we can get on the road." Strom was watching the snail-paced traffic as drivers rubbernecked to see the accident.

"I can do it."

Within seconds of everyone climbing into the car, Denny pushed the limousine back onto the crowded highway and they were off.

"You're beautiful, Candice," Strom said. "You're just beautiful. I couldn't envision seeing you as a wolf."

She climbed onto one of the seats and laid her head in Owen's lap. He stroked her head. "She is that." He was glad her uncle had something nice to say about her being a wolf. She didn't need any negative comments from anyone right now, especially her uncle.

"Denny will stay with you in the car while I ensure that the woman is arrested. I don't want anything to go wrong with this," Strom said to Candice.

"Do you want me to go with you, boss, or stay with them?" Jim asked.

"Why don't you come with me, just in case we have any trouble."

When they arrived at the courthouse, Strom and Jim left the vehicle, and Everett stayed with Owen, Candice, and the driver.

"I can't believe that Strom is a jaguar," Everett said. "Hell, he even owns the Clawed and Dangerous Kitty Cat Club company. Jim said it started out as a disco club in the seventies. I can't believe this is where Jim ended up either. Not a bad deal."

"I'd love to take Candice to the club…unless it's for jaguar shifters only," Owen said.

"No, it's even open to the public, so no shifting allowed on the premises. The biggest clientele are jaguar shifters, but all are welcome. I bet Strom wouldn't mind flying you both here just to visit, and he'd take you there," Everett said.

Candice was sitting up, staring out the window of the limousine, when she suddenly jumped off the car seat and began to pace. The three guys watched her now, trying to read what was going on with her.

Anxious about seeing the woman come out in handcuffs? Or something else?

She suddenly grabbed a mouthful of her sweater and shook it, looking at Owen as if he should be used to this by now.

"Hell, you're going to shift this quickly?"

She dropped her sweater and woofed.

"Everyone out of the car," Owen said. Though wolves got used to stripping and shifting in front of other shifters as a necessity, she hadn't been around others, so he figured they needed to be mindful of that.

As soon as the guys hurried out of the car and looked in the direction of the courthouse, Candice shifted.

"We've got to hurry." She yanked on her panties and then her pants as Owen grabbed her bra and handed it to her. As soon as she was sitting and pulling on her sweater, he helped with her socks and boots.

"How did you manage to shift so quickly?"

"I relaxed and started saying a mantra, anything to make me turn. I don't know. Maybe it's because I turned last night, and the only reason I did this time was because I'm so nervous about getting this over with without creating a scene. Let's go." She grabbed Owen's hand and led the way. She pushed open the door, and the guys all turned and smiled, but then frowned.

"Are you going to be okay?" Everett asked.

"I hope so."

Owen called her uncle and said, "We're coming in. Candice wants to join you."

"Are you certain?" Strom didn't sound real sure of her plans.

"Hell yeah." Owen wasn't sure she'd be okay, but

he was damn sure she wanted to be there. "Is the woman there?"

"No. She must have gone to the restroom or run off somewhere for a few minutes."

"Or gotten spooked that the police are there," Owen said.

"Well, the sooner we can sign off on this paperwork, the better."

"That's the woman. That's her," Candice said and jerked away from Owen.

Owen was afraid she'd knock the woman out for impersonating her. He didn't blame her for all the worrying she'd been doing over this whole situation. But he didn't want the police to arrest his mate.

Dora Emerson did resemble Candice to an extent, but she was taller and thinner, and if the part of her hair that she hadn't managed to fully color was any indication, she was a blond, not a redhead like Candice. Her jaw was a little longer, her eyes not as big, but if someone took a quick glimpse of the photo, all they'd really see was the hair and the color of her eyes. That's what stood out, and that's what looked close enough to convince anyone Dora was Clara.

"We see the woman and maybe Felix Underwood coming down the courthouse steps with her," Owen quickly told Strom. Felix was a blond, though his hair was darker, and he was older, but still tall and thin like his sister.

"I'm sending the police officers right down. Don't let Candice get into an altercation with her."

"I'm trying not to," Owen said. "Got to go."

The woman looked so similar to the photo he had of Clara, just a torso shot, and with the documents the woman had stolen—probably in the manila envelope she was carrying—she could have easily "proved" she was Clara Hart.

"Okay, hold it right there, Dora Emerson," Candice said, arms outstretched, blocking the woman's escape. The woman looked a bit startled that Candice knew her name. She tried to go around her, but Denny, Everett, and Owen stopped both the woman and the man with her.

"You have something that belongs to me...papers and photos stolen from my safe-deposit box."

"I don't know who *you* are, but get out of my way before I deck you."

"That's a verbal threat," Owen said, still ready to protect his mate.

"Yeah, assault," Everett agreed. "And she tried to steal an estate worth billions by pretending to be the heir. That's a federal offense."

"Maximum jail time because the real Clara's uncle is a good friend of the judge," Denny said, smiling.

The woman shoved Candice's shoulder, and Owen grabbed his mate to keep her from falling down the stairs.

Everett arrested the woman on the spot.

"You can't arrest me!"

"Actually, I can. Even if I didn't have a badge, which I do, I could make a citizen's arrest."

The PI tried to slip by them, but Rowdy and the two police officers were already racing down the steps to take over. Or at least Rowdy was there to lend a hand, since this wasn't his jurisdiction.

One of the police officers began reading Miranda rights to the both of them while the other handcuffed the PI and then the woman.

"She has the documents and pictures stolen from my safe-deposit box to pretend she was me," Candice said.

"She also shoved you, and we witnessed it." The one officer opened the envelope and searched through it. "Can you describe what you had in it?"

Candice folded her arms. "Mom and Dad holding me when I was a baby. She was wearing a blue dress. He was wearing a gray suit. They'd just brought me home from the hospital. There's a picture of me missing my two front teeth and holding my red pigtails out, smiling away. And I had the paperwork from the sale of my last home"—Candice gave him the address—"and my high school diploma, and the pearl ring, just a lot of stuff that would be important to me. And I'm a redhead, always have been. But this impostor is clearly a blond."

"We'll need the documents for evidence to prove she stole them from the bank safe-deposit box and to prove she was going to use them to steal your inheritance."

"Okay, as long as I get it all back."

"Guaranteed."

Candice got a call, and she answered it. "Yes, Uncle Strom? The police officers have everything in hand down here. The fake Clara and her brother will be going to jail for a very long time."

Not that Candice could know that for sure, but Owen loved that she got a dig in at the two attempted swindlers before she and the others headed up the remaining stairs to the courthouse.

"Thanks, Officers. Throw the book at them." Then she skirted around them, her hand on Owen's again as she headed up the stairs.

Denny said, "I'm going back to the car to wait."

"All right," Owen said. "See you in a few."

"I guess I don't need to come, but if you don't mind, I'd like to," Everett said.

"Yeah, you've helped us with this the whole time. Of course we want you to come with us." She glanced at Rowdy. "You too."

"Thanks," Rowdy said, and he sounded grateful they were treating him like one of the pack.

Jim was waiting just inside for them. "Follow me this way. Are you going to be all right?"

"For the moment," Candice said.

Everyone quickened their pace.

When they reached the judge's office, Strom ushered her in, and Owen and Everett waited in the outer office. Owen's palms were sweaty, and he couldn't tamp down his concern that Candice might shift while trying to sign all the paperwork.

"She'll be all right," Everett assured him.

Everett couldn't know any more than Owen could, or Candice even. The shifting was just so unpredictable during this time of month.

Jim said, "Hey, Rowdy, want to take a walk with me and tell me about some of your really interesting cases?"

Rowdy glanced at Owen, as if seeking his approval.

"We're fine. Go ahead. We'll see you in a bit." Owen suspected Jim wanted to take Rowdy someplace else in case Candice shifted again.

A few minutes after Rowdy and Jim left, *Owen* began to feel the need to shift. He could last, he told himself. Two hours. This was just the beginning. He wanted to be here for Candice if anything went wrong and to congratulate her on getting this done.

He realized suddenly that with her signing for her estate, he had also inherited a lot of money because he was her mate. Not that he planned to spend any of it. It was hers to do with as she pleased.

They needed to get married too, for the sake of their kids, when they had some of their own. If they could. Even though technically they didn't need to marry. He'd only been focused on getting this business with the inheritance done, but now they needed to sell her home in South Dakota and move whatever she'd like to their home in Minnesota. Hell, they hadn't even discussed how they were going to set things up. She could change everything as far as he was concerned. He didn't care as long as she was with him and happy.

The door to the judge's office opened and Owen stiffened, still concerned that everything had gone all right.

Candice came out smiling, but it was a sad smile.

He figured she was feeling bad about her parents dying all over again.

Her uncle said goodbye to the judge, and then they all left the outer office and headed for the stairs.

"Because of all the help Rowdy has been, I'm inviting him for dinner," Strom said.

Owen wasn't sure how well that would work, with all the secrets they were still trying to keep. He planned to sit it out if they didn't eat soon. He was certain he was going to shift. "I feel the shift coming on. I can hold out about an hour or so."

"We'll make sure we have dinner before then," Strom said.

Owen was again glad her uncle was a shifter. "And Rowdy?"

"I have a guest room you can use on the second floor, first on the right, if you need to shift. We can make excuses for you."

"And if I have to shift?" Candice asked.

Strom smiled a little. "Newly mated moment? I'll just make some comment about the lovebirds not being able to wait. At least he'll believe I don't know any better."

"Okay, sounds good." Owen wrapped his arm around Candice and kissed her cheek. "Are you all right?"

"Yes, but sad. I need to sell the real estate, and the land and other properties they owned. I won't be returning."

"We need to discuss your home in South Dakota too. And I want you to know you can get rid of anything you don't like at the house and decorate it your way."

"Hmm, what if we were to take some of the money from the sale of the estate and replace furniture in the house with stuff we'd both like? Though I love your living room set. And your dining room set. I'm thinking mainly of setting up the office so it works better for the two of us."

As far as Owen was concerned, he would love anything she loved. "That works for me."

"I suppose you want to marry me now," she said, smiling up at him, as if the money made the difference to him.

He was glad she was feeling better and not so anxious about shifting. He couldn't wait to get her home. "That goes without saying, especially when we have all the little ones."

"I think I could handle only one Corey."

"That's good. He only comes one to a package—one alpha, male or female. Usually."

She laughed.

"Rowdy, do you want to join us for dinner?" Strom asked as they met him and Jim at the bottom of the courthouse steps.

"Sure, I'd like that. Thanks. Then I need to be getting on my way. Leave will be up by the time I return home," Rowdy said.

Owen wondered if there was more to Strom's offer than that. Maybe he planned to question Rowdy about what he knew? Or how he perceived their kind? But then he would have played his hand, and Rowdy would think he was a wolf too. Right now, Rowdy was clueless about Strom and his staff. Owen really hoped he'd stay that way.

Strom called ahead to ensure his chef prepared something that would be ready when they arrived home.

As soon as they reached Strom's mansion, they were ushered into the dining room and Maggie began serving them dinner of bacon-wrapped filet mignon, lemon herb asparagus, and baked potatoes with little side dishes of butter, sour cream, bacon, cheese, and chives.

They finished the main course, and Maggie cleared away the dishes, then returned to serve slices of cheesecake topped with candy cane.

Owen couldn't last through dessert. To avoid being caught in his clothes in the middle of a shift, he had his phone set to ring him, and then he could make his excuses. "Mr. Hart, that's the call I said I needed to take—"

"Yeah, please help yourself to the guest room where you can take your business call in private."

"I'll probably be awhile." Owen leaned down and kissed Candice's mouth, then said to Rowdy, "If you have to leave before I can say goodbye, I just wanted to thank you for all your help."

"Sure thing." Rowdy smiled, but then looked at Strom as if he was worried he might learn what Owen was.

Then Owen left the dining room, glad he'd mentioned it to Strom earlier so he knew where to go to chill out as a wolf for a while. He hoped Rowdy wouldn't hang around, waiting for him to return.

Chapter 20

Candice had mixed feelings about Rowdy being here. She wanted to show she appreciated him helping them to such a degree, and she didn't want to send him off with just a thank-you, but this was nerve-racking. Strom and his household staff pretending they didn't know what Owen, Everett, and Candice were. Rowdy knowing, but trying to keep their secret. Candice feeling guilty about the whole charade.

She kept glancing at the clock on the wall, hoping Rowdy wasn't catching her looking, but she swore every time she did, she caught his eye. He'd finished his cheesecake—all of them had—and still Owen had not returned. She wanted to go to him, but not because he needed her assistance or moral support. She just wanted to be with him as his wolf mate.

An hour had passed, and she needed to encourage Rowdy to take his leave so he could head home to Montana. She didn't want him to feel he had to stay and protect them. She opened her mouth to say something about him getting on his way when Jim returned from an errand. "Mr. Hart, your lawyer needs to talk to you about some business matter."

"Thank you, Jim. I need to take care of this. I want to thank you, Rowdy, for your assistance to my niece. I won't forget all you've done to help her out." To Candice, her uncle said, "This might take a while. Feel free to make yourself comfortable before you leave. But I want to say goodbye first, so don't leave without me sending you off properly." He shook Rowdy's hand and then left the room.

Everett shook Rowdy's hand too. They were trying to be polite in sending Rowdy on his way, but Candice wanted to reassure him everything would be fine. "I'll see you off, Rowdy." She walked him out to his car.

She didn't know what to say, and she had felt the tension in the air when she even suggested going outside with him alone. Did they worry she would tell him that her uncle and his staff were jaguars? She had no intention of giving up their secrets.

"Are you sure you're going to be okay? What if Strom or his staff discover what Owen is really up to?" Rowdy asked her, standing next to his car and acting like he didn't believe leaving the wolves alone was a safe idea.

She wondered what he thought he could do if her uncle or anyone on his staff learned what they were, but she appreciated the detective's concern. "Owen is taking care of a business call. That's all." She smiled. "We'll be fine. We're leaving right after he comes down. I'm going to check on him after I say goodbye to you. Have a safe trip, and if you ever need our help—"

"During the new moon, right?" Rowdy smiled. "Take care of yourself, young lady."

"You too, Rowdy. And…you might want to be careful about who you let know you…well, know about things you shouldn't."

"I will. Allan raised hell with me for tracking you down, but…I just couldn't help myself. I was worried you and Owen would get yourselves into deep water, and I wanted to aid you in any way that I could."

"Why, Rowdy? Why would you risk your life over us?"

"The truth is, I raised a wolf from a pup. She'd lost her family, and I found her. I was a hunter before that. Finding her profoundly changed my way of thinking about animals in the wild. Then I ended up working in a job where I hunted real animals. The human kind. One day, I took on a new job as a homicide detective and was reviewing some old cases. Some people were involved in bizarre situations, when they appeared to be the good guys. The bad guys were dead, naked, bitten."

"By wolves?"

"Yeah. And I knew wolves don't kill people like that."

"And you automatically thought werewolves were involved?" Candice couldn't believe anyone who had a good head on his shoulders and relied on scientific facts to solve a case would come to that conclusion.

"Too many things didn't add up. In the end, I knew. I'm a big fan of the paranormal. I have an open mind. I didn't have any doubt as to what I'd discovered. And I wanted to help any of you that I could."

"What happened to your wolf pup?"

"I had her for sixteen years. She got sick, and putting her down was the hardest thing for me to do."

"I know what you mean. I had a golden retriever when I was a kid, and it was the same for me. You don't think raising a wolf is the same as being a wolf, do you?"

Rowdy smiled. "Hardly. The wolf gets the girl. Talk to you later."

What did he mean that the wolf gets the girl? Which girl? Candice had a sneaking suspicion he didn't mean her. "Wait. I want to give you something. Use it for whatever you think you can: donate it to a wolf reserve, use it to pay for your trip out here and have some to spare. Whatever you want." She pulled a check out of her pocket that she'd already made out to him.

When she offered it to him, he frowned and didn't take the check right away. "A bribe? I didn't look to get money out of the deal."

"We know that. I know that. It's something I want to do to say thank you. I'm serious when I say I couldn't have done this without you. So please, let me at least do this."

He took the check and thanked her. "Keep yourself out of trouble." He got into his car, waved, and drove off.

Candice sighed, relieved he was gone, and went into the house to see Owen.

Strom and Jim were waiting for her just inside the house. "Your business is done?" she asked her uncle.

"I didn't have any. I signaled to Jim to let me know I had business to take care of, hoping Rowdy would get the message it was time for him to leave so your mate could come and join us."

"Rowdy was afraid you'd learn what we were, and he wants to protect us. At least your ploy worked. I'll run up and check on Owen. I know Everett's ready to go home."

She hurried up the stairs, and when she reached the door, she knocked. "Just me. Rowdy's gone, if you want to come down and join us." She opened the door and smiled because Owen was sitting tall on the floor, looking handsome. She loved her white wolf.

Owen was so glad to see Candice. He hadn't expected her to join him and was just biding his time until he could shift back, but as soon as he saw her smiling face, she instantly cheered him. Instead of wishing he could shift now, he enjoyed being with her even like this, alone, having this private time with his mate.

"I had to tell everyone I was checking on you. I'm feeling fine, no urge to shift, but I wanted to keep you company. Maggie saved some of the cheesecake for you." Candice closed the door, crossed the floor, and lay on the bed. Owen jumped onto the bed and curled up with her.

"Everett wants to leave, because it's such a long drive home. Rowdy was eager to get started on his long journey to Montana too. I slipped him a check for ten thousand to thank him for all his help. He said he didn't do it for the money, but I told him if it hadn't been for him, I might have lost the opportunity to claim my inheritance. I know now that's not so because Uncle Strom knew me by scent, but we certainly didn't know it at the time."

She stayed with Owen for an hour, both of them taking a nap until he felt the urge to shift. He licked her cheek, and she smiled at him.

He leaped off the bed and shifted back.

Before he dressed, he pulled her close for a lingering kiss. "Thanks for joining me. It was a nice way to wait out the shift." He released her. "Be there in just a few minutes. I can't wait to arrive home and enjoy the holidays together."

"The feeling is completely mutual. Did you want to have that cheesecake now?"

"Sure, that would be great. And then we can get on our way."

"Okay, I'll let them know." When Candice went downstairs, everyone was in the living room having coffee. "Owen will be right down. He'll have some of that cheesecake before we take off, if that's all right with you."

Jim said, "I'll have Maggie cut him a slice."

"Thanks."

As soon as Owen joined them, her uncle asked, "Are you sure you don't want to stay a while longer? Overnight? Through Christmas?"

"I need to get home tonight," Everett said.

Owen left it up to Candice. He wanted to be home with the pack, enjoying the time alone with Candice as a newly mated couple. But if she wanted to stay with her uncle for a while longer to get to know him better, Owen was fine with that too. Maggie brought him a fork and a plate of cheesecake, and he thanked her.

"Thanks, Uncle Strom, but I'd rather come as soon as I can after Christmas. Then we can really visit and have fun. We can even check out your Clawed and Dangerous Kitty Cat Club. While Owen's eating his cheesecake, tell me how you came up with the idea of the club."

Owen had wondered about that too.

"I don't know if your dad ever told you, but when we turned sixteen, we inherited fifty million each from our granddad. He'd made it in oil, like Dad did, and then your dad and me. We were wealthy early on."

"Wait, Dad always said you did this all on your own."

"He probably wanted you to be your own person, make your own way in the world, and then leave you an inheritance when they passed. John was serious-minded, family-oriented. Me? I wanted to have fun. Had a Corvette and visited the pubs, and as tall as I was, no one ever thought I was just a kid. I met Cynthia, and she was one hot cat. When I turned eighteen, I bought my first bar. Overwhelmed with the urge to be a jaguar, I'd been taking trips to the Amazon to experience the jungle. I loved the exotic feel. The wildness. The heat and steam and green-and-vivid colors of the jungle. I started out with just one bar with a small dance floor… with a jungle theme.

"It was so successful, and because I was a cat, other jaguars began to fill it to capacity, so I ended up opening a much bigger place with floating stage shows featuring dancers and eventually replaced the fake plants with real. But then with some good managers and an assistant who oversees the whole operation, I ended up with a chain of clubs. I get requests from humans to buy a franchise, but the clubs are strictly jaguar operated, and I won't sell it as a franchise to humans. With all the money you have, you ought to open a wolf bar."

Candice smiled and shook her head. "But your club sounds like a fun and special place we'd love to visit."

Owen was thinking of what a headache starting a wolf bar would be. What if they ended up with a ton of trouble at the bar? Wolves who didn't get along. Humans that caused fights. They loved their peaceful coexistence.

"You'll get royal treatment. Don't be surprised if next month, a limousine picks you up at your front doorstep and takes you to a field where my private jet will be waiting to bring you home."

"We'd still love for you to come for Christmas," she said.

"Maybe next year." Strom didn't sound like he was interested in visiting a pack of wolves next year either. "For now, I'll have my pilot take you to Dallas, only about an hour-and-a-half trip that way. My driver will follow with Everett's car, drop it off, pick up yours, and drive it home for you. My pilot will fly you home tomorrow, and that way you'll be there for the holidays. He has family in Dallas, so he'll stay overnight with them."

Candice smiled. "Thanks. We'd love that, and Everett will be home with his wife sooner."

Owen finished the cheesecake and thanked them for it. He was thinking how much fun it would be to make some with Candice when they got home as their special contribution for Christmas dinner at Cameron and Faith's home.

After hugs and handshakes, Owen swore Candice's uncle was a little misty-eyed, and she was too. Strom's driver, Denny, drove them to the airport, while another driver took Everett's car back to Dallas. It was eleven that night when they arrived, and when they were getting ready for bed, they heard the two jaguars splashing in the pool again.

"I love them. They're so cute," Candice said, peering out the window.

"They've become family."

"We should do something special for them and for Howard, for driving us all the way here. I think a little nest egg for both," Candice said. "You don't think they'll see it as just paying for their services, do you?"

"I think they'd appreciate it, especially for when they have kids."

"Good. And for Howard, maybe to court a jaguar if he can find one he likes. I was thinking about selling my parents' estate. Uncle Strom offered to contact a jaguar Realtor he uses to auction off the furniture and such and put the house on the market. I told him that would be fine. He asked what I wanted from the estate, and I told him to just keep all the photos that they have in the house. Everything else can be sold off."

"Okay, sounds like a good deal. So tomorrow, we go home for Christmas, and then..."

"I need to return to South Dakota to pack and put that house on the market."

They climbed into bed and cuddled. "We need to do that. To think I married a *very* wealthy heiress."

She smiled and kissed his chest. "I'd like to donate some of the funds to the USF since they are supposed to help both shifter kinds to get along."

"I think that would be a great gesture."

"My uncle said he'd match whatever I donated to the cause."

Owen smiled. "He couldn't be shown up by a wolf."

She laughed. "I want to put the rest in pack funds. Faith was telling me about it over lunch one of the days you were gone, though she quickly said you all did it to keep the pack afloat when you couldn't work because you had so much trouble with shifting. Though she did say the pack was financially set. She didn't want me to feel in any way obligated to add my money to the pack funds."

"It's completely up to you. All anyone cares about is that you're with the pack now, money or no. Whatever you want to do."

She kissed his chest and snuggled against him. "I want to make love."

"Now that I can get on board with." He rolled her over on her back and began to kiss her.

After breakfast the next morning, Denny took them to Strom's private jet for their flight to Minnesota. When they got into the airport near home, Cameron picked them up. They told him all about what had happened, and he told them David wanted to make dinner for everyone on Christmas Eve. Tomorrow, Christmas Day, Cameron and Faith would prepare dinner.

Candice was ready to do the honors for Christmas Eve next year.

When they arrived home, they thanked Cameron and went inside with their bags. Owen immediately flipped on the Christmas lights, then built a fire. Candice turned on Christmas music and made a late lunch. After they ate, they wrapped presents for the rest of the pack and sat by the fire to write in their notebooks until it was time to go to dinner at David's place.

"Will David need any help?" Candice asked, thinking he shouldn't have to make the meal by himself.

"Nah, Gavin will be over there. And probably Cameron too."

"Not you?"

"I'm just where I need to be." Owen wrote further in his notebook.

They were sharing a big blanket, sipping peppermint schnapps cocoa, and writing away when Candice paused to think about her next scene.

He glanced over at her. "Need to brainstorm?"

"They just agreed to a mating."

Owen smiled.

She smiled back at him. "Okay?"

"Well, you know what comes after that."

"The mating, right. But do they do it in the bedroom or—"

"It's winter, right?"

"Yes."

"And they've got a toasty-warm, crackling fire going as they sit on the sofa drinking peppermint schnapps cocoa."

"They're not writing books."

"No, but wouldn't this be the perfect place to make love to the woman, or man, you just agreed to mate?" Owen set his notebook and pen on the coffee table, and she smiled broadly at him, suspecting what he was up to. He leaned over and kissed her cheek. "What could be more perfect than a place just like this? Christmas lights sparkling on the tree and mantel. Soft music playing in the background. Fire crackling at the hearth."

"It's not Christmas." She took his face in her hands and kissed his mouth.

He settled into the kiss, but then paused to rearrange the blanket so it was beneath them and covering the couch. They quickly stripped out of their clothes, tossing them everywhere.

Owen's kisses went from loving to hot and passionate, fiercely demanding. Candice matched him kiss for kiss, caught up in the heat of the moment. She savored every bit of his toned, hard body pressed against her, the feel of his cock fully aroused. Though they were mated and it was a done deal, she knew with every fiber of her being that this was right, that he was the one for her. That the overwhelming measure of attraction between them proved they were meant for each other. Raw desire filled her with need, and she wanted him inside her now.

She grasped his shoulders, pulling him even closer, wanting all that muscle and heat rubbing against her. He was eager to stroke her breasts, kissing them, suckling them, making her nipples bud and tingle. Then he began to stroke her between her legs, rubbing his erection against her thigh. It was the perfect place to make love—her cushioned on top of the blanket on the couch, the warmth of the fire and logs crackling, the heat of their bodies, the friction between them igniting her own fire and making her burn for him.

His name slipped from her lips, her breathing ragged, their heartbeats pounding as he carried her up…higher until she couldn't go any further. And shattered into a million splinters of ecstasy. He was irresistible, as she pulled him close again and kissed him as if she were a desperate woman. She was so thankful she hadn't answered her emails the day he sent her his contact form so he had to come see her in person. If he had never actually physically been near her, able to smell her scent, to know she was one of them, neither of them would have ever made the connection.

And he was ready to make that deeper connection as he maneuvered between her legs and pushed inside her, fulfilling her need to have him the closest he could be.

Owen penetrated her silky, slick heat, thanking his lucky stars Candice had agreed to be his mate. He pumped into her, deepening his thrusts. His body sizzled everywhere her soft, bare skin met his.

He held on until he couldn't any longer. He came

inside her and felt her inner muscles climaxing around his cock.

Candice was a dream come true. She completed him in a way no one else could, made him feel alive, and needed, and loved. He was glad they'd resolved the situation with her inheritance, and he could be with her like this, making love to her by the toasty fire, the lights sparkling on the Christmas tree, a joyous time.

"Ohmigod, you are so amazing," she whispered against his cheek.

"You are unbelievably good for me, and I'd love to take you right to bed so we could get in some naptime and more of this." He kissed her mouth and smiled. "Do you think the pack would notice if we didn't show up tonight for the Christmas Eve dinner?"

"Yes. Though I imagine they wouldn't be too surprised. On the other hand, if David has gone to all this work, he might be disappointed. The kids too. I'm not sure they would understand why we didn't show up."

Owen chuckled. "Okay. But just so you expect it, we're going to be doing a whole lot more of this now that we're home."

She laughed. "I would sure hope so."

He groaned. "I guess we need to get dressed and head on over there then."

As soon as they were ready, they took a walk in the woods to David's place. But halfway there, they smelled a cougar. They stopped dead in their tracks on the trail. The cougar was lying on the snow, his golden coat blending in with the tans and browns of the dead foliage on the dormant trees, the red pines towering to the sky, his gaze fully focused on them.

"What do we do?" Candice asked.

"Get on your phone and alert David we've got a cougar between his home and us. We don't run, and we can't climb a tree because they can too. Just keep your eyes on him. Usually when there are a couple of hikers, rather than someone walking alone, you're better off. We should have been making noise, just like you would to alert a bear, to let him know we were in the vicinity. Of course the old saying goes that if you've just noticed a cougar, he's been tracking you for half an hour already."

"Great."

"I don't think so with this one."

The cat stood, staring at them.

"He's got plenty of room to leave and if it's a she, no kits that I can see, we should be okay. While you're calling for backup, I'm going to lean over to get that stout stick off the trail. We want to appear big, so you never want to crouch down, and you always want to look menacing. Hold his gaze. With one of us standing erect, hopefully we'll be okay."

Chapter 21

Candice moved closer to Owen so when he leaned down to get the stick to protect them, she was still standing tall and protectively. "David? We're halfway to your place on the trail by the lake, and we've encountered a cougar."

"We're on our way."

Candice knew she could be scary looking to humans as a wolf, but as a human, that cougar was beautiful but scary looking too. As soon as Owen had the stick in hand, she said, "The guys are on their way."

Suddenly, New Year's noisemakers blasted the quiet woods from the direction of David's house and he, Gavin, and Cameron began shouting. "We're coming to your rescue!" "Never fear, the wolves are here!" "Don't run, whatever you do!"

She smiled at their words. The cat dashed off, way outnumbered by a pack of wolves. Candice had never had any moose or cougar encounters where she'd lived in South Dakota, but that didn't mean she wouldn't have if she'd continued to live there and walked in the woods alone. She was glad to have the full support of her new family, though she still wished her uncle had joined them. He was probably so set in his ways that he didn't want to be bothered with coming here to see them. Not to mention that the accommodations wouldn't be half as grand, and he would be outnumbered by a pack of wolves.

David laughed when he saw Owen with a tree branch in hand. "Glad we came to rescue you if that's all you had to defend your ladylove."

"Thanks for coming. Appreciate your show of support, as always," Owen said.

Cameron was already on his phone. "Yeah, honey. They're fine. We're headed back right now."

Before long, they were inside David's home, singing Christmas carols, playing games, having dinner, and opening one Christmas present each. Candice couldn't believe how different the Christmas holiday was with a mate by her side and a whole pack to enjoy the holiday spirit with. There was something to be said about their alone time, but quite another with seeing Christmas in a different light. The kids were a lot of fun, and she was even thinking about the day when she would have some of her own.

After the Christmas Eve celebration, Gavin dropped them off at their home, nobody wanting them to walk alone through the woods that night. Everyone planned to sleep in the next day, except for Faith, who said the kids would be up so early that she didn't expect to sleep in for the next few years on Christmas morning.

Candice had laughed about it, usually being a morning person herself, but with Owen making love to her in the middle of the night, she was glad they could just chill out in the morning.

The next morning, Candice woke to the aroma of bacon and eggs, toast, coffee, and tea, surprised her mate had gotten up and she hadn't even noticed. She must have been tired. She slipped on some pajamas and her robe, and pulled on mukluks, then left the bedroom to give Owen a Christmas morning hug and kiss. "You're up early after being up so much last night."

He chuckled and pulled her into his arms to kiss her. "I couldn't sleep… Too excited about Christmas. It's not just the kids who can't wait for Christmas morning."

She laughed. "Like when you were little?"

"Yeah, but not so much about presents like back then, though I hope you love yours. This time, it's all about you being here in my life. I couldn't be happier."

"I feel the same way about being with you. I couldn't be happier here, but I don't look forward to packing up the house in South Dakota."

"We'll tackle that together, and before you know it, you'll be completely moved over here. We could just pay to have it done for you."

"I still need to pack my personal belongings and decide what I want to get rid of first."

"Are you ready to eat? I didn't mean to wake you if you needed to sleep longer, but—"

"You couldn't wait to open presents."

"I can't wait for you to see yours."

"I'm ready." Candice wondered what he had gotten her that he was so excited about. His brown eyes were alight with happiness, and he smiled every time he mentioned it. Not only that, but he had a ton of gifts under the Christmas tree for her.

They ate breakfast, took turns picking out gifts from under the tree for each other, then sat back down on the couch to open them.

She laughed when she opened the Santa box and

found a winter wet suit for canoeing when it got colder in the fall and winter. "This will be perfect when I fall off slippery docks into the cold lake."

"There won't be a next time. But if we ever have the misfortune of flipping the canoe accidentally, you'll be prepared."

Owen opened a package containing a fine set of carving tools, sizes he didn't already have. He laughed and handed her a Christmas card.

She opened it, smiled, and handed him one. Each of them had given the other an IOU for one hand-carved hiking stick for walking in the woods, though she meant to purchase a hand-carved one for him, wolf head and all. "For protection against—"

"Cougars, bears, you name it."

"Sounds good." She opened boxes containing five sexy nighties—all lace and silk, from blue to red.

"Because you don't need the warm flannel pajamas when I'm heating you up all night."

She laughed. "I don't wear them that long anyway."

"Less is always better when it comes to nightwear," he said, squeezing her thigh.

She'd gotten him a butternut leather desk chair and new laptop for their office, for when they set it up just the way they wanted it.

"I'll put the chair together right after we finish here, and we decide where we want everything to go."

"Okay, sounds like a great plan." She really needed to have things set up for writing full time, so she was glad he wanted to do that next.

Owen gave her a hand-carved white wolf ornament to welcome her into the pack and to his life.

"I knew you were making one for me on the sly. Did you have many splinters in bed?"

He laughed. "I worked on yours at the office on my breaks."

"That's when you did it. Here I kept trying to see which one was mine, and none of them were. Well, I love it, and it's going to sit on my desk so I can enjoy it year round."

Candice gave him a hug, and he kissed her. Then he opened a Christmas box filled with ten narrow-lined notebooks to use to handwrite in bed or on the couch. He laughed about that. "Are you trying to tell me you want me to write lots of novels, not just the one?"

She smiled. "Practice makes perfect."

Candice also gave him one of those Zero Gravity Pens that wouldn't run out of ink if the pen wasn't tilted just right. He could write at any angle, underwater, over wet and greasy paper, and in a wide range of temperatures. Even in bed. Though she suspected as soon as they got into bed, that notion would fly out the window. He tested out the pen right away and gave it his seal of approval. It worked upside down and every which way.

And she had picked up a red apron for him—*Caution: Extremely Hot*—because he'd really gotten into cooking with her and for her, and she loved him for it.

"I will model the apron a little later when we're baking cookies, but only if you wear yours. Let's grab a cup of coffee—and tea for you—and walk outside to see beautiful Christmas Day on the lake."

"Sure." Candice made herself a hot cup of cinnamon tea and straight coffee for Owen while he cleaned up the wrapping paper. Then he led her outside, and she couldn't believe her eyes.

She cried. She couldn't help it. He had gotten her the most extraordinary gift of all—a gazebo right next to the lake. She couldn't believe she hadn't gone out on the deck since she'd been home and seen it. Now she wondered what he would have done if she'd said anything about going out to see the lake.

"Oh, Owen, I. Love. You." She threw her arms around his neck and kissed him generously.

He grinned and hugged her tight in the cold morning air. "Thank you for being my mate." And then he kissed her right back, lifted her in his arms, and returned to the house.

They couldn't finish Christmas morning without returning to bed and making love. "You are my best Christmas present of all."

"Same for me, Owen. I've never had such a wonderful Christmas."

After making love, they napped before they set up their office.

Then it was time for Christmas dinner. She'd dressed in a red-and-green-plaid skirt and a green sweater—because she thought it looked better on her than red—and was just putting on one of her boots when she felt the urge to shift. She *couldn't* believe it!

She ground her teeth and tried to fight it, wanting more than anything to halt the shift, though she knew if she stopped it, that didn't mean she wouldn't have the urge again while she was getting ready to eat at the MacPhersons' house.

She fought the tears, hating that she was going to ruin everything for everyone. Owen was gathering some last-minute presents for everyone else, and she just couldn't tell him, because she knew she'd cry and ruin the day for him. As a wolf, she couldn't cry like she did as a human. She started yanking off her clothes and tossing them on the bed.

Then she shifted.

Owen had boxed up all the remaining gifts for the other pack members and wondered what was taking Candice so long to join him. Last night, they'd baked some of that cheesecake her uncle's chef had served with the candy canes on top, so he brought it out of the fridge to take that too. When she still didn't come out of the bedroom, he suspected the worst. She had turned into a wolf. He knew she'd be upset about it and didn't want him to know. Not that she could hide the fact from him or anyone else.

"Candice?" he said, heading for the bedroom. He walked into the room, and sure enough, she was sitting on the floor, one woebegone-looking wolf. He crouched down and hugged her. "You know you are one beautiful wolf, and I'm proud to have you for my mate." He was certain that wouldn't make her feel any better, but he would do anything to cheer her up. Except shift. He wanted to, but he couldn't.

"I've got everything ready to go. I'll just take it out to the car now." He started hauling presents and the cheesecake out to the SUV, and while he was out there, he gave Cameron a heads-up. "Hey, just wanted to tell you that we're on our way in a few minutes, but Candice shifted and I'm sure she's upset about it."

"Tell her we've all been there, and we're used to it. No problem."

"I will, but I don't think that's going to cheer her up. I tried to call on the shift, but it's not happening for me."

"Okay, we'll ask if either Gavin or David can shift."

"Thanks. Got to go back inside and check on her."

"I'll let Faith and the kids know."

Which meant Cameron would tell the kids to make her feel better about her wolf half when she arrived. When Owen went inside, Candice was pacing across the living room floor, just like a caged wolf would do. He sighed. "Are you ready to go?"

He was prepared to skip the dinner, if she really didn't want to go, but he thought it would be good for her to be with everyone else and to see everyone was fine with her being a wolf for Christmas.

As a wolf, Candice glanced at Owen when he asked if she was ready to go, and then she paced in annoyance across the living room floor, hating that she had turned into a wolf, and that her poor mate had to put up with her irritability. It was Christmas Day, and she should be grateful to be among friends. She guessed it was because for the first time in three Christmases, she was going to actually celebrate a dinner with friends and family. Not sit alone, being whatever she was bound to be for the day—wolf or human. Back in her home in South Dakota, it didn't matter. Here, she was so looking forward to seeing everyone and being human when she did it!

She couldn't help feeling everyone might wonder what they were in for by taking her into the pack.

She growled and paced some more.

"I wish I could change too," Owen said. "I've tried, and it's just not happening."

She came over and licked his hand. He petted her head. She wanted him to know she wasn't upset with him. This was her issue to deal with, not his. When he went out to the SUV to load packages, he was gone for a few minutes more than needed, and she suspected he was probably alerting Cameron that he might be bringing an aggravated wolf mate with him.

Candice fought growling again. She felt like a little kid who didn't get what she'd wanted for Christmas, when the problem was anything but.

Owen went into the kitchen and pulled out a wolf dish for her, filling it with water, and set it on the floor. As much as she'd rather be drinking spiked eggnog, she was dying of thirst and walked over to the bowl and greedily lapped up a ton of it. She guessed she'd worked up a thirst from all that pacing.

"Sorry I didn't think of it sooner. We'll drive over so we can take all the gifts and a change of clothes for you for when you shift back."

She didn't want to eat as a wolf. If she had to, she wanted to take leftovers home and eat them later. It was one thing to eat as a wolf out of necessity. Another, when everyone was eating in celebration of the holidays.

Before Owen could convince her to go outside with him and get in the car, they heard snowmobiles, two of them. Instantly, she thought of the snowmobilers who had started the avalanche that had brought Owen and her even closer together.

Owen grabbed his jacket. "I'll check it out. You stay in the house."

She growled. On the one hand, she was thrilled they'd made love and opened their Christmas presents before she'd had to shift, though she still couldn't believe he had bought the beautiful gazebo for her and everyone had chipped in to make it happen while they were away.

The snowmobiles parked outside their house, and Candice wondered who would be visiting them now. She went to the front office and tried to push aside the blinds with her nose and stared wide-eyed at her uncle and Jim, who'd brought tons of gifts on two sleds. So thrilled she could barely think straight, she woofed and tore out of the office, then headed for the wolf door. Bolting outside, she raced around the house until she reached the corner and heard Owen say, "She's turned and not happy about it. Come on inside, and we'll make you something hot to—"

She darted around the house and jumped at her uncle, her paws landing against his chest in greeting, knocking him over in the snow. She licked his face, and Jim and Owen smiled.

"Merry Christmas to you too, Candice," her uncle said, laughing.

She woofed at him and they headed inside, carrying some of the packages with them. They left the rest on the sled, and she suspected they were for the others in the pack.

"We're due to go over and have dinner in about twenty minutes, and of course we want you to come with us," Owen said.

"Cameron and Faith already know. I wanted my coming for Christmas to be a surprise for the two of you."

Candice was glad she had sent her uncle Christmas

gifts from both of them already, but she hoped he didn't feel visiting them was a letdown from the way he normally lived, with a chef to prepare his meals. Not to mention that it was hard to have a conversation as a wolf.

"I'll show you the house first and the guest rooms." Owen took them through the house and Candice followed them, which made her think she looked like she was a puppy dog. But she didn't mind. She was so glad her uncle was here. And also Jim, who helped her uncle out so much.

Jim carried their bags to the two guest bedrooms, and Strom said, "I'll be out in a moment." Then he disappeared down the hall.

Owen fixed Jim a gin and tonic. "What would Strom like, do you know?"

"A Kentucky bourbon neat, but I don't think he has a drink in mind right now."

"Oh?"

Then a black jaguar joined them, and Candice couldn't have loved her uncle more for doing this for her. Instead of being annoyed that she was an Arctic wolf who had trouble controlling her shifting, he was showing her he loved her just the way she was.

She couldn't believe he was a rare black jaguar either. She'd envisioned one like Everett in a gold coat and black rosettes. Her uncle was beautiful. She nuzzled his cheek, and he licked hers. Then she saw Jim and Owen taking phone shots of the two of them—the white wolf and the black jaguar. Christmas couldn't have been any more special than this.

Chapter 22

"Is everyone ready to eat? It's time," Owen said, not sure how this was going to go over as far as feeding Candice and Strom was concerned.

Jim jogged down the hall to the back rooms, and Owen assumed he was gathering some clothes for his boss, just like Owen needed to do for Candice. Owen slipped the clothes she'd wanted to wear for the special occasion into a backpack and brought it with him.

Then he repacked their stuff on the other sled, and he and Jim rode the snowmobiles over to the MacPhersons' house while Strom and Candice ran behind them.

She even nipped at her uncle's tail twice, so thrilled he was here and no longer upset she was a wolf. Not when he wore his jaguar coat just for her.

She lunged for his tail a third time, and he turned so fast she wasn't expecting it—and tackled her! She woofed and growled with excitement, and attacked him right back, though he had the advantage of being a much bigger male jaguar. She barked in delight, and they continued on their way. Though at one point, she paused, lifted her chin, and howled with joy, telling everyone just how happy she was to be here with them, the rest of the wolf pack, and now her uncle.

Owen didn't know how the kids would react to seeing

Strom as a jaguar, though they'd loved playing with Everett and Demetria when they visited. He wasn't sure how Strom would react to them either. Owen got the impression kids weren't part of his lifestyle. Everyone was so welcoming, as if jaguars were part of the wolf pack, and Owen was proud of being one of its members.

"Merry Christmas," Owen said in greeting as Cameron and his triplets crowded around their father at the door. "This is Strom Hart and his assistant, Jim Winchester. They've come bringing presents."

"Oh heavens," Faith said, wiping her hands on a dish towel and joining them. "The kids will be spoiled."

Everyone was thrilled to see them, and the kids were excited about seeing Strom, telling him all about how Demetria was a black jaguar too. "How can you be Candice's uncle if you're a jaguar?" Corey asked.

"No, Corey, he was turned like Candice was. Except he was turned by a jaguar." Owen didn't bother to explain she had been adopted. To her, Strom was her flesh-and-blood uncle, more now that they were both shifters.

"A little jaguar like I met at the day care?" Corey asked.

"No, he was a little older." Owen smiled, unable to tell the pup what had really happened.

"I should have bitten him so he would be an Arctic wolf too," Corey said, eyeing all the shiny new presents.

They all laughed.

But then Faith said, "No biting to change people, Corey."

"I was just kidding," Corey said, as if he was afraid he was going to be in trouble again for the *last* time he changed someone.

Smiling down at him, Faith ruffled his hair.

"Can we open them now?" Nick asked, bouncing up and down on his toes.

"It's up to everyone else," Faith said in her strict momma-knows-best voice.

Strom and Candice shook the snow from their coats and came inside. Candice woofed her approval, and Owen said, "Candice votes for opening them."

"Kids should never have to wait," Jim agreed.

Everyone else said it worked for them, so the kids tore off the wrapping paper to see their new gifts. Everyone opened the presents Strom had brought for them before dinner, and Candice tore into several of her packages with her teeth, though if she thought the items might be breakable, she waited for Owen to unwrap them.

The kids gave everyone gingerbread cookies they'd helped make and decorate.

Everyone in the pack had gifts for Strom and whoever might accompany him in case he and someone else showed up for the celebration. They were more generic than anything, since the pack had not been sure what to give a billionaire who had everything. But he seemed thrilled they'd thought of him. Owen wondered if Strom never received gifts.

An hour later, Candice had the urge to shift back into her human form and headed to the guest bedroom where Owen had left her clothes. She was thrilled to be able to join the group like this. When she came out of the room dressed and ready to eat, Strom rubbed up against her and then loped back to the room to shift and dress.

Then she and Strom could eat with the rest of the adults. She hadn't wanted them to wait, but she was thankful they had. The kids had eaten earlier, and now they were playing with their new toys.

"We're going to South Dakota to sell my place as soon as it's safe to do so," Candice said as she dug into her turkey. "We should be fine then."

"If you want to go sooner, my jet can fly you there," Strom said. "Or I can have Jim handle everything for you so you don't even have to return there."

Candice smiled at her uncle. "Thanks, Uncle Strom. But I need to sort things out myself."

Owen couldn't believe how much Candice's uncle wanted to help them and was glad about it, but he didn't think they needed his help in this.

"We're going during the waning crescent moon."

"Okay. Well, if you run into any trouble at all, let me know."

"Thanks, Uncle Strom. We will."

Strom turned to Faith and said, "My chef could learn a thing or two from you."

Faith blushed and thanked him.

Though they tried to convince him to stay with them until they left for South Dakota, Strom had important business to take care of. Moreover, Jim was overseeing the sale of her estate near Houston, and they'd already had a couple of nibbles. But Candice and Owen promised to return to Houston next month and really spend some quality time visiting Strom.

"No telling where you might end up when you come to visit," Jim warned them, smiling. "One time, Mr. Hart said he wanted to go to this really great French restaurant. I was flabbergasted when we ended up in Paris."

Strom laughed. "It is my favorite French restaurant."

Several days later when they could safely leave Minnesota, Candice and Owen drove to South Dakota. The day after they arrived, they met with a Realtor and began packing up Candice's personal items and any food they could take with them. When she had left there to go to Minnesota with Owen initially, she had no real notion of moving, so she hadn't even considered the food she had in the fridge. She was glad she had Owen to help her move this time.

Because of weather conditions, it had taken them longer to arrive in South Dakota, and once they were there, it was going to take some time to pack everything and be ready to move. Candice had already scheduled a mover. That meant they were running into the next moon phase.

It was amazing how much she had to clear out, then remove everything from the walls, spackle and paint, and just plain…clean.

They'd spent another long day of it, but she really felt like she needed a wolf run before they crashed in bed and ravished each other. Sometimes they didn't wait until nighttime. It was sexy making a meal, her wearing her Naughty Christmas List apron, and him wearing his Extremely Hot apron—naked.

That usually meant meals were started and forgotten for a little bit. But they needed fodder for their romance novels too.

"Let's run before we go to bed, okay?" she asked.

"Sounds like a great idea. We've been so busy that we haven't had a chance. And it would be fun to have some runs before we leave here for good."

"Absolutely." She tossed her clothes in the bedroom, and he hurried to join her.

He pulled her into his arms and smiled down at her. "How did I ever get so lucky?"

"It all started with one little wolf pup—"

"I'll have to remember to thank him. But not in front of his mom and dad."

She smiled and kissed Owen. Then before they ended up in bed again, she said, "Last one out the door has to do the dishes."

She shifted and raced out of the bedroom and down the hall, across the living room, and bolted through the wolf door.

He was right next to her, running like the wind, nuzzling her, and she was nipping at him. They chased each other, tackling, biting, barking, and having a ball. Then they heard snowmobilers coming around the mountain, the telltale sound of them trying to best each other as they dove for the peak, and the rumble of an avalanche.

There were two of them this time, and she hoped the snowmobilers got away in time, but nothing could outrun an avalanche if they were too close to it. The snowmobiles were now silent, not a good sign.

She looked at Owen, and he barked at her. She licked his cheek. And then the decision was made, though she didn't think they would have done anything differently. Hopefully, they weren't two of the same men who'd thought they could cheat death. She hoped someone was in the clear so he could call for help, and no one had access to a camera this time.

When they reached the site of the avalanche, they

heard men shouting to each other as they started their engines. "Holy shit! Did you see that?"

"Hell yeah. Didn't think you'd make it out of there alive. Let's try on the other side."

"Okay." They tore off, away from the avalanche and where Candice and Owen were listening.

She woofed at him, and he agreed. It was time to enjoy each other in the privacy of her home, and let the risk-takers take care of themselves. She was glad that where they were going wasn't avalanche country. Yet, that incident was what had made her leave South Dakota in the first place, and she'd be forever grateful that the men had survived and she and Owen had found a new life together.

Owen would never let Candice know that if he'd been one of the snowmobilers, he probably would have done the same thing as them. He loved his mate and couldn't wait to make love to her again. He looked forward to being home with her, but he was having fun with her here too.

As soon as they were in the house, had reached the bedroom, and shifted, he tackled her on the bed, with packing boxes stacked everywhere. "Have I told you just how wild I am about you?"

"Every day. As much as I am about you."

Tomorrow was another busy packing and cleaning day—they were running out of time before her shifting problem returned. But for now, they were in wolf heaven. And every day brought a new adventure. Some would even be in their books, but who got which ones to write about was another story.

All that mattered to them was that *they* got to live their happily ever after.

Read on for an excerpt from the next book in Terry Spear's White Wolf series

Flight of the White Wolf

Coming soon from Sourcebooks Casablanca

Big Lake, Alaska

His first case just had to involve flying.

On his first day as a private investigator in Seattle, Gavin Summerfield had gotten a case that made him want to string the thieves up. Stolen pets were a lucrative market for criminals. Two male, champion-sired Samoyed pups, worth nearly three thousand apiece, had been stolen from their owner's fenced-in backyard. The owner and her two teen girls were in tears.

"I vow I'll find Kodi and Shiloh and bring them home safe." He hoped he wouldn't fail them. Sometimes, the pets ended up in lab experiments or were sold to breeders or puppy mills. Sometimes, the criminals who stole them were looking to return them for a reward.

Soon after he left the family's home with pictures of the pups and their favorite fetch toys, he had discovered that a white van had been sighted at their house and in the vicinity of four other dog-nappings. One of the neighbors had captured a photograph of the Alaska license plate on the same van parked in a friend's driveway when they weren't home.

Then he got a lead that the dogs had been flown to Alaska.

Now, he was trying to settle his stomach and pretend he wasn't flying high above the world on his way to see London Lanier, a retired police detective in Big Lake. Gavin's fear of crashing wasn't just some figment of his imagination. Six months earlier, while he was still serving in Seattle as a cop, he'd survived a plane crash after jewelry store robbers had taken him hostage.

The plane hit more turbulence and his stomach dropped. He closed his eyes, telling himself he wasn't going to crash. Not this time. That wasn't the only reason he hated to fly. He liked to be in control, and flying this high off the ground, he had no control over anything.

At least he had a lead on the pups. He wanted more than anything to return them to the family, safe and sound. The pictures of them reminded him of the dogs his family had raised when he was growing up. Their German shepherds had been as much family to him as his human family had been.

As soon as Gavin's plane landed, he picked up a rental car and drove to the town where his contact was located.

London Lanier was an animal rights activist, primarily concerned with the illegal hunting of wildlife in Alaska. When Gavin called him to tell him he had learned the pups had been flown to his neck of the woods, London had started checking into it.

When Gavin arrived at London's home, he thought the man looked like Santa Claus, with the white beard and hair, though he was a trim version of jolly old St. Nick. He was tall, fit, and eager to take on hunters with his bare hands.

"You look like a cop," London said, shaking Gavin's hand.

Gavin took the remark as a compliment. His hair wasn't as short as when he was in the force, now that he was a PI. Today, he looked more like a SWAT team member, with a black T-shirt, black cargo pants, and heavy-duty black boots. He was in a no-nonsense mood and ready to take these bastards down.

London served them both cups of coffee and then got down to business. "From what I've learned, one of the homes in this vicinity has tons of dogs barking all day long, and then a few days later, they're gone. Shortly after that, they have a new batch. Some of their neighbors are suspicious. Since I don't work on the police force anymore, you'll need to do some canvassing. Learn anything that will prove they really are involved in trafficking pets, let me know, and I'll call on the police. I'm still friends with several on the force." London handed Gavin a script map. "I talked to the locals, but everyone knows who I am. Maybe a new guy, just looking for his pups, might convince someone to share something they didn't tell me. Or maybe they've seen something new, or remembered something they didn't think of before. Good luck."

"Thanks, London. I'll let you know what happens. And I owe you."

London smiled. "Never know when I might need a PI. Besides, if you can help us take these bastards down, you've done me a favor."

Afterward, Gavin headed over to the Big Lake housing area: high-income homes, lakefront property, trees all around, and large yards for hiding a slew of runs for stolen pets.

He pulled into the driveway of a home three doors down from the suspect's house, parked, and went to the door. When he knocked, a gray-haired woman with bright-blue eyes greeted him with a smile.

"Ma'am, I'm a private investigator, searching for these two missing pups. They were stolen from the backyard while they were outside playing. Have you seen them? Or know anyone who might have them?"

"Oh, yes, of course." Her eyes were rounded and she licked her lips. "She's my next-door neighbor."

He frowned and glanced at his script. That wasn't the correct house. At least, according to London. "Are you sure?"

"Yes. She has dogs all the time. Not the same ones though. I see her out walking them along the road in the late spring, summer, early fall. Even in the winter when we're buried in snow. Always different dogs. I figured she fostered them or something. I saw her with two of the cutest little Samoyed pups earlier, maybe six months old? Not sure. They look exactly like yours."

"Do you know her name?"

"Amelia White. She lives alone. Well, except for the revolving door of dogs. I never considered that any of the dogs could have been stolen."

"What about the people at this place?" Gavin pointed to the house on the script map, the one London had targeted.

"Oh, yeah, sure. Did London send you? He already asked me."

"You didn't mention Amelia to him?"

"No. She's so sweet. I really didn't think she could be involved in anything so nefarious. But she does have two Samoyed puppies. And that's what you're looking for, right? I hadn't seen them with her before yesterday morning."

"And the other people?"

"Oh, the Michaels? Asher and Mindy? Yeah. I wouldn't be surprised at all about them. Not sure what he does. They don't seem to have a regular occupation, just...have money and lots of dogs. They don't walk them. The dogs just bark most of the time, and I've seen all of them rushing to the chain-link fence when I've taken strolls past the place. Different dogs all the time."

"What does Miss White do?"

"She's a seaplane pilot. Her family owns the business."

"Thanks." It would be easy to move stolen pets around as a pilot, wouldn't it? No paperwork hassle. Just fly them where they needed to go. What were the chances that both people were involved in the illegal trade of pets? Maybe Amelia took care of the overflow and the transportation. It would be convenient, with her living so close to the Michaels.

Gavin drove down to Amelia's house first, since she apparently had dogs like the ones he was looking for. He'd start surveillance on the Michaels after that.

He parked and headed for the door of the large, blue-vinyl-sided home, and climbed the stairs. No dogs barked as he approached, and the front door was slightly ajar. That's when two curious little Samoyed pups poked their noses out through the door, probably hearing his footfalls.

Before he could stop them, they nudged the door open, and one raced down the steps. *Hell!*

The second pup ran to join the first, and Gavin was

led on a merry chase. He managed to scoop up the one closest to him and finally reached the other, grabbing him up in his left arm. The puppies licked him as if this were just part of their playtime.

The problem was Samoyed puppies all looked the same to him. These two were both white, identical to each other. And they looked just like the photos he had of Kodi and Shiloh.

One pup secure in each arm, he hurried back to the house, ran up the steps, and hollered through the open door. "Miss White? Your front door was open and your pups ran off." If they weren't the right pups, he wasn't about to confiscate them and be accused of stealing *her* pets! On the other hand, he worried about foul play because the door was slightly ajar and no one was answering. What if something had happened to her?

Suddenly, a wet, naked woman streaked across the living room, glancing at him for a second as she ran, and disappeared down a hall. "Put them down, get out, and close the door," she called out.

Shocked, he stood there, his jaw hanging agape, the image of the gorgeous blond in the raw still imprinted on his brain. She was in great shape, her hands covering her bouncing breasts as she'd dashed down the hall. He closed the front door, not wanting to let the puppies run out of the house again, and set them down on the wood floor. "I'm leaving," he called. "Sorry—your door was open, and I was worried something might be wrong."

He needed to question her about the pups. He started to back away from them slowly so they wouldn't follow him. He'd almost reached the door when they came bounding after him. He was trying to figure out how to keep them from dashing out again as soon as he opened the door when the woman suddenly reappeared, a blue towel wrapped around her curvy body, and a Taser in her hand—and shot him.

Acknowledgments

Thanks so much to Donna Fournier for all the time she takes to brainstorm with me before, during, and after the process of writing the book—as always. And to Dottie Jones and Donna Fournier who were invaluable in critiquing. Thanks to Deb Werksmen and the cover artists who do an amazing job. And to my fans who remind me which characters I need to add to my next books!

About the Author

Bestselling and award-winning author Terry Spear has written over sixty paranormal romance novels and four medieval Highland historical romances. Her first werewolf romance, *Heart of the Wolf*, was named a 2008 *Publishers Weekly*'s Best Book of the Year, and her subsequent titles have garnered high praise and hit the *USA Today* bestseller list. A retired officer of the U.S. Army Reserves, Terry lives in Spring, Texas, where she is working on her next werewolf romance, continuing with her Highland medieval romances, and having fun with her young adult novels. When she's not writing, she's photographing everything that catches her eye, making teddy bears, loving on her first grandchild, and playing with her Havanese puppies. For more information, please visit terryspear.com, or follow her on Twitter, @TerrySpear. She is also on Facebook at facebook.com/terry.spear. And on Wordpress at Terry Spear's Shifters: https://terryspear.wordpress.com.

HEART OF THE WOLF
10TH ANNIVERSARY EDITION

The book that introduced readers to
Terry Spear's ever-expanding world of
sexy shapeshifters with heart

First published by Sourcebooks in 2008, *Heart of the Wolf* launched the immensely popular series of werewolf romance based on extensive research of how wolves live and behave in the wild, creating a fascinating world of nature and fantasy.

As a companion to Bella and Devlyn's story, this edition includes an exclusive, brand-new novella that brings the story of the *lupus garou* family full circle.

"The chemistry crackles off the page."

—*Publishers Weekly* Best Book of the Year

"A sizzling good time…Spear's writing is pure entertainment."

—Long and Short Reviews

"Enchanting romance with a unique twist…writing so superior that it felt real to me."

—The Romance Studio

For more Terry Spear, visit:

sourcebooks.com